THE
DEMON DEVICE

THE
DEMON DEVICE

BY SIR ARTHUR CONAN DOYLE

AS COMMUNICATED TO

ROBERT SAFFRON

A NOVEL

ILLUSTRATED BY
DON BOLOGNESE
AND
ELAINE RAPHAEL

G. P. PUTNAM'S SONS
NEW YORK

Library of Congress Cataloging in Publication Data

SBN: 399-12285-0

Saffron, Robert.
    The demon device.

    1. Doyle, Arthur Conan, Sir, 1859-1930, in fiction,
drama, poetry, etc. 2. European War, 1914-1918——
Fiction. I. Doyle, Arthur Conan, Sir, 1859-1930.
II. Title.
PZ4.S128De [PS3569.A282]   823'.8   78-9836

FOREWORD

The inconsistencies in this text, most of which I have clarified *(vide* Acknowledgements), and the vagaries of style tend to obscure a positive attribution of authorship. Often I have wondered whether the mind guiding my hand from the Other World was actually that of Sir Arthur Conan Doyle. Since the communications were entirely one way, I could not put questions to the unseen sender, and it seemed at times that this adventure was being transmitted by one of his host of imitators for some arcane, unimaginable game.

Conan Doyle, however, three years before his demise, forecast the mundane problems facing a posthumous writer. In *The Fortnightly Review* (Dec. 1, 1927, p. 721) he stated: "In the first place, he is filtering it through another brain, which may often misinterpret or misunderstand . . . In the second place, the writer has entered upon a new life with a new set of experiences, and with the tremendous episode of physical dissolution between him and the thoughts of Earth, this may show itself in his style and diction."

In any event, I have found that the narrative which follows is not wholly without verisimilitude, and the events which it reveals are sufficiently fascinating to merit wider dissemination.

Robert Saffron
New York
January 8, 1979

5

A NOTE FROM
SIR ARTHUR CONAN DOYLE

In the turbulent years since I departed my life on Earth, the meaning of the word "extraordinary" seems to have been debased in direct proportion to the value of the British pound. Nevertheless, "beyond the ordinary" is still a precise designation for the two events it is my pleasure to reveal herein.

For much of my adult years, I was deeply concerned with psychic phenomena, the manifestations of after-life: I communicated with my "dead" mother, brother and son, I beheld spirits stroll about a séance and engage the group in conversation, and I experienced the unique odour of ozone, which identifies ectoplasm. In the course of the First World War, I became convinced that a psychic religion, based on the return of and communion with the dead, was the only one which offered sublime hope and serenity; for convenience, we believers called it Spiritualism.

Being in myself now proof of the immortality of the soul, I searched for the path to communicate this exultant news from my glorious Summerland to Earth. But, just as my five senses were attuned to the material world when I inhabited Earth, here, in my etheric body, I am attuned to the sounds and visions of the etheric world, and it was exceedingly difficult to find a sympathetic receptor to whom I might transmit my thoughts.

Now at last I have crossed that awesome barrier, and for evidence to silence the ever-present scoffers, I have conveyed to Mr. Robert Saffron, as my amanuensis, this chronicle of my espionage activities in the First War. As to the method by which my words were transmitted, I shall elucidate all this and more in a two-volume work upon which I am now engaged, recounting my voyages of discovery in the extraterrestrial world.

My purpose in ventilating this German adventure is to contribute to an understanding of our grievous errors in 1917, which I felt I might have prevented and which led to the calamities of 1939 and, possibly, to consequent wars. The reports of my findings were buried or destroyed, and could not be published, even posthumously, by orders from the very highest level of government, on the assumption that truth at that time was one eccentricity the English could not afford.

My memory, fortunately, has remained as comprehensive as ever, and my correspondent has added a few notes, with my approval, to bring the historical events into a current perspective.

Occasionally, someone here wonders if I actually possess the attributes of my fictional detective. The truth is, a writer creates a character who is accepted as a living person not so much from observation of others but out of his own wellspring of conflicting hopes and desires, and since I have also delineated numerous enemies of society, I can only reply—*Mea culpa.*

CONTENTS

In *"His Last Bow: The War Service of Sherlock Holmes,"* Conan Doyle at last identified Holmes with himself. . . .

Now it need not be stated, even with a suppressed grin, that he himself did not take cocaine, did not fire revolvers indoors, did not keep cigars in the coal scuttle. . . . But there are more personal characteristics than these. His fondness for working in old dressing gowns, for clay pipes . . . for compiling scrapbooks, for amassing documents, for keeping a magnifying glass on his desk and a pistol in the drawer form a more presentable domestic picture. . . .

Many of the identifications, of course, were unconscious. . . . We can scarcely dip into the stories anywhere without finding Holmes telling us how unemotional he is, and in the next behaving more chivalrously—especially toward women—than Watson himself.

The deliberate identification with Holmes, at the time of all the endless queries at the top-side of success in 1892, Conan Doyle slipped into his Memories. Who could resist some references to Holmes's early struggling days on his arrival in London? Holmes took rooms in Montague Street; his creator . . . took rooms in Montague Place. And the family background?

"My ancestors," says Holmes in *"The Greek Interpreter,"* *"were country squires."* So were his creator's. . . .

There are seven other identifications, but the Sherlockian will have found these for himself.

—JOHN DICKSON CARR
The Life of Sir Arthur Conan Doyle

THE
DEMON DEVICE

CHAPTER ONE

African Witchery in the Centre of London

The deadly adventure which snatched me from a life of desuetude, confecting propaganda articles while friends and family were dying on the Western Front, began bizarrely enough in London on a marrow-chilling March night in 1917. Zeppelins were raining their foul eggs on the West India Docks, where, amidst the uproar of crashing bricks and timbers and anti-aircraft guns, rose the screams of the wounded and burning. Over all hung a sulphurous miasma of smoke and flame, a portent of the cloud which might yet wipe out all Britain.

Across the Thames, where Limehouse Reach narrows down below the Foreign Cattle Market, Butcher Row lay blanketed in serene darkness. But within a disused livery stable there was fire and wailing and deep booming, as of distant cannon. The last was created by the reverberation of African jungle drums while frenzied, chanting blacks squatted around a great wood fire. In the centre of the group, stomping in and out of the flames, moaning incantations to resurrect the dead, whirled the Obeah, a huge, wrinkled witch-man draped in a lion's skin surmounted by a wooden mask of the beast, ferocious with fangs and mane, claw bracelets and anklets. He brandished a hunting-spear at a sweet-faced Devon country girl, squirming and screaming in the circle of blacks.

At her side, somewhat more restrained, swayed a tall, slender white gentleman of indeterminate age in rumpled tweeds; his face hawk-nosed and cadaverous, his deep-set, piercing eyes darting over the entire circle but always returning to focus on the woman beside him.

The Obeah scraped a magic symbol on the dirt floor in the centre of the group, while an assistant pulled in a quivering goat. With a slash of his horned knife, the Obeah cut the animal's throat and, as the blood gushed forth, cupped it in his hands, then daubed the gluey red over the white woman's face and arms. She writhed in an eerie passion, as if possessed by an inner demon. "He come now!" the Obeah hissed. The figure of an elderly white man, grey as a wraith, materialised from the dark of the hay-loft and floated down towards the fire.

Screaming "Father! Father!" the woman rushed towards him—and collapsed suddenly on the floor. The gentleman in the tweeds instantly knelt at her side and took her pulse. It was scarcely beating.

"A doctor!" he cried out. "Where's the nearest doctor?"

To comprehend this grotesque manifestation of jungle sorcery in the very centre of London, the reader must journey backwards in time to that same morning in my rooms in No. 15, Buckingham Palace Mansions. Shortly after my marriage to Miss Jean Leckie and the purchase of our home, Windlesham, near Crowborough in Sussex, I had taken this flat as a *pied-à-terre*. It enabled us to enjoy occasional evenings in London with friends, but it served mainly as a headquarters when my plays were being produced, and as a depository of research for my literary projects.

On the morning of 5 March I sat smoking a pipe in the study to calm my railing at the fate which had kept me from active participation in Britain's most debilitating crusade against despotic evil since Napoleon's day. Mine was a comfortably cluttered den, overflowing with mementoes and remnants of previous habitations. Bristowe's *Principles of Medicine* and the pipe-stand from my first practice at Portsmouth, where I'd lived on a shilling a day, shared space atop a mahogany table with a magnifying-glass and a microscope, which verified the chemical wizardry of my omniscient sleuth. The table was salvaged from my consulting-room off Harley St., into which not one client ever ventured.

Over the fire-place I'd crossed the cricket-bat that had scored my first century at Lord's with the leather gaiters and pith helmet of my wanderings as war correspondent in Boerland. One closet was stuffed with boxing-gloves, envelopes of manuscripts and correspondence, my old Norwegian skis, and the residue of my physical-development course with Sandow, iron weights and bars, which I occasionally hefted to relieve moments of exasperation.

Book-shelves covered three walls, and despite the best efforts of my wife and our former housekeeper, now a conductorette, my note-books and clippings of crimes from Albania to Zanzibar, together with scientific periodicals from Europe and America, spilt on to the floor. So much of my life and thought had been channelled towards order and logic that here I luxuriated in the freedom of clutter.

My particular delight, which conjoined all these loose ends even though it stimulated my wife to occasional spasms of laughter, was J. Foot & Son's patented adjustable chair, a wondrous variation of a dentist's "iron maiden." A detach-

17

able front table of wood could be set flat for writing or inclined for reading. Both velour-tufted arms lifted up and turned outwards, forming side-rests to hold books and research notes. A second wood tray telescoped out on a brass arm at the left, so that I could swiftly refer to information at either hand. A small, round oak table, on a brass arm at my right, held the pen and ink-pot employed in the *accouchement* of my first detective tale, "A Study in Scarlet," with space for a coffee-cup or whisky-glass. The upholstered back-rest, its cushion contoured to fit my head, could be adjusted by the touch of a button to any inclination desired, as could the foot-rest, thus converting the chair into a comfortable lounge for my bulky six-foot-two frame. The entire contrivance rolled on wheels to face the window, fire-place or bookshelves. It was truly a marvel of comfort; wrapped in my old red dressing-gown, I could work, eat and sleep without need to leave this velour womb.

That March I was occupied in interviewing survivors of the devastating Somme campaign, seeking the truth, the heroism and blunders, behind our losses of 420,000 men for my history *The British Campaign in France and Flanders,* begun in the first months of the war with the permission of Sir John French, the commander-in-chief. This project kept me from suffocating in a slough of disuse which affected me most keenly, for my entire family were actively engaged in reply to the atrocious German onslaughts. My son by my first marriage, an acting captain in the First Hampshires, had been invalided out after the fighting on the Somme. My younger brother, Innes, only forty, was adjutant-general of a corps. My brother-in-law and two nephews had been killed. My daughter worked overtime to assemble shells at Vickers, and my wife had set up a home for Belgian refugees in Crowborough.

And I, in the full vigour of my life, had been denied

permission even to help evacuate the wounded in France because I was a bit beyond the age for military service. I organised the Crowborough Volunteers, who became a unit of the Sixth Royal Sussex Volunteers, the home-guard which did release some men for active duty. I put my pen at the service of the government. After visiting the war fronts in France, Belgium and Italy, I wrote optimistic articles for the press; even a new munitions plant in Gretna engaged my enthusiasm. But it was particularly galling not to be in the thick of it when from my windows at Windlesham I could hear the faint rumble, rising and falling like the break of surf, from the guns in Flanders, one hundred and fifty miles across the Channel. To be so near and yet so far!

When my door-bell sounded, I was in Foot's chair, expanding my notes on a pilot's-eye view of a skirmish. My caller was Sgt. Matthews of Scotland Yard, whom I had met but once before, a clean-shaved young man with a generally florid complexion, the nephew of the woman who had faithfully and lovingly looked after my children for many years. At the moment, he was in such a state of apprehension and haste, for he had been ordered to board a train to Carlisle within the hour, that his words tumbled out one atop the other as he implored my aid in a matter "too delicate" to bring to the attention of the Yard. His was indeed an exotic quandary.

His wife, Cora, an unsophisticated country girl, had taken employment the year before, in order to augment the sergeant's modest income, as a typewritist for the Society for the Propagation of Health and Education in the Congo. Her heart was too weak, the sergeant said, to permit work in a war plant, which offered more money. Her entire personality had changed somehow during that year with the Society. As he put it, "She displays little interest in me—or life around her!"

"Withdrawn into herself?"

"Not even in the same room with me! I snap my fingers in front of her eyes—no effect, sir! Not the dear girl I'd married—almost as if another soul occupied her body!"

His hand quivered as he displayed recent photographs made on holiday at Brighton, the usual gimcracks taken against painted back-drops: the couple seated on the hump of a camel, or heads poked through holes atop barely clad bathers. The pictures revealed a placid, round-eyed, quite attractive young woman, with a rather prominent laryngeal cartilage, ungracefully known as the Adam's apple.

"Is she given to fainting? Or high blood pressure?"

"No."

"What do you wish me to do?"

He had been ordered to Carlisle, some three hundred and fifteen miles to the north, to present evidence for the prosecution in a theft from the home of a textile-mill owner there. While the sergeant was walking through St. Pancras station, an elderly woman had stumbled into him, causing her cheap hand-bag to pop open and spill out Georgian silver and jade cabochons; the "lady" was, in fact, a man. The sergeant implored me to keep watch on his wife while he was called away.

"Why? Where?"

"Some coloureds she met at the Society claim they can bring her father back from the dead. Voodoo or witch-doctor, I think. And Cora's attending their séance tonight."

I knew of the Society as a responsible organisation, with a wealthy Liberal baronet as chairman. "Witch-doctor?" I repeated incredulously. "Not a medium?"

"An Obeah, she calls him. I beg you, sir, accompany her tonight. You're the only one I can turn to—she has no relatives in London."

Over the years I have received hundreds of requests, ad-

"Not the dear girl I'd married—almost as if another soul occupied her body!"

dressed to me or my ever-ready investigator, supplicating, occasionally demanding, aid for individuals in deep distress; but only a few cases seized my attention, particularly those in which the law had miscarried.* Although I had explored psychic phenomena for some years, an African witch-man had never appeared in a sitting, and this compelled me to attend.

Two hours after Sgt. Matthews' departure, a military motorcycle roared up to the entrance of my flat. Peering out from my oriel window, I observed a three-striper leaping off his machine, and in a few moments his sharp knocking

---

* The George Edalji affair (1906): A young Parsee solicitor, residing in a village near Birmingham, was convicted of a bizarre crime—ripping open the stomachs of farm animals. Dr. Doyle's analysis of the blood-stains and mud on his clothes, together with the depth of the cuts, which could only have been inflicted by a special instrument, proved Edalji was the innocent victim of race hysteria.

The case of Oscar Slater (1911): A gambler and procurer, Slater was sentenced to life imprisonment for the murder of an elderly spinster in Glasgow. Even though a policeman later admitted that the prosecution had suppressed evidence which would have proved him innocent and that their main witness had perjured herself, Slater languished in jail for years. A fellow prisoner, when released, smuggled out Slater's plea for help in a hollow tooth. Conan Doyle responded with an eighty-page, finely rea-soned exposé, and carried on an unpopular crusade in behalf of Slater, who was not released until 1928.

The problem of the abandoned nurse, Joan Paynter, was in some aspects similar to the author's tale "A Case of Identity." She had been engaged to a Dane, who had wooed her with gifts and persuaded her to leave her position at the hospital. After the wedding arrangements had been made, he vanished, and neither Scotland Yard nor the Danish police could trace him. Conan Doyle deduced, from the nurse's correspondence with the man, not only his whereabouts but the peril of her further association with him.

Conan Doyle undertook even more peculiar cases, including the theft of the Irish crown jewels, which involved homosexuality so close to the throne that the probable culprit could not be brought to trial. —R.S.

rattled my door; here was a messenger from someone of importance in petrol-poor London.

I opened to confront the apotheosis of the recruiting sergeant: flat nose and square chin, puttees wound to perfection, and a clarion voice which made clear how he had intimidated many a youth in Trafalgar Square into accepting the King's shilling.

"You are Sir Arthur Conan Doyle?" He called out each syllable.

I was forced to agree.

He thrust an unmarked envelope into my hand. "I am ordered to wait for an answer, sir." He followed me into the sitting-room, shut the door and stood smartly at attention. Since the man was obviously free of disabilities, while so many wounded rankers had been returned to France, I could infer only that the person whom he served had the unconcern of a Pharaoh for the opinion of ordinary people whose sons were serving on the battle-fields.

Under the green, fluted lamp-shade, the note created the eerie semblance of hieroglyphics, and I needed a minute to decipher them into English. They were the product of either frantic impatience or advanced *paralysis agitans*.

SIR,

Gen. French recommends I see you tonight on a matter of interest to His Majesty's Government. Messenger knows time and place.

The signature was an initial—*D*, or possibly *A*.

"I have a pressing engagement this evening. Inform your superior that I am available to meet with him at his convenience tomorrow."

The courier requested the use of my telephone, and repeated my message with parade-ground weight. He called out his superior's reply. "Available only tonight dinner at twenty hundred hours. What is your pressing engagement, sir?"

The unseen interrogator's arrogance nettled me. "An investigation of psychic phenomena," I averred.

Puzzled, the sergeant carefully repeated my words, then his superior's reply: "Ours is a matter of higher importance. An experienced, trustworthy observer, C. B. Plumsoll, will appear in your stead. Expect him at your quarters within the hour for instructions."

Higher importance? I saw no course but to accept. The messenger ordered, "Present your card to the doorman at the Beefsteak Club at twenty hundred hours. I am instructed to advise you to be prompt, sir."

I climbed into Foot's chair and lit up a pipe to consider this turn of events. The Beefsteak was favoured by the old propertied, ecclesiastical and financial oligarchs and fertilized by the new money of brewery and patent-medicine barons. A demonstration of its constituency, as relayed by one member who insisted it was more than apocryphal, allegedly occurred the year before, when whisky was sold between noon and twelve-thirty P.M. and brandy was legal only on a physician's prescription.

A quartet of members spilt out into the night with sufficient jollity to persuade a constable and a sergeant that it was a house of ill-repute. The merry foursome were requested to identify themselves. One elderly gentleman replied that he was Governor of the Bank of England. A second certified that he was Lord Chancellor.

"Are you now?" asked the sergeant, losing his indulgent grin when the third gentleman insisted that he was the Foreign Minister. "And you, sir," said the officer to the fourth man, "are no doubt God himself?"

"Oh, I do speak to Him on occasion," replied the Archbishop of Canterbury.

I assumed, therefore, that my secretive dinner-host must be situated at the most exalted level of government.

Mr. C. B. Plumsoll, the "experienced, trustworthy observer," arrived fifteen minutes before the appointed hour; he could reveal nothing about my peremptory correspondent because he had never met the man. I was astonished by Plumsoll's resemblance to the American actor William Gillette, who had so successfully played my unshakeable shadow on the New York and West End stages: tall, lean, the face appropriately intellectual and emaciated. But Plumsoll's windy emanations, leading to seemingly logical *non sequiturs,* his ejaculated "By Jove!" and "I say!" revealed the ill-stuffed mind that had more than once inflamed me with the urge to kill off not my sleuth but his only friend. Plumsoll was now employed in an amorphous capacity enforcing loosely drawn regulations of the Defence of the Realm Act; in short, one. of the smaller wheels in the intelligence machinery and subject to slippage. He made elaborate notes in a lizard-covered notebook, and spent five minutes intently memorising the face of Cora Matthews from the photographs her husband had left with me. Twice Plumsoll repeated questions I had already answered, then departed after emphasising that he, too, had studied medicine "for a few years."

Dressing for dinner, I was not buoyed by the realisation that my substitute was a man who heard but did not listen.

The cabman ferreted out the Beefsteak in a run-down structure off Leicester Square; still, after I climbed the dismal stair-case and presented my card, I was scarcely prepared for the ordinariness of the accommodations. There was simply one long hall with a high-pitched roof, under which some old prints, Hogarth and Rowlandson, made a small effort to enliven the décor. Members dined at one long refectory table and were seated at places selected by the waiters themselves. It was all what is termed in the theatre "underplayed," proof that the members were so certain of their position and wealth that they disdained the usual adornments.

A blond-haired waiter, resplendent with Guardsman's moustaches, led me to one end of the table, where my mysterious summoner sat in a wheel-chair. He extended his left hand languidly, and his first words were, "This is Charles. For some whimsical reason lost to history, all our waiters are named Charles."

"A blessing for short memories," I replied. His speech betrayed no regional or occupational clue, but his tie whispered Balliol.

Charles adjusted my chair opposite the host, and advised Dover sole and a rationed mutton-chop.

The enigmatic gentleman and I accepted automatically, and we faced each other in silence. His appearance was totally unremarkable except for the almost opaque, unlined skin, tinged with the sallowness which indicated a career in the tropics of Asia or Africa, where our administrators hide from the viciously hot sun, avoiding contact with the natives they govern and ingesting great quantities of quinine. The face was as bland as a junior manager's at the Royal Exchange Assurance, revealing no hint of his age (I conjectured between forty and fifty), and his eyes exhibited no interest in me or my reactions; they were simply hazy, hollow green receptacles for absorbing information, possibly by osmosis. He co-ordinated all intelligence services; I shall call him Arachne.

Charles set a snifter before him, filled with cracked ice

and a liquid which, from its clarity and low viscosity, I took to be fine gin. I contented myself with whisky and a splash, and waited for the man to begin.

"You don't look like your detective," he said flatly. "More like the other fellow."

The banality, the utter predictability, of a man in his position shocked me. I gave him my reply reserved for such fatuousness. "Despite my total abstinence from cocaine, I have managed to confound the police in several cases where justice had not been done."

"I'm not really concerned with justice," he said, with the weary sigh of a don for a failing student. "I'm searchin' for a man with more emphatic qualities for covert entry into enemy territory, a formidable and exhaustin' job. You've displayed some admirable derrin'-do: boxer, footballer, cricketer, a balloon ascension, pilotin' a heavy biplane at Hendon in 1911—"

He took up his glass for an extended sip while Charles served the sole. The elided *g* was another aristocratic affectation, and from the evidence that his right arm was an inch shorter than his left, I judged that he had suffered a birth defect. He would, therefore, have risen to his present eminence by qualities which did not require physical prowess, possibly family or school connexions, multiplied by the indomitable will concealed beneath his languid manner. Still, he was not completely in control; he displayed a peculiar tic, impatiently flicking the pendulous end of his nose with the tip of his left forefinger, all of which combined with the fixed curve of his tight lips to create the impression that he was confronting an unfortunate odour. It enhanced his already insufferable assumption of inbred superiority.

"—but you're now approachin' fifty-eight. The reflexes have slowed a bit."

"I still march fourteen miles' drill with the Sussex Volunteers, full pack on my back. And my weight is the same as twenty-five years ago—fifteen stone."

"I refer to the calcification of the mental processes." He pressed his fork into the fish and half-heartedly lifted a few flakes. "You were also endorsed by the PM—an old dear, Asquith, but his retirement can never compensate the nation for total inadequacy. He is sixty-five. Your General French commanded the cavalry with great dash against the Boers and therefore employed similar tactics for infantry, ordering attacks with bayonets on Jerry machine-gun nests. French is also sixty-five. It's quite empyrean to sit in one's study, Sir Arthur, spendin' weeks to concoct dazzlin' intuitions and disablin' counter-blows, but Mauser bullets are speedier than even your super-human hero's brain."

He'd certainly known of my age and acquaintances before to-night. I sensed two under-currents, not necessarily to my benefit. One was that this mission had been set in motion by someone other than Arachne, and that he sought to despatch a man to forestall future complaints of inaction. Secondly, that he did not welcome my auspices: if this project were to go seriously awry, General French and Asquith (both of whom I knew but slightly) were sufficiently powerful to ask disturbing questions. He was playing a charade, to appease them while searching for cause to disqualify me.

"Your age, combined with certain dangerous notions you've expressed, could be fatal—"

"Dangerous notions?" I was astounded by what followed.

"Mawkish romanticism. I agree with Ludendorff: one cannot conduct war with sentimentality. Your public campaigns—sheer soft-headedness. Supportin' those chambermaids at Brighton when their wages were cut. Really! The poor can never be improved by money; they merely produce more children and sop up more drink to endure their wretched jobs." He flicked his nose impatiently. "As for your brouhaha to release the Jew Slater, that's a sickly refusal to see life as it truly is. Courts can never admit mistakes, don't ye know?—undermines confidence in law and order."

His vituperative scorn aimed to bait me into an angry outburst; I reined myself in.

"And you campaigned to keep Roger Casement from hangin'. Good Lord, man, he was a traitor!"

"A simple gaol term would have been more practical. Now he's a martyr to the Irish."

"No, the endearin' qualities I require for this job are mental agility combined with ruthlessness." He withdrew a blue file folder from a despatch case on which his right elbow rested. "First day's report, but it demonstrates the evil of sentimental slop, my man."

I would not endure "my man." It was as much a display of contempt for an inferior as dubbing all the waiters Charles. There was still time, fortunately, to reach Mrs. Matthews before the séance concluded, but first I would have my say. "The true matter which divides us is not sentimentality but the chasm between your Oxford and my University of Edinburgh."

He lashed back while Charles served the chop. "It's not my fault, ye know, that your father was a clerk in the Office of Works while mine inherited fifteen thousand acres and a draughty castle. Sheer accidents of birth."

"Dreadful accidents for the nation. Hundreds of thousands of good men have been slaughtered in this war, led by aristocratic faces who secured their commands through family and royal connexions. After three years in which so many ships have blown up in our own Thames, you still have no defence against mines! You have provided no dinghies or vests, *nothing!* to keep our seamen afloat when your 'unsink-able' dreadnoughts go down. And you all know, deep within your bones, that armoured tanks can never replace brightly costumed cavalry. These blunders are not the result of age but of congenital deficiency of grey-matter, caused by in-breeding. The destinies of our great empire are in the hands of wilful amateurs who have never grown beyond their uni-versity years!" I pushed back my chair and arose. "Surely you can find someone who meets your peculiar specifications more exactly than I. Good night, sir."

"All that may be quite true," he replied, in a tone so flat as to verge on the negative. "But you owe me the courtesy of hearin' my case. Do sit down."

"You owe me the good sense to make your lecture brief." I continued to stand; my height emphasised his infirmity and it was cruel, but I'd really had enough of the man.

He stared up at me, revealing for the first time a glow of balefulness in those empty orbs, while he waited for me to sit. I would not do it.

He continued grimly, "This matter reeks of sentimen-tality. Our most effective agent in a neutral country, one Sardanyi, Hungarian, age fifty-four, has just murdered his good friend and will no doubt hang. Seems the friend's wife persuaded Sardanyi that her husband, though a rather small man, beat her, and Sardanyi pushed him out of the hotel's eighth-floor window."

Pushed out a window? The case assumed an intriguing aspect. "You believe Sardanyi was her lover?" I asked.

"Of course. Why else would a man be so obligin'?"

"What specific conduct provoked the husband to these alleged beatings?"

"The wife objected to his sellin' tinned ham to the Austrians."

30

Small loss, but the wife's political conviction loomed large. "Do the police have a witness to the alleged push from the window?"

"No. However, Sardanyi was seen by two people, a waiter and a lift man, enterin' the room shortly before the body was discovered in the courtyard."

"Aside from these two observers, do the police have one scintilla of evidence against the fellow?"

"None so far."

"Then I suggest that the Hungarian is innocent."

Again the despairing sigh. "Come, come. Are you now unable to distinguish between fiction and reality?"

"As a physician I was trained to diagnose by the unique smell, the singular skin colour, the enlarged vein under the eye; in a crime I search for the peculiar fact that marks this death or that criminal as different from all others. Does it not strike you that the *method* of the murder—defenestration—is quite significant?"

"Perhaps."

"That Sardanyi is Hungarian is the second significant fact."

"Indeed?" He sniffed while he sliced into his chop. An aide entered and placed at his elbow a folder similar to the one he already held.

"What was the wife's name?" I asked.

"Madame Reutlinger."

"I require her *maiden* name."

"I fail to see the import of that."

"If you had, you might have solved the entire puzzle yourself."

"My dear sir, do you presume to assert that if I supply you with this woman's maiden name, you shall have positive evidence of the actual murderer, even though the police on the scene have the prime suspect, you are seven hundred miles away and have never seen the principals involved?"

"You have stated my case exactly."

He searched with some irritation through the sheets of flimsy. "Madame Reutlinger's maiden name was Capek."

"A native of—?"

"Prague."

"A Czech. Each detail is illuminating, but as they accumulate, they have an irresistible logic. The police must be up to their usual level of incompetence; they should have discovered that someone was in the room after Sardanyi departed and before Reutlinger plunged to his death."

Arachne pondered what he had overlooked in his analysis. "And you claim to know who pushed him?"

"Yes. Madame Reutlinger."

"Why do you insist that she, not Sardanyi, killed him?"

"Because of her name—Capek."

His fork hung arrested in mid-air. " 'pon my soul! What does *that* have to do with it?"

"Everything. Defenestration is a rare form of political killing. It first appears in recorded history after Jan Hus, the Czech patriot, was burned at the stake by orders of the Council of Constance in 1415. Four years after that, the hotly nationalistic Czechs revolted and hurled the pro-German councillors out the town-hall windows. The second case occurred two hundred years later, 1618, the notorious Defenestration of Prague, when Czech rebels heaved two imperial commissioners out a castle window—"

"Yes, yes!" he muttered impatiently. "Set off the Thirty Years' War. I am quite familiar with European history."

"Then you should be able to recall any other case of defenestration."

After a moment's consideration, he admitted, "None."

"And as you said, Reutlinger was an Austrian sympathiser. This was an affair less of passion than of politics—the Czechs hunger for freedom from the Austrian yoke."

"But why should only Czechs employ this form of killing?" *

"Why did only Hindus force their widows to cremate themselves on their husbands' funeral pyres? Why did only the Chinese bind the feet of their women so that they could not walk? These are questions best left to anthropologists."

"Your entire case, dear chap, is based on the assumption that the woman murdered her husband because she is a Czech patriot?"

"Precisely."

"Let us see." He produced several sheets of paper, and after scanning them with swift determination, regarded me indulgently. "The report states that Madame Reutlinger is *not* of Czech descent."

I was confident of my interpretation, but in the next moment a poisonous suspicion percolated through my entire body: had he decoyed me into this trap in order to eliminate me? Since only he could decipher the code, I was at his mercy, unable to challenge whatever evidence he chose to reveal.

"That folder at your elbow is your second-day report," I declared.

His reply was faintly derisive. "And why is that significant?"

"Because I shall stand here until you decode it."

The minutes crawled by like inch-worms while I grasped

* In 1948, Jan Masaryk, Foreign Minister of democratic Czechoslovakia, was alleged by the Communists to have committed suicide by jumping from the window of his third-floor bathroom in Prague. *Time* magazine (May 9, 1977) revealed that former employees in his ministry have sworn that Masaryk was pushed to his death as part of the Communist political coup. —R.S.

the back of my chair, searching his face and body for clues to his train of thought. He sat shrouded in silence; from time to time his head tilted petulantly, or an Olympian smile curved his thin mouth. Nothing so surely consolidates one's sense of god-like certainty as a tumbler of gin.

At length he looked up bleakly. "Our cipher-clerk over there has been sacked. Madame Reutlinger is indeed Czech, and she has sworn Sardanyi left the room ten minutes before her husband leaped in suicide."

His lips curled open, in a rictus usually associated with *rigor mortis.* "Sit down. Let's get on with it."

2

CHAPTER TWO

On the Trail of Dr. Einstein

"Our man in Berlin came across information that the Jerries were perfectin' an awesome weapon of terror which could win the war and create Prussian hegemony over all Europe. This device—we don't know its shape or size—is presumed to create a tremendous explosion and fire which can't be quenched by water. It may be something which focusses X-rays."

"A huge burning lens?" I asked sceptically.

A vague grimace admitted his uncertainty. "We recalled our man to present his details to our scientific people, Rutherford and Moseley, who've been experimentin' with X-ray radiation at Manchester. The day he arrived, there was a fire in his Brompton hotel, wouldn't ye know?—and he was asphyxiated in his room. A neat German job, and of course our entire network there is now compromised. We require an immediate investigation in Germany by a man they won't expect at 70 Königergratzerstrasse—you. The amateur you so thoroughly despise."

"Did your man leave any papers, notes?"

Arachne drew from his pocket a wrinkled envelope and gingerly extracted three charred bits of paper. They read:

BOMBARD WITH X-RAYS

BUCH [here fire had obliterated the intervening words] HAS EINSTEIN

I.A. (PARIS) VON RINT?

If I.A. represented a female's initials, I had known a brilliant schemer in Paris who made me an unwitting accessory to a crime, but I dismissed this connexion as far-fetched.

" 'Von Rint' I assume is Captain von Rintelen, who was posted to America to sabotage aid to us. Was it your people who trapped him on the Dutch ship?"

"The case is closed." He sniffed and ordered the trifle.

I declined dessert. "No doubt you questioned Professor Rutherford on X-rays?"

"At the moment, he's developin' submarine-detection devices. He insisted there's absolutely no possibility of focussin' X-rays in sufficient strength to kill soldiers or burn through armour-plate. That, he said, is a Wellsian fantasy."

"All science is fantasy until one man proves otherwise— often by accident. As for 'Buch,' there are countless combinations—'book-binder,' 'book of—' "

"Our cipher department is listin' them."

Charles served the trifle together with two demi-tasses. "And the '96 Niepoort," Arachne added.

" 'Einstein' would be the German who has proposed some rather abstruse theories," I said. "One has to do with the constancy of the velocity of light and the inter-relation of time and space; the other extends this special theory to the phenomenon of gravitation and by implication to all natural phenomena. What did Rutherford make of that note?"

I detected a glimmer of surprise in Arachne's marble eyes. "I wasn't aware you're so keen on physics."

"I peruse many scientific publications to keep up with future projects for my malevolent villains."

His manner was now almost benign. "You writin' chaps do have some serviceable qualities. Sir Ernest told me that this Einstein has a profound mind, but neither of his theories has been proved."

"Or disproved. And it would be a rather tall order to question Dr. Einstein on the military application of his theories: he's engaged in research at the Prussian Academy of Science in Berlin."

"Most regrettable."

"But, of course, all these clues could have been planted on the deceased agent to divert our scientists from vital war research. Nothing is so blinding as the obvious. Why should the Germans eliminate your man here, when they could have accomplished it much more neatly on their home ground, without exposing their presence in London?"

"Agreed. Still, we must explore all possibilities."

"In short, you wish me to track a weapon that may or may not exist, its size and shape unknown, through some hundred thousand square miles of enemy territory, to bring back its secret or destroy it?—for which, if apprehended, I face certain death or other unpleasantness."

"A bit sticky," he agreed.

Without the trace of a smile I said, "I had hoped for something more challenging."

He managed a thin grin. "But 'tis enough, 'twill serve."

"I require a focus, a point of departure. I shall think upon it to-night, and be prepared to leave upon one day's notice."

He dismissed me with a slight bow of his head. "Good night." Instantly his sergeant and a corporal took battle stations on either side of him; they carried the wheel-chair down the stairway as if it were a throne, fulfilling the Pharaonic vision of him I had perceived before we met.

Plumsoll dashed into the doorway at the foot of the stairs in a highly excited state, and, seeing me on the way down, cried out, "Mrs. Matthews is dead!"

Arachne, now being borne through the exit, did not turn his head.

"*Dead?*" I echoed. "How?"

"Collapsed at the séance—no pulse-beat. We summoned a physician from nearby—Dr. Joseph Williams. Native of Jamaica, a light-skinned man. He verified it was heart failure. Coronary arrest."

"Where is the body now?"

"At the doctor's, I assume."

"You assume but do not *know?*"

He shook his head helplessly. "One of the white men from the Society said she had but one sister, in Devon. Both parents are dead. Since her husband was not available, Dr. Williams volunteered to notify the sister."

"Not quite good enough, Plumsoll." I required a study of the body and the place of the death before any clues to this extraordinary demise cooled into conjecture. I hurtled up the stairs and beckoned to our waiter. "Charles, a torch and two sardine tins."

He hurried off to fill my order. Plumsoll asked, "Will you have further need of me?"

"Certainly." In actuality, his khaki-coloured staff car, which I'd observed through the club's door, was more needful, for swift transportation.

After the waiter returned with the tins on a salver, I snapped off the two slotted-rod openers and handed back the sardines; Charles did not lift an eyelash at this. Plumsoll drove off for Butcher Row at the maximum speed possible in the blacked-out streets.

I questioned him as to the configuration of the symbol which the Obeah had scrawled on the stable floor.

"By Jove! I didn't pay it much heed—I was concentrating on the woman."

"The figure of her father—you say it floated?"

"Oh, yes. Like a child's balloon."

"Even genuine materialisations walk as they did in previous life. . . . I always suspect chicanery when drums and shouting overwhelm a sitting. The eye is an intricate, finely tuned but unreliable instrument; its view can be lulled into conveying visions to the brain which do not, in fact, exist. African Obeahs are skilled in group hypnosis."

"But to what purpose—to frighten a sweet little lady?"

"We shall see."

We searched the narrow ways surrounding Butcher Row for a door with the brass plate of Dr. Joseph Williams. It was a deserted area of warehouses and a few squalid houses renting beds to sailors; a doctor in this area would be hard put to earn a few pounds a week, tending to the accidents that afflicted low-paid dockers.

I flashed the torch up and down Deptford Green, Hughes Fields, Watergate and Dacca Streets; we found no Dr. Joseph Williams. "In this poor area he may not have a sign at all," I said.

"I recall the interior of the house," Plumsoll emphasised. "Wall-paper peeling, several coloureds clustered in the hallway, jabbering. And the examining-room: well, not much, a table and some chairs, a kerosene lamp, which I held over her."

"I must ask you to return here tomorrow morning, Plumsoll, since your responsibility continues in this matter, and press the search for Dr. Williams. Most particularly, make a copy of the death-certificate."

"Certainly, Dr. Doyle," my companion replied, in a manner which indicated he felt some dereliction of duty. We now proceeded to the stable. Though disused, its brickwork was solid, the hay-loft entry nailed shut, and the carriage doors were secured by two heavy chains through the wood, clasped by a new Chubb lock. The premises held something of value to someone. In the side wall I found a narrow door, now fitted with a bolt-lock.

In years of research, verifying procedural details for my mystery adventures, I had acquired several obscure skills. One was picking locks. The rods from the sardine tins I bent into the shape of an *L;* Plumsoll held the torch as I lifted the spring of the door-lock with one rod and felt for the notch in the bolt with the other. The bolt was rusty; only after a few minutes of probing and scraping would it slide open.

An acrid smell of burnt logs in the centre of the floor could not overpower the still-permeating odour of horses and old leather; African rites had not been conducted here frequently. My torch lit up a circular symbol, about two feet in diameter, scratched into the dirt in front of the former fire. Some elements had been obliterated by the Obeah's stomping, but I could piece together sufficient portions to re-create the talisman.

It was West African, of a Calabar River tribe. The three-pointed arrows, older than Triton's spear, represented the weapons of King Umbuda, who ruled and guarded the world of the dead. To bring back any one under his rule, it was necessary to appease his power by a sacrifice, and since his arrows were omnipotent, only the opposite ends could be turned aside. The cross-bars on the arrows hindered the ability of King Umbuda to employ his weapons accurately, and thus the dead could escape, in the direction indicated by the single-headed long arrow.*

All this indicated the work of an authentic African magic-maker, but could there have been an actual manifestation of the woman's deceased father? The long arrow pointed to the crude ladder of the hay-loft. By the light of the torch we searched for prints in the earth around the ladder, since Plumsoll was most certain that the father had appeared barefoot.

"Did that not strike you as worthy of note?" I asked. "It is still winter—surely even the black men wore shoes or sandals."

"Confound 'em, so they did. . . . I must confess, I was so startled by that wraith, I had no sceptical thoughts."

The prints resembled the jumble around a water-hole in the veldt, but when I examined them at close range, stretched out on the ground, I discerned a large bare foot, toes splayed and very little arch between them and the heel. It was the print of someone who had walked for much of his life without shoes.

"If the father were barefoot, he would make very little sound. Still, as the print reveals, he must have walked like

* After receiving his medical degrees, Conan Doyle earned money to help set up his practice by signing on as ship's doctor in October 1881, aboard the *Mayumba,* a passenger-carrying freighter. It stopped at West Coast ports from Tenerife to Monrovia, Liberia; and the doctor, an insatiable enquirer, managed to explore the interior. —R.S.

any mortal man, not floated. Could you describe the apparition exactly?"

Plumsoll hesitated. "Well, it's impossible to recollect details in all that noise and flickering fire-light. . . . Husky man, I'd say. Greyish colouring. Coarse features of a farmer. Country clothes—old sweater, wrinkled corduroy trousers . . ."

"You have omitted one essential—his height. This is a large foot."

"Oh, rather short—about five feet five or so."

Short men can have large feet, but it was quite clear, from my assessment of the evidence, that the apparition had been staged, with the drums and fire and chanting employed by the Obeah to envelope the on-lookers in some form of mass hypnosis.

"Dear me! But the motive?" Plumsoll persisted, as we returned to his motor-car.

"Perhaps Mrs. Matthews' death. That's based merely on intuition, acquired after many years spent in the study of crimes and their rationale. But murder is a most grievous charge. In this instance, one must prove *intent*—pre-meditation. Between my assumption and proof sufficient to satisfy a court of law lies a vast gulf of unknowns. Mrs. Matthews did, after all, attend the séance of her own volition—and her husband did not forbid it. Could one convince a jury that the Obeah, when he produced his fraudulent apparition, *intended* to excite her heart sufficiently to kill her? This emerges as a grotesquely fascinating riddle, and I regret I cannot now focus my entire energies upon it, particularly since Mrs. Matthews was placed under my protection."

Plumsoll shook his head glumly. "I've let our side down."

I could only say, "Something evil, out of the eternal heart of the jungle, has been released in the centre of London!"

* * *

Since Plumsoll resided in Wimbledon, I invited him to spend the night at my flat for a convenient start to Butcher Row in the morning.

I manned the telephone. The duty officer at Scotland Yard conveyed the name of the sergeant's hotel in Carlisle, and a sleepy desk-clerk at the Crown and Mitre roused him from his bed. In his drowsy state, Matthews at first could not comprehend my dreadful news.

"I can't return now!" he exclaimed in despair. "I'll be giving testimony tomorrow and the next day." After a sob of frustrated anger, the trained officer gained control: he would telegraph his wife's sister to arrange for the funeral in Devon, and he would obtain permission to attend the funeral, from the Commissioner of the Yard if necessary. I informed him that I was investigating the particulars of this tragedy, and hoped to have further information tomorrow.

Pipe in hand, I curled up in Foot's chair to analyse Arachne's charred clues. My guest, promptly lighting up his amber-stem briar, stretched out on my cordovan couch to consider his case and, I suppose, what he might have arranged differently to preserve Mrs. Matthews from her fate. With the black air-raid draperies drawn, the room was soon beclouded with the blue swirl of tobaccoes, and even though we raised the windows, the foul fog slipping in, combined with our puffing pipes, made the room so stiflingly dark that we flung the heavy curtains open, quite certain no street-warden could discern a violation.

I turned my attention to the most intriguing clue: I.A. (PARIS) VON RINT?

Paris ... Isabelle Andros. This vexatious encounter was so indelibly engraved in my mind that even now, twenty-six years after, the precise details of her clothing and smile reassembled before my eyes.

March 1891: On the way home from Vienna, where I had

studied diseases of the eye, I stopped off in Paris with my first wife, Louise, in order to consult with M. Landolt, the foremost oculist of Europe. We took rooms in a small *pension* near the Louvre so that we might enjoy its wondrous treasures.

As we unpacked, I heard a rather accomplished pianist practising Chopin *impromptus* across the hall. Shortly after Louise ventured out to a nearby shop, for the purchase of a fur muff, there came a timid knock at our door.

I opened it to face a startlingly lovely girl of seventeen or so, shifting from one foot to the other. She was French, she said in excellent English, which indicated training by an upper-middle-class mother or governess. She trusted her piano practice had not disturbed me; I replied that I had, in fact, enjoyed it.

She had heard my name from the *concierge* and, having read some of my early mystery tales, she now took the liberty of introducing herself: Isabelle Andros. Her hair and eyes glowed in the same raven black, and the oval face displayed the creamy olive colouring of a Renaissance madonna, though un-enhanced by paints. I detected no perfume other than the natural freshness of a newly bathed youngster. Her costume consisted of a simple dark-blue serge pinafore over a red paisley-pattern blouse, and her legs were masked by black cotton stockings.

She chatted quite perceptively about my tales, revealing how she had unravelled some of the puzzles from the clues long before the *dénouement*. After a few minutes she wished to show me something. I assumed it would be a fledgeling melodrama, like those with which I had once bedevilled adults, but I waited never-the-less; the girl was a welcome flower of gay colour in that wan Paris after-noon.

She returned with a thin paper-wrapped packet. These were love letters from a boy, she admitted shyly, and she begged me to hold them because her "tyrannical" mother was searching for them. The girl's eyes scampered from gay sparkle to hurt to pleading in swift succession; Romany blood must have been inter-mingled with the French. I had no wish to serve as an accomplice to a child's romantic adventure, but the helpless urgency of those eyes melted my reserve. Impulsively, she threw her arms round me in gratitude, and ran from the room. The packet I slipped under the pile of note-books in my portmanteau, and I said nothing to Louise.

Two days later, insistent, sharp rapping on our door awoke me. Drawing on my dressing-gown, I admitted two gendarmes, one tall and rotund, the other, short and thin, bearing a disconcerting resemblance to a provincial music-hall team.

Had I possibly heard any sound of an intruder in the hall or perhaps through the wall the night before? asked the short one; his moustaches, waxed to spiky points, quivered like a mouse's.

"I heard nothing," I said.

The tall one, with the appropriately beaming face of the comedian in the duo, asked if I was aware that the rooms across the hall had been ransacked.

I surmised that someone other than the mother had a desperate need for those letters, but I felt no compulsion to interfere in the ways of young love.

The police departed, and I turned back to the bedroom, hoping that Louise was now awake so that I could relate the morning's adventure, when I heard a familiar light tap at the hall door.

Isabelle had come to collect her letters. She thanked me profusely, but now I observed an obvious delight, a self-assurance of a worldly woman twice her age. The letters, she revealed, had been written by a wealthy young gentleman;

in the final note he admitted that he had caused her pregnancy, and since he was about to enter into a family-arranged marriage, he inclosed one hundred francs to abort the child.

She murmured knowingly, "Aren't there severe laws against killing one's child? And suppose his family hears of this? He will pay two thousand, don't you think?"

Her eyes glittered; her entire body vibrated with sensual intensity. I was appalled. True, the young man had wronged her; but this was blackmail, and, most exasperating, she had made me an accessory to her crime. I demanded, "Are you certain you are with child?"

"Edouard believes it," she replied blithely, "and now I shall have three paid years at the *conservatoire.*"

She truly savoured her triumph, for she had duped both her lover and me, the embodiment in her mind of the omniscient detective. She approached closer, whereupon I noted a musk perfume that had not been present at our previous meeting. Measuring me up and down with a Romany glance, she kissed my cheek. "Thank you, Dr. Doyle—I regret you can't stay a few more days."

She glided out the door. I turned around to see my wife, wrapped in her peignoir, staring at me with the eyes of a startled doe.

If Isabelle had collaborated with von Rintelen for German Intelligence, she would do so not only for money but also for the glorious opportunity to manipulate men.

Plumsoll by now had brewed coffee and settled on the floor, restlessly thumbing through the piles of journals and papers scattered there. I cautioned him not to disturb the various strata, for I had filed them in my own private order.

Sipping the coffee, I considered "bombard with X-rays." Prof. Rutherford was, after all, not the only authority on radiation. Dr. Niels Bohr worked in Denmark, and Mme. Curie was still active in France. Scientists, like theatre critics, have the lamentable habit of neglecting new concepts when they are not one's own.

And what relationship did "Buch" have with Dr. Einstein? The savant's name prodded me into recollection of an item in a recent newspaper, whereupon I immediately shuffled through the most up-to-date piles but found nothing.

"Oh, I say!" Plumsoll broke in. "Here's a Swiss paper in English! Didn't know they spoke it."

"May I suggest that you turn in for a good night's rest? I shan't disturb you—I require only a few hours of sleep." And I resumed my search.

Plumsoll gasped occasionally as he pored over the Swiss reports from the Western Front. "Why, this Zurich *Intelligencer* gives our planes the worst of it, when the *Times* said—"

I snatched the *Intelligencer* from his hand and found my item in the social notes: "Dr. Albert Einstein has arrived in our city for a visit of two weeks with Prof. Sanger. . . ."

The paper was dated 27 February, affording me less than a week to reach Zurich and find Dr. Einstein; well, I could depart immediately, and Plumsoll would carry on with the Matthews case. As I assembled my kit in the Gladstone, I was aware that Dr. Einstein, engaged in research for the Prussian Academy, might well be reluctant to divulge information; never-the-less I looked forward to an encounter with one of the most penetrating minds of our century.

CHAPTER THREE

Swift Reply from Enemy Intelligence

The gallery of the Ritz vibrated with the chit-chat of the colourful, the beautiful, the well-born, as if all Belgravia were assembling for a pre-war luncheon in a great country house. Despite food shortages so severe that arrangements had already been made for the Queen to open a communal food-kitchen in Westminster Bridge Rd., nothing had dimmed the glitter at the hotel. The women were gowned in the very newest "flapper" mode of high heels and skirts up to the knee, to meet brightly uniformed, bemedalled officers or arrange benefits for the Red Cross and entertainments for the wounded in hospitals. It was all quite necessary "war work," and provided an opportunity for society to dress and dine well without guilt.

I restlessly awaited Arachne, in order to secure his speediest facilities for my journey to Zurich, and he could see me only here and only at thirteen hundred; like the Romans, he conducted his councils of war as one interminable banquet.

Plumsoll had reported back to me smartly before noon. Through a boy in a baker's shop, he had tracked down the home of Dr. Joseph Williams, just one block from where we searched. The copy of the death-certification specified coronary arrest. All seemed to be in order: the certificate had been sent to the Register of Births and Deaths, and a notice sent to the sister as Informant. The body was already on the train to Devon, Plumsoll said, and the funeral had been arranged for two days hence.

I telephoned Sgt. Matthews; he had already been informed of the time and received permission to attend. I asked, quite casually, why he had not forbidden his wife to attend the African séance.

"Women these days are strong-willed, sir. It's the war."

Since I could not, in all conscience, raise even a suspicion that his wife's death might have been planned, I did not enquire whether she had any enemies.

Arachne was wheeled in promptly at thirteen hundred hours. He greeted me with his usual curtness, and I formed part of the procession to his table in the Palm Court, facing the fountain of the monstrous gold nude. Here he turned his attention to the menu: turtle soup, salmon in aspic, partridge with morels, a brandy mousse, all gentled by an excellent Loire wine and a claret. I had little stomach for all this and ordered duck and roast potatoes.

Arachne stated as his opinion that consulting Einstein was of little consequence; if the German's theories had any military application, he would certainly not be fool enough to reveal it to me. "By the way, how did you acquire German?"

"With an Austrian accent. A Jesuit academy in Feldkirch."

"You're a *Catholic?*" His right eyebrow rose ever so little, as if I were a Freemason.

50

"No, I couldn't swallow all of it, so I rejected it all. But I do affirm my belief in God and King."

He stressed that the mission was now entirely in my hands and he would back me with the full resources of his command. I would communicate directly to him from the Zurich consulate by wireless, in a private cipher.

"And your cover?" he asked.

"Simply myself, on the way to Davos for a bit of skiing."

He nodded half-heartedly and added, "I have arranged for Plumsoll to accompany you."

"Plumsoll? Why do I need him? The man's hard-working but he has the mind of a fox-hound—follows only one scent at a time."

"Still, he's a dear fellow with a pistol, and knows our procedures. Workin' alone in a foreign country leads to depression, the urge to act simply to get somethin' done. And it's much easier to sleep while the other stands guard, don't ye know? I must advise you, finally, that none of our allies can be requested to assist you in this venture."

His demand left me puzzled and affronted; did Plumsoll have an un-specified function of which I was being warned, or was he simply a body-guard or accountant?

"I do not want Plumsoll," I repeated.

"I must order you to accept him. He does speak German— was married to one. After all, what would excite less remark in Zurich, infested with spies of all civilised nations, than two English slackers on holiday?"

I drew in several deep breaths to settle my vexation. "Can he ski?"

"I doubt it." After which he concentrated on his partridge.

And so the mission was duly put in train for departure on Friday. I remained "A. C. Doyle" on the passport, which Arachne's organisation arranged together with our sportsgear and transport to Le Havre. Knowing of Dr. Einstein's interest in justice and political rights, I managed to despatch by diplomatic courier my book *The Case of Oscar Slater,* as an entry to conversation. I explained to my wife that I would be in Switzerland for a week or so, writing a propaganda piece.

Plumsoll's passport read "Dr. C. B. Plumsoll." "You hadn't told me what medical degree you attained," I remarked.

"Oh? It's DVM."

"Doctor of Veterinary Medicine?"

"Exactly," he replied, his lean face suffused with dignity.

Thursday, 8 March

Having boarded the Great Western at Waterloo for Exeter and Mrs. Matthews' funeral, I was startled a moment later to discover Plumsoll, in an Inverness cloak, seating himself beside me with a friendly but abstracted "Good morning." He had come, I supposed, to appease some feeling of culpability.

Scheduled time for the journey was four and a half to five and a half hours, but troop trains and truck convoys at crossings added another hour. At Exeter we were met by a veritable cloudburst; finding no transport available to the village church-yard, some twelve miles away, we fretted at the station, and after ten minutes I was all for hiking it, despite my lack of a waterproof. Fortunately, the station-master prevailed upon a reluctant farmer to convey us in his ancient two-wheeler. The collapsible top leaked at the seams, and it was difficult to determine which was the elder, the carriage or the horse.

They brought us to the village a half-hour late for the scheduled ceremony, and the sodden burial-plot, adjoining a Gothic church of the sixteenth century, lay deserted. We discovered the mourners sheltering themselves inside the church while they awaited the arrival of Sgt. Matthews. They numbered but a dozen, mainly farmers gnarled and toil-worn. Apart from this group, and examining the stone carvings of the altar, stood a tall, slender Negro, dark but with features almost Caucasian, accoutred in the latest Bond St. mode, a Burberry draped over his shoulders.

We paid our respects to the relatives grouped around the closed coffin. Cora Matthews' sister, Rebecca, a wan, pinched spinster of forty-five or so, wearily questioned us for details of the death, but Plumsoll and I had agreed it was best to say only that the fatal occasion had been a séance, not a display of African witch-craft.

Did she possess a photograph of her late father? I enquired.

"I carry it with me always." From her reticule she produced a brownish, faded studio portrait, two and a half by four inches, made some fifteen years before. The father's face was surrounded by luxuriant mutton-chop whiskers and displayed none of the coarse features Plumsoll had described.

He exclaimed, "Good heavens! That's—"

I nudged him into silence. "How tall was your father?"

"As tall as you are, sir."

If Plumsoll's five-foot-five estimate was accurate, the wraith was an utter fraud, and yet Mrs. Matthews had cried out "Father!" I could only posit that both she and Plumsoll had been overwhelmed by the Obeah's hypnotic powers. That the elaborate deception had been staged especially to involve Mrs. Matthews, I did not doubt; still the tormenting questions remained: Why, and for whose benefit?

The sergeant arrived, dripping water, in an open hired car, and the coffin was borne out to the grave, by now a pool of sloshing mud. The minister delivered his few words hurriedly, in a low voice overwhelmed by the beating rain. As the coffin descended into its final home, in the water and slime, I could not restrain an abysmal sadness; could this be all, the end of God's promise of redemption in a glorious, shining after-world? I experienced a wrenching stab of premonition, such as I had never sensed before: I would cause great destruction in a foreign land, and I would be put under ground but not be buried!

Walking away from the grave, I was cheered somewhat by the inscription on the stone of Felicity Pool, born 1742, died 1831.

> "There is a place of eterne rest,
> Far, far beyond the skies,
> Where beauty smiles eternally
> And pleasure never dies."

The black man introduced himself to Sgt. Matthews as Joseph Mombeya, secretary of the Society which had employed his wife. Expressing profound regrets, he told the bereaved husband that his wife had been a devoted worker, missed by all who knew her, and that no members of the Society had been involved in the "barbaric mumbo-jumbo" at the stable. The sergeant shook his head abruptly and stalked away without a word. Mombeya spoke in the Oxonian tones so dear to Arachne; he evidently came of a wealthy family, for very few coloured men reached that university on scholarship.

While we awaited the train at Exeter, I considered placing the new evidence of the father's photograph in the expert hands of my friend at Scotland Yard, Inspector Neil. Four years before, building on some facts I accumulated, he had neatly brought to justice the murderer in the notorious "Brides in the Bath" case.* He was prudent enough not to

---

* George Joseph Smith *alias* John Lloyd *alias* Henry Williams persuaded two consecutive wives to sign away legal rights to their capital and property, in the Kent coastal town of Herne Bay, and soon after he came upon them dead in the bath-tub. Smith was accused of doing in a third woman, but the jury felt two were sufficient to hang him. —R.S.

embarrass Sgt. Matthews, and I could not in all conscience abandon this mystery simply because I was unable to pursue it myself. I determined to turn the investigation over to Neil as soon as I reached London.

Joseph Mombeya returned on the same train, and made himself known as soon as we had settled into the compartment. He had heard me on a platform ten years before, he said, with E. D. Morel and Roger Casement, in the campaign that brought reform to the wretched rule of Belgium's King Leopold in the Congo State.*

As our train plunged across the withered countryside, Mombeya revealed what he termed a bizarre return to the old misery of the Congo. In the Katanga area, a Belgian-French copper-mining syndicate were now mining pitchblende—from which both radium and uranium are refined—at an astonishing rate with forced labour.

"Forced? Precisely how?" I asked.

"A new refining-process was installed early in 1913, in an area of several square miles, surrounded entirely by a barbed-wire stockade and armed guards. Families, as a condition of employment for a pitiable franc a week, must sign an agreement which they do not comprehend, and so an X-mark binds them to live and work within this stockade for two years. If they do not complete assigned duties, they are whipped!"

"Wretchedly unfair way to do business," Plumsoll muttered.

"Do these processes concern radium or uranium?"

* Conan Doyle's own investigation led him to write a dramatic exposé, *The Crime of the Congo* (1909), which focussed international attention on King Leopold's exploitation of what was virtually an immense private estate, operated for his own profit. Entire families were chained to their work in the mines or fields and confined in labour camps; if they did not fulfil work quotas, they were often beaten to death or their hands were cut off. The Belgian government soon took over Leopold's holdings and abolished forced labour. —R.S.

Mombeya shook his head regretfully. "My friends there do not comprehend the difference. The Germans call it *Spezialmetall.* The process concentrates the ore, reducing one ton to one-fourth its weight. It is crushed and ground fine, then mixed with water. This is agitated with paddles, causing the finer grains to drain off through filters. It is then treated with an acid—sulphuric, I believe—which burns the hands. At the same time, the ore is roasted—"

"Like coffee?" Plumsoll enquired.

I explained that the metallurgical term was "sintering."

"But the Germans did not have the means to build large ovens to create the intense heat they needed," Mombeya continued. "Africans, however, have been building small crucibles to make bronze for centuries. And so thousands of these pots, the size of large melons, have been set up in the stockades, and the ore moves slowly over the intense heat in round metal pans, centred on a metal post and revolved by cranking a handle. Twenty-four hours a day, thousands of pans are rotated above these furnaces by thousands of men, women and children. It is almost beautiful. As my people chant the old work-songs—their rhythm sets the timing for the rotation—the fire-pots project the shadows of the workers among the trees overhead, creating fantastic fire-flies and bird-like creatures whose shapes are continually changing. It could be an elaborate setting for the ballet at the Paris Opéra—unfortunately, the performers are whipped if their timing is not exact. Oh, Sir Arthur, I beg you!—help free us entirely from Belgian rule."

I was not prepared for this outburst, yet it was a supplication that in all justice could not be ignored. "At the moment I am engaged in an enterprise which may have a link to your plea. If it does, that refining will be stopped, by force if necessary. But I must know where the concentrated ore is being shipped."

"Down the Congo River to Boma, where it is loaded on to ocean freighters flying Swedish and other neutral flags. The port of destination I do not know. ...."

It would be Hamburg; German engineers, haste and secrecy signified the military importance of the ore, and they had been accumulating it since 1913. I now had little doubt that radium or uranium was the primary component in the terror weapon.

"Will you help us, Sir Arthur? You have friends in high places," Mombeya concluded.

"I have one who could conceivably help."

I had not the slightest inkling of how that chance meeting with the black man would burden my future.

Arachne pursed his lips, uncertain it was worth the pother: "Of course, we have a man or two down there. We and the French have some troops sloggin' away at the Jerries in the Cameroons. It bears lookin' into. ... Oh—*bon voyage!* And best of British luck." The last came in an after-thought, as if he had neglected to answer his doorman's "Good night, sir."

Friday, 9 March

Before first light, Plumsoll and I boarded a swift destroyer of the latest class at Newhaven, and some hours later we debarked at the quai in Le Havre. Arachne had booked us on the de-luxe express to Lausanne from Paris; a *rapide* from Le Havre to Paris made the connexion, according to *Bradshaw's,* but knowing the mercurial shifts in war-time schedules, I applied immediately for places on the first train out, and we were fortunate to find seats in second-class.

The ironies of war-time surrounded us as we waited. While women and ragamuffins hawked sheets of sentimental ballads, known as *"Fleurs de Guerre,"* by croaking the lyrics to the accompaniment of mandolins or accordions, our train was hitched to approximately half a mile of waggons, bearing the true flowers, the deadly night-shade, of combat: ammunition, lorries, British tanks. About a dozen *poilus* boarded for their return to the front, their musette bags bulging with *charcuterie,* sweets and wine; those arriving on leave carried in the same bags enemy helmets, parachutes to be sewn up as women's handkerchiefs, and large-calibre shells that would be transformed into vases for flowers.

The train lurched off an hour later at approximately eighteen miles per hour. The only other occupant of the compartment, seated opposite us, I took to be a Frenchman: in his fifties, with close-cropped full beard, his eyes under heavy beer-mug lenses fluttering about like tropical fish; the soft felt hat and worn but well-preserved black clothes indicated the civil servant or teacher. He immediately absorbed himself in the second volume of Macaulay's *History of England.*

"By Jove!" Plumsoll exclaimed suddenly, observing the town recede ever so slowly, "can we trust them to provide a restaurant-car?"

"Permit me, sirs," our companion said, in accented but precise English. "There is such a car, but, unhappily, because of our shortages, the food will be banal."

I avowed that most of English cooking had always been so. "As Heine put it, we have four hundred and fifty different religions but only one sauce. Do you object to smoking?"

"Never!" he replied, and drew out a half-smoked Gauloise from a packet in his coat. Plumsoll and I lit up, and I settled into a physics journal which analysed several of Dr. Einstein's speculations.

"Are you continuing to Paris?" the Frenchman asked.

Plumsoll nodded.

"I, too. Oh, it is a wretchedly cold, hungry city. . . . Permit me to introduce myself—Dr. Etienne Salcrou, professor of English history at the Sorbonne. It is a double pleasure to travel with you, to hear the true English spoken."

We introduced ourselves as friends with aged relatives in Paris whom we intended to take back to refuge in England. When Salcrou heard that Plumsoll had never visited this land, he elaborated upon the historical points of interest we passed at a crawl. . . . "Harfleur, taken by your Henry the Fifth; he contributed the foundation for that elegantly carved Gothic church. . . . Barentin—here we leave the fertile land of the Pays de Caux. . . ." As the train jerked to a halt at Rouen, he lectured, "Here, William the Conqueror fell off his horse and met his death. . . ."

"Ah, yes," Plumsoll sighed. "The greatest of men are brought down by the smallest miscalculation."

The conductor announced a stop of one hour here, which Plumsoll and I employed to advantage by visiting the magnificent cathedral, now serving as a hospital. "Plumsoll, I strongly doubt that the fellow is a professor of English history, or any sort of teacher. William died here, but fell off his horse at Mantes."

"Might it be a lapse of memory? We all have them occasionally."

"I applaud your sense of equity, but have you considered the middle fingers of Salcrou's hands? Teachers write a great deal, books or lectures, and the pen presses against that finger, creating a callus." I displayed mine. "Neither his right nor his left hand displays such callosity. More evidential is the way he marked the page when he closed Macaulay. Teachers, who live by the printed word, have respect for books: they do not turn down the edge of the page—that destroys a book. Caution, Plumsoll, caution."

"Harrumph! Of course!"

Upon our return to the compartment, I instantly observed that my Gladstone and Plumsoll's canvas carry-all had disappeared from their rack. The astonished professor had not seen any one move them and immediately offered to find the train-master in order to conduct a search. "It is the wartime," he sighed, deeply mortified by this insult to an ally.

As he hurried ahead of us in the corridor, I whispered to Plumsoll, "Search his bag," and followed Salcrou.

I had made certain to leave nothing in my Gladstone that might reveal our purpose or destination, but I was troubled by a possible oversight on Plumsoll's part.

A porter discovered our luggage in a corner of the baggage waggon, where, strangely enough, I had not seen it a few minutes before. I examined mine quickly and pronounced all in order; the professor and I returned to the compartment with Plumsoll's bag, and he found nothing amiss.

Salcrou joined us for a late lunch in the restaurant car, and the friendly history lecture continued all the way to Paris, where we arrived at St.-Lazare four and a half hours late. The Frenchman, presenting his card, urged us to visit him if we had an available moment.

"Any thing gone?" Plumsoll asked instantly.

"A letter from my brother, with his corps at Amiens. Purely personal. Salcrou or his confederate may have thought it would have value to military intelligence."

"The buggers!" He had found a note, penned in English, in our companion's shave-kit. It instructed Salcrou to watch for A. C. Doyle and Dr. Plumsoll and ascertain their final destination and purpose. The description of me was distressingly accurate: "six feet, broad chest, brown hair, grey eyes, bushy moustaches, face rugged and tanned, genial country gentleman."

We gazed at each other in shock and alarm: how could

enemy intelligence have zeroed in on us so swiftly? The leak had to spring from someone close to Arachne, perhaps an underling who'd arranged the passports or transport. My perturbation was not assuaged when our express chuffed out of the Gare de Lyon and I glimpsed, behind a copy of *Canard Enchaîné,* the felt hat and magnifying lenses of Salcrou. Lausanne would now be on the alert for us. If Arachne continued to operate so porously, we were doomed.

CHAPTER FOUR

The Phantom of Isabelle Andros

Our de-luxe train was neutral territory, where the demi-mondaine and espionage agent, the old-rich and the war-rich could meet on equal terms: all had paid the same fare. Rolling, often tottering, across the land, it resembled an Edwardian mansion whose fortunes had faded with those of all Europe. We were enveloped in rosewood marquetry, velvet arm-chairs and damask draperies; we ate from Limoges plates, and water was poured from crystal decanters, but the napery was flecked, dust hazed the windows and the few waiters barely maintained their balance. Still, despite war-time exigencies, the restaurant offered two soups and nine dishes; the *tournedos* of beef in wine sauce were indeed exquisite (I suspected an equine lineage), and not one harsh, shriveled *haricot vert* marred the plate, for the chef would have deemed this as much a betrayal of *La Patrie* as the surrender of Verdun.

The English lady ate with gusto; she was not particularly

handsome, yet the translucently clear skin and indestructible energy that are the legacy of Albion's aristocracy gave her a certain glow. She had dedicated her estate in Suffolk and her house in Paris for hospital use, she told her companion, "and now I do deserve some quiet at my chalet."

The gentleman with her, dark-bearded and virile, a Sikh major in white silk turban, with the dignity of a rajah, agreed that Paris was impossible. "I wore a fur coat, yet I was so frozen I abandoned Molière after the first act."

At another table, one of the vulpine profiteers, his up-turned moustaches forming parentheses around the exclamation point of the nose, explained to his *vis-à-vis,* who might have stepped off a Mucha poster, "The gowns are still made in Paris, the labels are changed in Zurich, and we sell them in Berlin—'Made in Vienna.' "

Nearby, an American diplomat's wife in the sheerest silk wore an aviator's cap and replicas of wound stripes on her sleeve, considered very chic in Paris. "—I have it on reliable authority that Krupp is building a gun to shoot from Calais to Dover!"

Other voices, from other tables, reverberated off the domed ceilings:

"At first the French spread straw in the churches for the wounded. Then they discovered it carried the tetanus! . . ."

"—to-night, my dear?" a gentleman asked.

"Why not?"

"—from Princess Blücher herself! The Germans found this handsome Russian officer in a trench, sitting up, smiling at a photograph of his lovely wife and two small children. He was stone dead."

While passengers boarded at Dijon, a troop train waited on an adjoining track; it consisted of waggons for "40 men— 8 horses," carrying troops north to the front, chalk-marked with *"A Berlin"* and rowdy epithets of bravado. Two soldiers, peering through the horizontal bars that barely provided ventilation for the beasts, hurled empty wine-bottles at the windows of our compartment. Only the bottles shattered.

Saturday, 10 March

Changing at Lausanne for the local to Zurich, we were closely observed by a man in a black great-coat and bowler hat, the beefy sort destined to become constable or patrolman in any European city; this one had advanced to plainclothes. Without further incident we arrived in Zurich before sunset, and as we registered at the Hotel Pelikan in the Pelikanstrasse I noticed the same bowler-hatted fellow, or his twin, peering in from a street window.

"A Swiss detective?" I asked the manager.

The surprise that flickered across his face was almost virginal. "Oh, no, sir. All that talk of our land as a battle-field of spies is malicious nonsense. Spread by *hôteliers* of the Côte d'Azur."

We established ourselves in a suite affording a pleasant outlook on the Botanic Garden and the snow-laden Alps in the far distance, and turned in for a good night's sleep on immobile beds.

Sunday, 11 March

The consulate being closed, our hotel operator put me through to the home of our Consul-General, Mr. Henry Angel, who promptly invited us to late breakfast.

A tense man in his forties, he weighed his words carefully and did his best to please, even though he had no hint of my purpose. (I would work with the consulate's Intelligence Officer.) My enquiry about the ubiquity of bowler-hatted men evoked a forbearing tilt of his head. "Most are Swiss detectives, some are Swiss informers, and some are simply foreign spies. The Swiss guard their neutrality with a two-year prison sentence for espionage—inevitably the police are over-worked." He located the address of Prof. Sanger through the telephone operator, and a motor-cab ferried us to his quarters, in a four-storey house much like the others near the Polytechnic School. I steeled myself, for if my mission was not to die on the vine, I would need to bend the prodigious intellect of Dr. Einstein to my purpose.

The plump maid-of-all-work took my card, and we waited in the tiny reception hall. It was a most ordinary flat of dark wooden wainscotting and duck's-egg wall-paper; through an open door down the hall came the pensive variations of the Bach *Chaconne* for violin.

The girl ushered us into Dr. Einstein's bed-room, where he was peering myopically at the music on the brass stand in such concentration that for several minutes he did not see us. I judged him to be approximately thirty-eight years of age; his face was ovoid and quite blank, with black moustaches that drooped at the ends, and eyes large and gentle as a spaniel's, over-shadowed by a large shock of black hair, salted grey. From the loose-fitting collar and folds of skin under his chin, I estimated that he had lost fifty or so pounds quite recently. Since only profiteers and German aristocrats, with game on their estates, were eating well, he must intensely have loved that country or his work at the Prussian Academy, in-as-much as he retained his Swiss citizenship and could live more abundantly here.

At length he looked up, somewhat annoyed by our interruption. I introduced myself and Plumsoll, as my secretary, in German and enquired whether he had received my book from England.

"No, I have not," he replied gently, "and since I have never heard of your work, Herr Doyle, I can not recommend you for any academic position. What is your field—mathematics?"

66

"I write mystery tales, using a scientific genius of a villain. Your theory of motion as energy opens up a new world for me; if the bonds of the atom could be broken—or my villain could bombard the earth with X-rays—why, he would have the world in his grasp!" I enthusiastically outlined the most outrageous possibilities ... "rays that propel vehicles to other planets! and—"

"Herr Doyle, please," he broke in. "I never read such stories—they will not let me sleep. You must excuse me." He took up his violin, and to my astonishment instantly, completely withdrew from that time and place; a vague, apologetic smile remained and the music slowed, as if he were weighing each note, yet his eyes, though wide open, revealed no lustre, like a blind man's. It was a form of meditative trance. He found tranquillity and insight for his scientific problems in music, much as I imagined my sleuth would; indeed, the works of Bach have a mathematical logic in their tonal progressions.

But then, a few seconds later, a chain of observations revealed that his was a problem of a very personal nature and I had interrupted at a most grievous time in his life.

On the dressing-table at my right lay a letter, dated two weeks before, from Zurich. I glimpsed, in my peripheral vision, MILÈVA AGREES TO THE BOYS' SCHOOLING, and below, the signature TOBY. Portable photographs of two boys rested on a shelf above; both resembled the scientist, but their faces were plump. One, signed WITH AFFECTION, EDUARD, was framed in thin, plain walnut; the other, inscribed simply HANS ALBERT, had been fitted into an oval, elaborately inlaid with mother-of-pearl designs common to the Near East, and topped by a brass Greek cross. Milèva, then, would be the wife, but her face was nowhere displayed. Her name was Balkan, possibly Serbian, and since her husband was of the Hebrew faith, she must have supplied the Greek-cross frame.

This suggested that she practised the Greek Orthodox religion and was probably nurturing Hans Albert in that faith, a further source of family strain.

These details, combined with two other assumptions (the boys' serene, round faces, indicating they were well fed, together with schooling arrangements, made not by the mother or father but by a friend, Toby, in Zurich), led me to conclude that the wife and children lived apart from the father. And the lack of friendly salutation from Hans Albert, in the mother-of-pearl frame, implied that he stood fast by his mother and might not even correspond with his father in Berlin.

Had Dr. Einstein come here for reconciliation? On the mantel-shelf I observed a small pile of women's jewellery, not new or expensive: two gold chains, a small ring, an amber brooch with a gold letter *M* set in its centre. Milèva had returned her husband's gifts, leaving me but one conclusion—divorce proceedings.*

And I, a stranger, was trapped in the midst of his emotional turmoil, attempting to pry loose answers for complex questions under a rather thin pretext. I did not dare come out into the open; given his obvious devotion to the work in Berlin, he could be engaged, as was Rutherford, in war research, possibly on this very weapon I sought. Since the two-week visit announced in the *Intelligencer* could end today or tomorrow, I needed to break through his withdrawal swiftly. The boy under the Greek cross would be the stimulus.

"Doctor Einstein!" I exclaimed sharply. "Doctor! I regret—"

As abruptly as he had withdrawn, he returned to us, murmuring, "Why do you interrupt . . . ?"

* Two years later Dr. Einstein married his cousin Elsa. —R.S.

I continued gently, "I sincerely regret that your son Hans Albert has stopped writing to you, but I, too, have sons, and know it is a phase that will pass."

He was appalled that I had fathomed his innermost hurt. "*Ach!* Are you a music-hall magician?" Suddenly he asked, "English, yes?"

"Quite so."

"English gentlemen play billiards?"

"I have some skill."

"Excellent." He rose and opened the door of a room down the hall. "Sanger!" he announced. "An Englishman is here to play billiards with you."

Prof. Sanger greeted me in a striped wool robe; over its quilted collar flowed a wonderfully full, square-cut beard off an Assyrian frieze which was trivialized by small, tortoise-shell spectacles; his head shone bald white, and an ample stomach protruded from under the robe.

"Here is Herr Doyle," Dr. Einstein said, and to me, "Now, please, leave me to myself."

He walked back to his music. Prof. Sanger stretched his arm over my shoulder and exclaimed in English, "How good of you to come! My German friends consider billiards frivolous, and the Swiss, despite their genius with tiny clocks, are clumsy with the cue-stick." He ushered me into what had been the dining-room, now furnished only with a professional table and lighting, worthy of Thurston's old room in the Strand.

Prof. Sanger gave me first turn, as guest, and I played for time, to evolve a method of re-engaging Einstein in conversation. I was an above-average billiards player who once reached the third round of an amateur championship by the luck of a bye and the alcoholic quivers of my first opponent, but my mind focussed on the outer room. I had once attended a séance in which strongly willed messages had been conveyed, and received, throughout an entire house; I concentrated my thoughts to call Dr. Einstein to this table—and broke a pitiable twenty-eight.*

My host soon made it clear why a professor of elementary mathematics at the Polytechnic had invested in such expensive equipment: it was his obsession. He broke ninety-six.

I did not relish losing in life or sport; even when I played against champions in cricket and football, I always believed I had a chance to be victorious. I put my eye and arm into it, and broke eighty-one; where upon Prof. Sanger, no longer obligated to be the gracious host, ran off one hundred eight.

I had scored five twenty-five to Prof. Sanger's five sixty-three when the door groaned and Dr. Einstein put his head into the room. He watched my forcing shot quizzically, then, unwilling to break my concentration, asked my opponent in a whisper, "What is so fascinating to push three balls around the table with a stick?" From his melancholy tone, I knew he could no longer bear to be secluded with his marital dilemma.

Prof. Sanger replied, "It demands both talent and skill. Much like the violin."

Dr. Einstein's eyes glimmered in curiosity, and he followed the red ball as I struck a white hazard off the right cushion. "It seems simple enough—the angle of reflection equals the angle of incidence."

"Approximately," Prof. Sanger stated. "The nap of the table and resistance of the cushion are variable."

"Of course," his friend retorted impatiently. "But it is

* English billiards was played on a six-hole table with three balls: one plain white, one white with a black spot, one red. The player's ball was the cue-ball; the other two were object balls. Points were scored by striking and holing combinations of these balls. A succession of scoring strokes was a "break." —R.S.

70

fundamentally a problem of one sphere in motion striking another at rest, and if the angles before and after this interaction can be calculated accurately, the path of the struck sphere must lead into one of the holes. Is that not correct?"

"But the striking force is so variable."

"Can't it be measured?"

"Yes," I replied. "By Joseph Bennett—on a scale of one through seven."

"Then I should be able to play this game," Dr. Einstein said quietly, rubbing his hands. "Since you two have the advantage of experience, you will allow me the advantage of exact measurement?"

Prof. Sanger and I glanced at each other in puzzlement. "Of course," our host replied.

"But you can not overcome experience," I insisted. So long as he played this game, I had an opportunity to put queries to him; I put out the bait. "Indeed, I'll wager an English pound that even with a week's practice, you would be unable to score up to Professor Sanger or me."

"I accept," he said instantly.

Prof. Sanger shook his head regretfully. "It is not a fair wager, Albert."

"If I do not try, I shall never know." He left the room and returned shortly with a pad and pencil, a slide-rule, a steel rule, and a protractor borrowed from his host which was a work of art, in polished box-wood and brass fittings.

"The influence of the table nap must be reduced so far as possible," Dr. Einstein said.

The maid was called to iron the felt, while I instructed the savant how to stand at the table and make a bridge for the cue. "If I can manipulate the violin bow, I can manipulate this," he said confidently. I informed him in brief of the rules and the scoring, which he absorbed instantly, and I demonstrated the techniques of "side," "screw," and "massé," and the degrees of force applied in Mr. Bennett's strokes.

"Aha! Now, we compute the path of the red struck by the white as a simple rolling motion. . . ."

Pad in hand, he swiftly set down a series of symbols. As I translated them, over his shoulder, they were:

Let velocity = V.
Velocity of rotation = V/a where a is the radius, with no obstruction to the rolling.
Origin is centre of ball at impact.
Axis of x, horizontal parallel common tangent.
Axis of y, normal to both balls.
Axis of z, vertical upwards.
Angle between direction of motion of striking ball and common normal = θ.
Co-efficient of friction between the balls = f.
Modulus of elasticity = $1-e$.
Mass of ball = 1.
P is normal impulsive force operating so long as balls touch.
Then frictional impulsive force will be

$$-f\text{P} \sin \theta /\ /x \text{ and } f\text{P} \cos \theta /\ /z$$

"We now proceed," Dr. Einstein continued, "to investigate the instant result of the impact. . . . Let the velocities of the striking ball, when impact is completed, be u_x, u_y, u_z, $\bar{w}_x$, $\bar{w}_y$, $\bar{w}_z$. Or, neglecting second powers of e, f and μ . . ."

At this point, I abandoned all hope of comprehension.

Dr. Einstein set the red ball on the top spot, made his calculations swiftly with the slide-rule, lined up the cue with his angles calculated on the protractor, and applied the

Dr. Einstein made his calculations swiftly and set the protractor for the angle of his cue.

correct Bennett stroke. The ball rolled to within two inches of the destined hole.

"I have over-looked another variable. Ah, yes!—the effect of the cushion." He revised his equations, making the reflexion of the ball a parabola instead of a straight line, and again the ball fell short. He persuaded the maid to brew coffee, and patiently refined his computations until he holed a red hazard for three.

"Good shot!" I exclaimed.

He beamed at Prof. Sanger. "You see, Maurice? I might have become an expert years ago if I hadn't been put off by your talk of the game's complexities."

My one-pound challenge expanded into one of the most sublime tournaments of my life. I was privileged to engage the Newton of our century in full-hearted play, turning lightning-swift calculations into billiard strokes and concentrating on the three balls as if they held the secrets of the universe. But he waved aside my enquiries concerning X-ray weapons.

"Play the game!" he exulted, as he broke nine.

Poor Plumsoll, who had no inclination to learn, fell asleep on the sofa in the sitting-room.

We drank demi-tasses of excellent coffee as the hours passed, and Dr. Einstein refused to stop. At length, Prof. Sanger firmly set his cue into the rack and announced, "Time to eat." A long-time widower, our host was his own chef (the maid having departed long ago), and whether because of faddism or simple apathy, the meal set forth on the kitchen table consisted in its entirety of meagre portions of hard-boiled eggs, cucumbers in a dill sauce, and boiled potatoes with sour cream.

Again I turned the conversation to my villain and Dr. Einstein's theories. Was there possibly a military application?

His impatience now was as palpable as the soggy cucumbers. "I don't know. They are mathematically logical, but practical applications do not interest me."

I pressed on. "Since X-rays burn the skin, is it possible for my villain to concentrate them with a lens, in order to penetrate armour plate?"

"I have no interest in warfare; Germany is starving; they have already lost the war."

I wondered at the distant "they." "Are you not concerned with the fate of Germany?"

"Of course. I am a German. But the militarists and the Kaiser are in control. I pursue my own studies and feel only pity and disgust for my country."

"Your studies are not involved in the war?" I asked.

"When I agreed to come to the Prussian Academy, my contract stipulated that I could work on any subject I chose. I am a pacifist—I choose to have nothing to do with war. But why do you raise questions of my work, Herr Doyle? Are you a writer—or an *agent provocateur?*"

"Good heavens!" Plumsoll exclaimed. "You can step into a book-shop anywhere in Zurich and see a copy of his work!"

Dr. Einstein roamed about the room, upbraiding us more in sorrow than bitterness. "Why should a writer bring his secretary when he calls on a stranger? Are you employed by the German police? Is he your witness? It does not matter—they know my opinions. Go now, Herr Doyle—or whatever your name may be." He stalked out of the room.

Prof. Sanger silently opened the front door, and we departed. This was cold porridge indeed. I had not imagined that the coercive Prussian war machine would permit such a creative intellect to wander on his own way in the midst of a war that threatened the Fatherland's very existence. And now I paid a heavy forfeit: after a seven-hundred-mile pilgrimage, I had alienated my most precious source of information.

We returned to the hotel on foot; I breathed deeply of the cold night air as I pondered my next move, for I could hardly return to London with nothing to show for this elaborate expedition. Out of the dark trees across the street, a great-coat and bowler hat emerged. We doubled back through a park, and eventually climbed into a motor-cab. As we walked through the hotel door, the hat and coat arrived outside.

Germany had scored twice tonight; Britain, zero.

Plumsoll's only suggestion for a proper counter-thrust was a superlative restaurant to alleviate the taste of Prof. Sanger's kitchen. Still hungry, we dressed for dinner and descended into the dining-room of the Grand Hôtel Bellevue-au-Lac. A gold-carpeted marble stairway, its gilt wrought-iron rail displaying the glowing-ray emblem of the Sun King, Louis XIV, curved down like an elongated S to a magnificent room modelled after the Hall of Mirrors at Versailles, though mercifully on a somewhat smaller scale.

The orchestra of a dozen or so, outfitted in costumes recalling the Grenadier Guards, could not still the chatter and laughter. Some of the dancing faces I recognised from our train, but most of these men in black tail-coats owned the mines that fed the locomotives as well as the mills that had rolled the track. Here swirled the princelings of the old regimes, silver-haired men with self-contained faces who wore authority as a birth-right; swarthy South Americans, holders of lands as large as duchies, waltzed among stolid Americans, proprietors of gold and silver lodes, and nobly moustached Russian nobility, shrunken in their pale-blue uniforms. The women were weighted down with necklaces, tiaras and stomachers, more than enough to outfit a Buckingham Palace reception. The immense candelabra cast a golden radiance over all, reflected from one mirrored wall into another to create a grand, glowing world dancing on and on into infinity.

To aerate my set-backs, I ordered a Dom Pérignon and a robust old Pomerol for a joint of genuine British beef, now, alas, seldom seen in London, and I encouraged Plumsoll to partake of an elaborate French concoction, a galantine of pheasant.

The dancers having seated themselves for serious dining and gossip, the orchestra modulated into a listless medley from "Chu-Chin-Chow." Gradually, the voices and the clatter of glasses faded as heads rotated towards the great stairway to observe an incredible procession.

First waddled a man of grotesque obesity, entirely overstuffed: a huge sack of grain, tied in at the appropriate places to form neck, wrists, thighs and ankles; convexities swelled under his eyes, a knob protruded from his nose and out of various slits in this huge bag, diamonds over-flowed.

But all eyes converged on the woman gliding a step behind. She was, as the French say, of a certain age, yet of such supreme beauty and glorious figure that the musicians lost tempo as they, too, turned to marvel. A long, black jewelled cigarette-holder preceded her like a trumpet, heralding a gown of black velvet, around which curled a peacock of metallic embroidery and jewels; the bird's head rested on her *décolletage,* its neck and body wound about her waist, and the tail of purple, red, green and blue stones formed the train. Her black hair, plaited like a wreath and crowned by a diadem, framed a proud oval face lit up by sparkling eyes the colour of her hair; only a slight smile acknowledged all this reception. Her neck and arms were studded with diamonds so that the entire effect, magnified by the mirrors, was that of a sun-goddess, emblazing dawn into day.

It was one of those singular occasions when I could not believe the evidence of my own eyes.

Plumsoll sucked in his breath. "Who—who is she?"

"She may well be Isabelle Andros." I summarised our Paris encounter as she was seated with her gargoyle at a table nearby. Our waiter identified them as M. Alexandre Helphand and Mme. Inessa Armand.

I.A.!

But which I.A.? Or could all three conceivably be the same?

5

CHAPTER FIVE

Ulyanov, the Messiah

"Preposterous co-incidence!" Plumsoll exclaimed.

"I never reject co-incidence. Life, birth itself, is a co-incidence of genes. The death of the Archduke Ferdinand was an accidental sequence—the assassin's bullet could have hit a half-inch off target. But this woman is unique. Let us put my hypothesis to a test." I could not suppress an ironic smile as I wrote a note on the back of my "A. C. Doyle" card: THE WRITER, WHOM YOU MET IN PARIS IN 1891, WONDERS WHETHER YOU COMPLETED THE THIRD YEAR AT THE CONSERVATOIRE.

Our waiter passed it to her and stood by for her answer. Her dark eyes flickered over me from across the room, and an eye-brow rose in a scornful "ridiculous," as she turned back to her companion.

Soon after, M. Helphand lumbered over to our table, and as my fork lifted the long-awaited beef to my lip, he clapped me on the back as if we were old school chums.

"What the devil!" I cried, just short of stabbing my cheek.

"Dr. Doyle!" he roared, in explosive bursts, like the back-fire of a motor-car. "Sure you remember me! *Helphand!* One of those Congo meetings! I contributed five hundred guineas!"

"You have made a mistake." I would certainly have remembered that gargantuan sack, and particularly the voice, a harsh, rasping dialectical stew, flavoured with Russian, French, German and a pinch of Scandinavian.

"The world makes mistakes—not Helphand! You are Conan Doyle, the writer, correct? Incredible stories, but I enjoy!" He pulled up a chair from an adjoining table and ordered the waiter to bring two magnums of Dom Pérignon.

"My dear friend," he continued, his arm, heavy as a ham, now resting on my back, "you are a realist, correct? Now your British Empire, it has brought much good to the world: law, honest civil service, sanitation—!" He laughed as if choking of apoplexy. "But the sun has set on your Empire! Tell your friends in Whitehall they must accept now a just peace—!"

Plumsoll broke in. "Would you be good enough to let us eat in peace?"

Helphand hammered away relentlessly. "Helphand also has friends, in the Wilhelmstrasse! The Germans pray for peace, not just for themselves—for you also! You must unite with the Germans against the greatest danger—from the East! Russia and China!"

"Sir, I have stood twice for Parliament and lost. Politics is now a matter of supreme apathy to me, one that borders on a coma."

Helphand howled in disbelief. "After you and the French and Germans destroy each other, the barbarians—*six hundred million!*—again will pour out of Asia to the gates of Vienna!"

"That's sheer nonsense," Plumsoll muttered.

"The Mongols turned back from Vienna only because Genghis Khan died!" Helphand roared. "This time the West will not be so lucky! Tell Balfour! Lloyd George! The King! You must have peace to unite—"

Mme. Armand undulated to our table and took his arm, tilting her head to us in apology. In the golden glow of the candelabrum overhead, I discerned a stunning resemblance to the girl who had duped me years ago in Paris.

"Forgive him," she said. "Champagne makes his head pop."

As she led him to his table, Helphand roared above the orchestra, above the dancing and laughter, *"Six hundred million Asiatics* will burn all this! The comedy is ended!"

He was not intoxicated; years of treating town and navy drunkards at Portsmouth had given me insight into this disease. Yet why should he appeal to me? And so publicly?

A grand alliance with Great Britain against the East was an old German dream. In certain British circles, rumours circulated of a secret meeting in 1911, in the Kaiser's hunting-lodge in the Black Forest, attended by his highest military and naval officers together with Winston Churchill, First Lord of the Admiralty, and Viscount Haldane, then Lord Chancellor. Presumably plans had been discussed to turn France into a neutralized Switzerland and thus jointly rule Europe, the East and Africa. Both Churchill and Haldane publicly laughed at this tale.

Only last July, after tremendous victories over Russia, Germany had lost four hundred thousand prisoners at Lutz. Perhaps the stratagem now was a separate peace with England, so that the Teutons could overwhelm Russia. But would the Wilhelmstrasse place any trust in so gross and flamboyant a figure as Helphand? Did he actually expect me to put such a proposal to Churchill and Haldane, whom I had never met?

I took another sip of champagne. Under the glass lay a corner torn from the menu, on which was written in a precise feminine script:

> *Boat at Alpen-Quai station*
> *1:30 tomorrow*

Monday, 12 March

That infernal bowler hat bobbed behind me as I strolled to the station. The hills in the distance now excited my interest, and I turned my back to the quai. Just as the stream-launch pulled out for its tour of the Zürichsee, I hurdled aboard, leaving my shadow behind.

Mme. Armand sat on a bench by a window, attired in a lively yellow wool suit, fetchingly completed by a hat of the fabric adorned with osprey plumes. She smoked her cigarette in a short black holder. In the sharp spring light pouring through the glass, I was even more certain she was Isabelle Andros.

"Forgive the subterfuge, Sir Arthur—Helphand need not know." She spoke softly, almost playfully, with the easy assurance of high beauty. I detected an un-necessarily derisive note in her "Sir Arthur."

"And what is your game today, Miss Andros?"

"Game? Oh, dear! Your meeting in Paris must have been most un-rewarding. I am Inessa Armand."

I did not recall the slightly rolled *r* from our first meeting. "Your accent and the Vionnet costume stamp you as a Parisienne. Are you still operating over there?"

Puzzlement wrinkled her nose. "I was *born* there."

Only four passengers, at the other end of the cabin, were viewing the lake on this cold day. I ordered a pot of coffee.

She turned to me with a smile, as faint as the first glimmer of sunrise. "You are seeking a German weapon, I hear."

82

From Helphand? Or was she actually von Rintelen's "I.A."? "Rubbish, madame—I'm on holiday, skiing in Davos tomorrow." I parried with, "What precisely *is* Helphand?"

She dismissed him as too clever by half. "Under the name of Parvus—that means 'little one'!—he was active in the Russian under-ground, and collaborated with Leon Trotsky in the 1905 uprising, so cleverly that both were sentenced to Siberia. Afterward he engaged in complex international deals with rifles and machine-guns in Constantinople, where he survived two attempts on his life: pistol and grenade. Through trading companies in neutral countries, he now enjoys a mansion in Copenhagen and a house on the Côte d'Azur—the Marxist Midas!"

"And the German Foreign Office is aware of this?"

"They deal with any one."

"Why should he choose to babble about peace to me?"

Her smile expanded into a light laugh. "He is involved on so many sides he will one day meet himself crossing from opposite borders."

"Then what is your rôle in all this?"

"Helphand is a vulgar bore. And impotent. But since he must display an attractive woman on his arm, this arrangement permits me to devote my entire time to work for the socialist revolution."

I could not restrain a surprised "Humph!" which shook my cup.

"More coffee, Sir Arthur?" She poured before I accepted.

"Socialist? Come now, madame!—or is it still Miss Andros? Beautiful women don't call for workers of the world to unite—they already have the world at their feet."

"I am flattered, but not amused by your chauvinistic sophism." Her tone changed swiftly to firm chiding. "The future of this century lies not in the West but the East. However, I never debate with Helphand—I merely accept his money. It is certainly more dignified than the way our great intellectual mis-leader of world revolution, Trotsky, lives—he earns one dollar a day playing small parts in American cowboy movies."

It was all very plausible and most un-likely. Why should that hedonistic French child be transformed into an apostle of violent revolt, financed by an obscenity? "Then you agree with Ovid?" I suggested, with a tinge of incredulity. " 'So long as he is rich, even a barbarian is attractive'?"

She sipped her coffee, then replied, "Correct!" in the encouraging manner of a school-mistress. " *'Dummodo sit dives barbarus ipse placet.' *"

An astonishing *riposte.* But surely Isabelle could not be capable of honours in Latin. Who, in fact, was this woman? "What is your business with me, madame?"

"There is one man in Zurich who has ears every where in Germany. It would be in your interest to speak with him."

"His name?"

"Ulyanov."

"Lenin? The Bolshevik exile?"

"The leader of the Russian masses." It was a statement of fact which brooked no contradiction, like the sphericality of the earth.

I had never encountered a self-anointed messiah. Possibly he wished to sell a morsel of information; exiles were notoriously poor, and my hand was ready to seize any thread that might lead through the maze to that weapon. This time I was prepared for the woman's wiles, whether she was Isabelle Andros or Inessa Armand or Medusa.

"When, madame?"

"Now. And you may call me Inessa."

"I prefer to call you I.A."

A motor-cab took us up the Spiegelgasse, a hill of run-down white-painted houses, and stopped in front of a café that labelled itself RESTAURANT JAKOBSBRUNNEN. A breeze from the top of the street wafted the odour of a slaughter-house or leather-tannery. I.A. led me to No. 14, the doorway beside the café, and up the squalid squeaking stair-case to the top-most storey, where she opened a door.

Three women crowded the tiny kitchen. A sad, bulky peasant stood at the stove boiling a small pot of thin soup. Behind a round table, covered by oil-cloth, sat an officious *Frau* who from her thin pursed lips and the bridling at our interruption I took to be the landlady of these rooms. The third, about thirty, could only have been a low-paid woman of the streets. My guide asked a question in Russian of the woman at the stove, who made an affirmative reply in a bronchial cough. I.A. led me down the hall, revealing over her shoulder that the cook was Ulyanov's wife, who had never learned how to cook; she then scratched twice on the second door.

It was opened a few inches for the occupant to examine me; he removed an old cap he'd been wearing to keep warm, then ushered us into the room with a mock bow. Lenin was a few years under fifty, his moderate height over-weighed by the powerful, baldish head of a Roman patrician, adorned with inconsequential moustaches and a spade-pointed goatee. Yet even in silence he displayed what the military term "command presence."

The small bedroom also served as his study and library—it was, in fact, the couple's only room, for they shared the kitchen. The manifestations of a most orderly person were obvious, though the room was stuffed full with two cheap beds, a chest, a pot-bellied iron stove, rush-seat chairs, a table—all cast-offs, but in good repair. Books were carefully arranged in packing-cases, piled one atop the other; the table-desk had been nailed together from the same rough-hewn wood. A political agitator, banished from country to country, carries no furniture.

Lenin dusted the table with an old hat-brush while he

simulated disinterest in me. He shifted several manuscripts and a pencil into place, exactly parallel to the table edge. I lit up my pipe. Then he spoke in Russian, translated by I.A.: "I can't stand the stink of smoking."

He waited until I had tamped out the embers. "May we speak German?" I asked.

After the translation, he weighed the dangers, then agreed. His aspirates were more guttural than mine, but we quickly adjusted to each other's intonations. Sticking his thumbs into the arm-holes of his waistcoat, frayed but neatly mended, he lectured like the pedants in Edinburgh, enumerating each point. His words, however, flowed out with overwhelming energy and conviction, his eyes glittering, his head back, chin high and goatee probing every sentence like a jemmy.

"First, I have received reports from my comrades in Germany of a new weapon, a cannon-shell or incendiary device, but I do not know if it is fully developed, or its place of manufacture. I—"

"Does this weapon require radium?" I interjected.

"Do not interrupt, please. I shall answer questions when I conclude." The light seeping through the room's single dusty window gave his face the sallow, un-worldly look of a monk.

"Second: the Prussians must be destroyed. Therefore, any enemy of my enemy is my friend. The Hohenzollerns and Hapsburgs will collapse, just as the Romanovs must inevitably fall, to make way for a truly democratic workers' and peasants' government. War is the mid-wife of revolution. The German people are desperate to end the slaughter. Sixteen-year-olds are being called up—women riot for bread in Berlin—miners are striking in the Ruhr. History moves in its inevitable course, yes!—but only for those who see it. At this cross-roads—now!—you and I must collaborate to destroy German militarism.

86

"Third: their secret service already know you are sniffing on the trail. Their fork is in every stew-pot; their agents are here, too. Has your chief explained the workings of the German police?"

"No . . ."

"He is either lazy or a fool. The Germans have the world's most effective police, divided into five branches. First, the regular police examine all who enter. Second, the *Geheim-polizei—Gepo—*the secret police, follow movements of strangers inside their country. Third, the secret service keep their eyes on political activities. Fourth, the military police, and fifth, the *secret* military police, spy on the other three branches. Thousands of civilian informers and *agents provocateurs* can accuse any one of treason or espionage, and those are put under 'protective arrest.' None of your bourgeois democracy's *habeas corpus—*you stay in gaol for a year or longer. You vanish from the face of the land."

Possibly Arachne assumed I knew all this, but certainly he might have hinted.

". . . you have written police tales, but I can assure you, you know nothing of the true secret-police mentality. I do. For many years I evaded the Russian *Okhrana—*one learns to fight rats in their burrows. But you?—you are a strong, fearless, fair-minded Englishman—you may enter Germany, but *you will never come out alive!* Therefore, here is my proposal. My comrades have formed a dedicated secret network under my instructions; many are collecting arms and know how to use them. They will guide and shelter you. In return for this aid, I must have:

"Twenty-five thousand pounds sterling, deposited to my account in Zurich. In advance.

"A transit visa, arranged by your government, for me and a few comrades, so that we can return immediately to Petersburg by way of France, England, Norway or Sweden. I have reports of riots and mutinies in Russia—the Romanov government is disintegrating. My party seek only land for the peasants and control of the factories by those who labour there. I will give your government mineral and oil concessions to guarantee its loans. . . ."

I wrenched my mind free from his hypnotic harangue. Here was one man, in one dreary room, convinced he could over-turn the government and change the economic structure of a polyglot empire numbering one hundred fifty million people, stretching over eight and a quarter million square miles, from Europe across Asia. His audacity beggared the imagination. Was he mad? Madmen can be most logical if one accepts their premise.

". . . a triple alliance," he concluded, "Britain, France and Russia, would rule over all Europe and the East, for we could then control the sleeping China." He sat down on the bed to accept questions.

Surely he was aware that our intelligence net-work in Germany had collapsed and our allies could not aid me. I asked, "How many of your people will work for me?"

"Enough."

"That's not sufficient. Furthermore, before I can even consider presenting your suggestions to my government, I must have a direct answer to one question."

"What is it?" He stood alertly before me, his thumbs once more jammed into his waistcoat.

"Once I am in Germany, your comrades will hold my life in their hands; I shall be a hostage, a guarantee that Britain fulfills its agreement. What is your guarantee?"

He pointed his thumb at Mme. Armand. "She will go with you."

I masked my astonishment with a shrug. "I already have a confederate."

"Your man is a fool. And she speaks better German than you." He spoke of her as though she were not in the room.

Lenin's words flowed out with overwhelming energy and conviction: "You may enter Germany but you will never come out alive!"

"This is not work for a woman," I insisted. "They do not have the male consistency of logic, being governed by emotions, and they can not endure the physical hardships."

He shook his head with a grim curl of his lip. "She has been in prison twice—escaped from Archangel, and that is like Siberia. She is my most trusted courier."

"The inconvenience of travel with her would out-weigh the advantages."

Her eyes glistened with anger and frustration, but she did not dare interrupt Lenin.

I continued, "I shall put your proposal to my superior in London, although in my own mind I am far from certain of its usefulness. But two sticking points must be resolved. I shall not enter Germany, under any circumstances, until I know the approximate hiding-place of the weapon or its factory."

Lenin nodded. "I shall make enquiries."

"Secondly, Mme. Armand is un-acceptable to me."

Lenin knitted his brow and exhaled a grunt of despair. "Can't you understand that my comrades in Germany risk death if they help you? They will not identify themselves or work for you without Inessa—they know and trust her: We meet at a rare, brief inter-section of immense historic forces that can change the face of the world. Why do you quibble over a woman?"

He bowed stiffly; the meeting was ended. I replied with a similar bow, and descended the stairs, I.A. behind me.

If Lenin indeed controlled a devoted, clandestine network, he could be of immense assistance. But tomorrow, he might discover the path of history taking a different turn, and I would be stranded—or sacrificed. The ascetic, professorial face indicated a man who enjoyed the give and take of argument, but when he turned those small Mongol eyes, dark and cunning, upon me, I realized there was no give.

His fanatic certainty of revolution, his learning and manipulation of logic, combined with the remorselessness of the Inquisition, made him more dangerous than a madman. And the woman was even more un-knowable; female hearts and minds are forever inscrutable to a man. Although the Bolshevik's scheme presented formidable dangers, I was forced to weigh its possibilities.

Outside No. 14, I.A. turned to face me. "You mis-trust me because you believe I am Isabelle Andros. What must I do to convince you other-wise?"

I indicated the café. "Take tea with me."

"I take brandy."

CHAPTER SIX

Return of the Bald Bolivian

The café, like the rooms above, was drab; the tile floor reeked of ammonia. The dismal sandwiches consisted of greyish bread with bits of herring, sardines, dry cheeses and wretched sausages, reminiscent of the saveloys on which I had subsisted during my first years of practice. And I.A. puffed cigarettes through it all, inter-mingled with glasses of brandy. I accepted only the tea.

She spoke openly and readily, with none of the kittenish sparring of our previous encounter. M. Armand was a textile magnate and land-owner whom she had met through her grandmother, an English tutor to his family in Moscow. Life with him had opened her eyes, she said, to the vicious exploitation of children in factories, the starvation and flogging of peasants, the total moral corruption of Armand and his class. She joined the Social Democratic Labour party, and was imprisoned for handing out leaflets to workers. "The questioning of the *Okhrana* was much worse than the sentence."

Un-able to endure her husband, she returned in 1910 to Paris, where she met Lenin. Because she spoke five languages, she translated his political articles and served him as special representative to meetings in other countries.

"And his wife?"

"She has other duties."

With her exceedingly quick and fertile mind, Isabelle could have acquired her facility in languages at a special training-school for espionage; we operated one, as did the French and Germans and probably the *Okhrana.* Still, her fluency in Latin puzzled me, because it was not the usual study for a woman, except in the fields of classical scholarship or the Church, and she most certainly had no vocation for nunhood.

"Did you seek me out at Lenin's behest?"

"Oh, dear! does it matter? You mustn't under-estimate him because he does not live in the style you bourgeoisie consider a proof of accomplishment. He has dedicated his life to his vision, like an anchorite. He studies all day at the library in the *Predigerkirche,* lives on oat-meal and stew, and he gives way to temptation only once a week—with his wife he shares a chocolate bar. He is a very difficult man, like all messiahs. He's fought with all the exiles at the Café Adler, and he has fought with me."

"Ah, now we reach the arcanum inside the mystery: why should I trust *you?"*

"It is not my fault that I have the same initials as your *bête noire,* Isabelle Andros. I've read many of your stories, and the women you depict are all images of the Victorian gentleman's sexual fears. . . ."

Isabelle Andros had also read my fiction.

"Men of your class can not conceive of women as human beings, equal in courage and intellectual power. There are only two kinds of women in your world: breeders of sons, to keep your property intact, or whores, whom you patronise because they are more fascinating than wives. Now—"

"I have never—"

"I am certain *you* have not. I have studied your history, just as you are enquiring into mine—my life is at risk, too. You felt a great affection for Jean Leckie—whether you are capable of genuine love, I do not know—but you never consummated that attachment while your invalid wife was alive. You waited *ten years!* until she died, then married Leckie. That respect is noble, but I can hardly admire it. . . ."

Physicians have long known that changes in the size of the pupil indicate hidden thoughts and emotional states; I.A.'s now indicated a high degree of pleasurable excitement as she luxuriated in her catalogue of the iniquitous man's world.

"You state it bluntly in your tales: women are grains of sand in the precisely adjusted gears and levers of a man's brain. Nonsense! I am your equal in every way for this mission. I do not possess your physical strength, but I have fortitude and determination and I know how to protect myself."

"The fundamental quandary remains—you are dedicated to Lenin and his Bolshevik revolution. Why should I have faith that you will be dedicated to my task?"

"Because they co-incide. I have donated my life as bond for you—"

"—if I am alive to claim it. In Germany, surrounded by your armed friends, you would have a few advantages over me."

"I, too, can be seized by the police in Germany. If it helps you feel less imperilled, you can carry a pistol—I shall take no weapons. You can carry the compass, the maps, and I will accept all your orders. . . . Can't you recognise that

Lenin needs you as much as you need him? He wants that visa most desperately. The old regime is disintegrating—mutiny in the army and navy—while he sits in Switzerland, two thousand miles away, a stateless person. He is now forty-seven, his faction is small but resolute, and he's the only man with the courage and fire to raise Russia out of the mud."

"And you are willing to sacrifice yourself for him?"

"Yes! He has given me hope for the future."

"It does not follow that such hope extends to my future."

"Don't be a bloody fool! You have no other realistic alternative. Your Austrian German is excellent but larded with Englishisms. All your stories are translated over there—your face is known!" Her voice, though low, had expanded in passion and bitterness. "You are an English sporting gentleman, a foot taller and twice heavier than I—were I a man, you would accept me. But because I'm a woman, you insist I *must* be treacherous!"

She rose from the table and laughed aloud. "It's in your eyes!" she exclaimed, as if she had read my previous thoughts. *"You fear me!"* Gathering up her cigarettes, she drained the brandy and strode away.

A remarkable woman: the five glasses of brandy had no visible deleterious effect on her. As I departed, I noted over my shoulder that Lenin was taking a call on the café's telephone.

In the motor-cab to our consulate I analysed the vexatious dilemma created by Lenin's proposal: if this woman were indeed Isabelle Andros, I could never trust her; if not Isabelle, the astonishing Inessa could be most useful to me, unless the Bolshevik Messiah had some self-serving plan not yet evident.

I despatched to Arachne in our private cipher the details

of Lenin's tender, together with my impressions of the man: magnetic leader, keenly analytical mind, great will and energy. His excessive neatness, everything in perfect order, indicated an autocratic bent. I also advised delaying the visa, since it could debilitate an ally, and requested immediate enquiries into the family and whereabouts of Isabelle Andros as well as Inessa Armand.

Cablegrams for the same information went out to William J. Burns, the fore-most American detective, who had visited me at Windlesham, and to an inspector of the French *Sûreté*, a source of secret information for one of my tales.

That evening, over dinner, Plumsoll enquired if I had made progress in our mission. Since in truth I had not, I kept my own counsel on Lenin and I.A. and replied in the negative.

"By Jove! I do wish you would take me into your confidence more, as a partner, a litmus-paper whom you may use to test your ideas."

"You can be most helpful on a certain matter," I replied, and made out a list of supplies I required—electric-light bulbs, sockets, wire, *et cetera*—to be purchased next morning.

Tuesday, 13 March

Plumsoll, dressed in my coat and hat, created an approximation of my moustaches with a bit of shoe-blacking and went out on his shopping-errand into the dark, rainy morning. The bowler hat hesitated a moment, but trailed after him.

I donned Plumsoll's checked coat and set out on a reconnaissance of the city, first stopping at the consulate. Arachne had replied, L'S PARTY WELL-ORGANISED IN G. MUST CONSULT PM ON QUID PRO QUO. I HAVE NO OBJECTION TO L'S ASSISTANCE. TO FIND WEAPON, WOULD DO DEAL WITH KAISER.

Upon my return to the hotel that afternoon, Plumsoll had

accumulated every item faithfully, all wrapped in a neat parcel. Again he asked if he could be of further assistance, and I urged him to keep watch over our rooms; the room-maid had been pawing through our belongings.

As I made my way out through the lobby with the parcel, a swarthy man in an Astrakhan coat and hat arose from a wing-chair to accost me.

"Good afternoon. You are Sir Arthur Conan Doyle?" he asked in excellent English, over-laid with a very un-Castilian Spanish lilt.

I replied, "Good afternoon," and moved aside to resume course. My stay here could certainly not have been better advertised had I inserted a notice in the *Intelligencer*.

He slipped directly in front of me in small, graceful steps, to proffer his card. He was a few inches shorter than I, and even though the open coat added bulk, his body displayed the massiveness of a mountain-bear. The hand holding the card, however, had particular interest for me: Sandow, the strongman, had developed extraordinary power in his hands by squeezing and releasing a heavy U-shaped steel spring, and the card of Gen. Miguel Cordova was held by a hand as spectacular as Sandow's.

"Would you give me the pleasure of a few moments of your time?" he asked in a surprisingly gentle voice. "It is a matter of mutual importance and honour." He gestured to a chair beside him.

I preferred to stand, and retorted with some sharpness, "What importance? Whose honour?"

He draped his coat over the chair, a movement which sprayed the air with a sweetish perfume akin to rose-water. He began with an ingratiating grin. "Mr. William Somerset Maugham, the writer, and I were engaged in some ticklish work for your government here, two years ago."

"Maugham? What do you mean by 'ticklish'?"

The bland smile turned into an incredulous frown. "Come, come, sir, he was an agent of your secret service."

Having met Maugham at a literary tea, I was now in turn the disbeliever: would that stammering, fragile aesthete collaborate with this *bravo?* "You're greatly mistaken, general."

"Oh, no, sir. He operated out of Geneva, starting in 1915. He even wrote a play as cover; left the pages lying out on his desk so the maids would see them—"

"Play indeed! What was the title?"

"The Unattainable."

I had seen it in London the previous year; not my dish, but my wife was amused. What an extraordinarily compartmented soul Maugham had, to write a successful drawing-room comedy while working as a full-time spy.

"He was a man of peculiar humour," the general went on. "In the interest of harmony I permitted him to address me as the Hairless Mexican. I am neither hairless nor Mexican. I am a Bolivian, and although I am bald"—he lifted his hat—"I am not hairless." He opened his tie and three buttons of his shirt to reveal a mass of hair which could indeed have adorned a bear.

"Quite right," I said. "Could we come to the point of honour?"

"I am a sensitive man, and so 'Hairless Mexican' caused me great personal anguish, coming as it did from a man whose own face resembled, if you will forgive me, the rear of a hen before it lays an egg."

"General, I must tell you I have an engagement—"

"Si! I now come to the purpose of my call. Mr. Maugham and I journeyed to Naples, where he had been ordered to pay me one thousand American dollars on completion of the work for your government. He refused to pay."

"Did he say why?"

"He claimed I eliminated the wrong man!" *

"Good heavens! I can't remedy that!"

"But this involves the honour of the British government!—they owe me one thousand American dollars."

"Why don't you take this up with whoever it was hired you?"

"He is deceased."

"General, I can do nothing. I am not a government agent."

"Come, come, *señor*. Zurich is small—we all know who is who. I ask you to lay the facts before your superior. The Greek agent I discarded had been identified *incorrectly* by British Intelligence. It was *their* fault, not mine. My work was impeccable. In our profession, a man's honour is his only capital. Now, because of your government's error, I can no longer find work in the espionage community. I do not ask one cent of balm for the humiliation Maugham has caused me. I ask you only to procure what is due me—one thousand dollars. Preferably in a day or two."

I emphasised that I was here on a ski-holiday, leaving tomorrow, and I could not be involved in this matter.

"*Señor*, if you will reflect for one moment, you will realise why you should help me."

As a for-hire assassin, he would work for any one, in particular the Germans.

"Do not make the same error twice," I warned. "I am quite able to protect myself. But in the interest of justice, I shall contact my government today."

He inclined his head gracefully. "I accept your word. I shall be here tomorrow at the same time."

---

* In Maugham's account of these years, published as *Ashenden, or The British Agent*, in 1927, "The Hairless Mexican" is one of the episodes. —R.S.

"That will not be necessary. I have your card—I shall telephone you."

I took up my parcel and walked to the hotel door. He followed me. *"Señor,"* he said, tapping gently on my shoulder, "there is a fellow outside keeping a crude eye on you. I know him—passes for Swiss but actually a German *Hanswurst* named Schrank. Permit me to remove him."

"Gracefully," I cautioned.

"Of course."

We walked out together; the general approached my bowler-hatted shadow and growled in German, "You idiot! You've got the wrong man!"

In the ensuing confusion, I leaped into the only waiting motor-cab and sped away, pondering how I could possibly procure one thousand dollars in a few days; the mills of wartime bureaucracy ground with Asiatic torpor, if at all. I stopped first at the consulate, where the duty-officer handed me three cablegrams.

One, from William J. Burns, reported no knowledge of either Isabelle or Inessa in America, and enquired if I cared to collaborate on a case involving a snake-love cult in Mississippi. The inspector from the *Sûreté* responded that Inessa Armand's birth-certificate showed she was a French citizen, born in Paris, 1874. (This would make her seventeen when I visited in 1891—and that was approximately Isabelle Andros' age. At the present time, either woman could be forty-three.) The report stated that Mme. Armand had come from a vaudeville family, married a Russian and run off later with his brother. But, the inspector warned me, these records meant little, for they could be altered by forgers to derive passports for determined travellers, such as criminals and professional revolutionaries. In short, Isabelle Andros' name could have been erased to create Inessa Armand.

The third cable was signed by Inspector Neil: NO VIABLE

CLUES MATTHEWS CASE. INVESTIGATION CONTINUES. Neil would hang on, by his teeth if need be.

I wirelessed Arachne: MIGUEL CORDOVA, CLAIMING SECRET WORK FOR MAUGHAM, ASSERTS DID NOT RECEIVE 1000 U.S. DOLLARS FOR DISPOSAL JOB.

Wednesday, 14 March

I dressed before Plumsoll arose and took breakfast on the terrace adjoining the hotel for an early start on my exploration of the city. The Bald Bolivian had evidently been very persuasive, for my shadow, Schrank, did not so much as glance at me; perhaps he was now concentrating on Plumsoll.

By mid-afternoon, I made my way back to the consulate, and Arachne had replied with his usual alacrity: VOUCHER SHOWS M PAID VILLAIN TOTAL MONEY. WHY YOU INVOLVED? WHAT PROGRESS L?

My reply: WILL CLARIFY SOON. But I had not the slightest intention of paying the Bolivian one dollar when we were being taxed for the war at the cost of £5 million per day.

Returning to the hotel, I enquired of Plumsoll: "Have you noticed a bulky Bolivian in an Astrakhan coat in the lobby?"

"No. But a fellow answering that description pounded on our door two hours ago. Claimed he had an appointment with you. He appears to be capable of indiscriminate mayhem."

"You've hit it exactly, old man. If he appears again, tell him 'the money has been authorised.' Nothing more."

"Right. A dangerous game, eh?"

"I'll be out late again. Good day."

Within a few minutes after I strolled out on to the Pelikanstrasse, I became aware that Plumsoll was following me. I had never fathomed why Arachne had foisted him on me;

102

possibly he had been ordered to keep close watch; never-the-less, it was unsettling to discover that he could not be depended upon to obey instructions. I determined to test his competence at hare and hound.

Turning left on the Bahnhofstrasse, then into the station, I wandered through the throngs on the platforms, doubled back on a bridge and saw, some distance behind Plumsoll, the bowler hat of our indefatigable Schrank. I slipped out a baggage-room to the rear of the station and into the National Museum, circling the rather limited exhibits of Swiss culture. One of the large cabinets, displaying Alpine peasant dress, had been left ajar; I squeezed down behind a six-teenth-century costume. To no avail: Plumsoll was waiting for me at the exit door.

After crossing the Wlache bridge into the centre of town, I picked up the pace. Swiss city streets have no regular pattern, such as New York or Paris or much of London, an idiosyncrasy that makes Zurich ideal for hiding-places. I weaved in and out of alleys, abandoned a café through the kitchen door, hopped on and off tramways, climbed a rear fire-escape ladder, popped into a dust-bin. Plumsoll stuck to me like a limpet, but we had lost Schrank.

In a dank hallway I climbed silently to the second landing, braced myself in the darkest corner, and waited. Plumsoll entered warily and crawled the stairs laboriously. When we met face to face, I could not restrain a "Boo!"

Possibly I should have eluded him, as my private investigator might have done, by slipping into a woman's hat shop and exiting dressed as a lady's maid, laden with parcels. But by now I recognised that I was on the wrong side of town for hats, and much too bulky for that rôle. I contented myself with the reality that Plumsoll, though a decade younger, was gasping like a man with a bone in his throat.

103

"I must compliment you on your doggedness and ability," I said in the darkness, "but you have disobeyed my express instructions. It must not happen again."

Somewhat abashed, he replied, "You have my word on that. My talents have lain disused so long, I wished to exercise them a bit. But I do hope you will include me in your calculations as to your expedition. I may not be a flash of inspirational lightning, but I do carry a steady torch."

"I've led you here in a sporting chase, not only to relieve the tenseness that has gripped both of us in the past days, but also to reveal my method of ascertaining the latest twist of events." So saying, I opened the door of the tiny front room I had rented in No. 12 Spiegelgasse. Here I had suspended a shaded electric bulb from the ceiling to light a wood table, on which rested a wireless head-set; this was connected, by wires running out my window, to the house telephone-line, attached on the wall outside. The same line also served the café where Lenin put and received his calls. To demonstrate how I had been eaves-dropping these past days and evenings, I lifted the head-set. *A convulsive electric shock surged through my body!*

Dropping the head-set instantly, I took a moment to recover, then rushed to the window; a live electric wire, tapped into the city's street-lighting system, had been clipped to my telephone connexion. This tap bore the familiar trademark of A.E.G., the giant German electrical combine. Retracing my own line back to the head-set, I found that the connexion into the insulated ear-phones had been by-passed by two tiny black wires, which connected instead with the steel head-spring. Had I picked up the head-set by the metal spring instead of by the Bakelite ear-phones, I would have been electrocuted.

Departure from this earth had beckoned to me twice before: once by way of the enteric in South Africa; again when

104

my motor-car over-turned, pressing its ton of weight on my neck and shoulder. Now it was borne in upon me that the enemy would employ the most intricate means to remove me.

I detached the death-dealing wire and, finding no other snares, adjusted the ear-phones so that I could listen to one and Plumsoll the other. The café's line was occupied by dialogues in German and French among amiable women and male visitors to the city. Plumsoll whispered that he was fortunate to have learned German from a former wife. "I must say, the women do sound ... voluptuous," he added.

My purpose, I explained, was to hear and judge Lenin's unguarded views; this required identifying the Bolshevik, his objectives and fellow conspirators to Plumsoll.

"But that I.A. woman? I've had experience with more than one wife, Doyle, and few of them can be relied upon beyond the kitchen door."

"Our very civilisation is threatened, Plumsoll. We must be prepared to take bold steps, even into the drawing-room."

We heard Russian voices, then Lenin demanding in German, "No! No! Parvus, speak German. I have two comrades from the Berlin committee here—they want first the news from Russia, then Zimmermann."

"Germany's Foreign Secretary," I whispered to Plumsoll.

Parvus, telephoning from a café in Bern so that he would not be over-heard, revealed in bursts of shouting and curses that the news from Russia was, as always, confusion. His sources, his own trading company's office in Copenhagen and "friends" in the German Foreign Office, were convinced that with the military in full revolt, the Tsar must abdicate shortly. "Kerensky's Mensheviks, SR's, anarchists, Kadets, are cracking each other's skulls instead of the old regime." Kerensky, the "right-wing faker," would probably become the compromise head of government, and he would carry on

with the war. Kamenev and Stalin, "those b-----d opportu-
nists" who had control of the Bolshevik party, were seeking
to find places in that government, and "the coward Trotsky"
was already on his way to Russia from America.

Lenin exploded into violent Russian epithets. "The visa! I
must have a transit visa! I expect one from England—"

"—England be damned! German U-boats will sink you in
the Channel. Listen to me—*Zimmermann has accepted my plan!*"
For the benefit of his German comrades, Parvus explained
his influence with the Foreign Ministry: his trading companies in Denmark and Sweden had been trafficking in
potatoes, grains and caviar from Russia to Germany; in
exchange, he sold German pharmaceuticals, scalpels, electric
lights, machinery to Russia. It was beneficial to both sides.
Now the General Staff realised it could win only by disen-
gaging the Russian bear from its back, so that Hindenburg
could transfer several hundred thousand troops from the
East to overwhelm the Allies, and Parvus claimed he had
convinced Zimmermann that the only man capable of creating a revolution was Lenin!

A chorus of "Correct!" from the comrades.

Nudging my ribs, Plumsoll murmured, "Outrageous
brass!"

"But the visa!" Lenin complained. "I must break out of
this Swiss prison."

Parvus roared happily, "My friend Arthur is planning to
send you by train! With visas! All costs paid! You, your
wife, Zinoviev, Radek, all your people. This was confirmed
to me fifteen minutes ago by Baron Romberg, the German
ambassador."

Silence from Lenin, then: "A *German* train? *Across Germany?*
We'll be branded traitors!"

"Three days and you'll be in Petrograd. So fast nobody
will know! Anyhow, you can swear the Swiss government
ordered it, to get rid of you trouble-makers!"

On the ear-phones we heard a German offer to Lenin—twenty million gold marks.

"This is a very dangerous move," Lenin grumbled.

"Listen to *me*. Zimmermann says he can persuade the General Staff and Hindenburg to grant as much as *twenty million gold marks* to help you grab control of the government, if you'll take our country the h--l out of the war! Do you lap that up?"

"What a slimy nest of vipers!" Plumsoll exclaimed.

"Twenty million?" Lenin echoed in utter disbelief.*

"*Five* million to start! We've already got about a million in the Petersburg branch of the Bank of Moscow, because we always sold more goods to the Germans and kept the balance in rubles! And *I*—Parvus—did all this while your fatheads and theologians were sitting on their a---s in Adler's café, arguing how many peasants can work on the head of a pin!"

"Ah, my dear friend Parvus, you are a true genius!" Lenin exclaimed with his mordant laugh. "You will be my Foreign Minister *and* Finance Minister—if we ever see one of those millions."

This was followed by silence at Lenin's end. Parvus demanded irritably, "What in h--l are you saying?"

"Our German comrades think Zimmermann is p-----g on you!"

Parvus denounced them with foul abuse. At length, Lenin said, firmly and calmly, "This is all talk. As soon as the visas—I will send a list of comrades—and the train and the marks are in hand, I will accept. Furthermore, dear genius,

---

* The magnitude of the funds supplied to Lenin was revealed when the Foreign Office's secret files were opened after World War II. More than 26,000,000 marks had been spent by 31 January 1918. Of this 11,500,000 was paid out to the Bolsheviks in Russia before Lenin even seized control, on 7 November 1917. This was the equivalent of £600,000, or more than $2,000,000, but in terms of today's purchasing power, those sums should be multiplied by ten. —R.S.

where is the factory for that secret weapon? Your company ships the ore, and you don't know where is the factory?"

"I only know the ore is off-loaded in Hamburg."

"If you continue to ship, Germany may win the war before I get to Petersburg!"

If he stopped shipping, Parvus countered, alternating each word with a curse, he would lose his acceptance at the Foreign Ministry. Lenin replied in kind, and rang off.

I set the ear-phones on the table. "Well, Plumsoll, what a breath-taking plot! One must admire the sweep and grandeur of it. The capitalists, whom Lenin despises, the enemies of his homeland who have captured or killed a million of his compatriots, now offer to finance the achievement of his life's dream. To this obscure agitator, a failure at forty-seven who has never governed any one except his wife, Germany says, 'You need only to betray your government and the memory of your own dead and you can be the new Tsar of all the Russians! All we desire is peace in the East, so that we can destroy those imperialists in the West.' Now, what opportunities for us does your good steady torch reveal in this black intrigue?"

"Opportunities? Why, any one who collaborates with these monsters would be, with all due respect to you, totally mad."

"Parvus, who hatched this diabolical conspiracy, is not mad; neither is Lenin, and neither am I. But the political conspirator, like the master criminal, is so blinded by the brilliance of his complex scheme that he always over-looks the one detail required to make it succeed. Zimmermann's plan has not yet been approved by the General Staff or Hindenburg, granting us a bit of time to un-cover that one detail. Consider: what does Lenin desire most of all?"

"Position. Power in Russia."

"Shrewdly put, but it requires much more illumination. I

109

have spent a few hours in a book-shop here, hacking my way through one of Lenin's diatribes. He insists revolution can not occur in Russia alone—it must be world-wide. His concepts must dominate the planet. *That* is his obsession."

"All the more reason to drop him—"

"No, no. All the more reason to *use* him. You recall he enquired of his chief benefactor, Parvus, where the weapons factory is located. I'm quite certain Parvus does not know. But if there is such a weapon, Lenin *craves* it for his world revolution."

Plumsoll tapped his chin for a few moments. "Well, that would explain why he wants to send his clever witch with you."

"Exactly. An extraordinary woman—*sui generis*. I venture to say she is as consummate an intriguer as Parvus or Lenin, and she may have the better brain. She will undoubtedly attempt to steal the secret of the weapon."

"That's as may be. The opposite could also be true—she may not want it at all."

"I welcome an opposite view; like a mirror, it may reveal an aspect one has not seen before. What is her motive, then?"

Plumsoll accented each word with his left fore-finger, pointing directly at his temple. "If Parvus is Lenin's double-agent in Germany, could not I.A. be the German agent planted among the Bolsheviks? The Jerries are certainly the equal of the Russkies in double-dealing."

"If she worked for the Germans, they would not undertake the trouble and danger of electrocuting me here—they could simply nab me as soon as I crossed the border. Your point about equality in conspiracy is well put. We must assume the Germans know Lenin will attempt to radicalize them, just as Lenin knows I would extend a hearty slap to keep him from reaching Petrograd. Each side understands the other perfectly, and that makes for a comfortable feeling all around. Now, I must warn Arachne of Zimmermann's game—"

"But Dr. Doyle," Plumsoll interjected. "You've overlooked an important detail."

"What might that be?"

"If I.A. accompanies you to Germany, what shall I do?"

"That, I'm afraid, is in Arachne's hands. But you have been most helpful to-night. As the result of your steady torch, all my problems have been narrowed down to two simple questions: where is the weapons factory? and who is I.A.?"

Thursday, 15 March

At dawn Prof. Sanger's breathless maid rapped at the door to present a note from Dr. Einstein: COME AT ONCE. She added, "He must go back to Berlin."

CHAPTER SEVEN

The Master Forger of Bern

The motor-cabs had not yet lined up at our hotel-stand. I boarded a No. 6 tram of the Marionstrasse line, which dawdled in an exasperating crawl to the Central Station and then to the Polytechnic.

Dr. Einstein, waiting in a trembling Hispano-Suiza cab, beckoned me to accompany him to the railway station. He was in the grip of a tormented anxiety that obviously had overcome his sleep that night, and his first words were, "Please, let me see your shoe."

Taken aback, I repeated, "Shoe?"

"Yes, yes! Take it off, *bitte*."

I removed the brogue, and he peered inside, searching for the maker's name. "Ah, yes. . . . And now, may I see your glove, please?" Puzzled, I handed one to him while I re-tied the shoe. He nodded. "Rainproof. Thresher's, 152 Strand," and returned it. "Forgive me, Sir Arthur. There is no leather for civilians in Germany, and I needed to make certain you are British."

"I am flattered you accepted my German."

"It is the phrasing of an Austrian who has lived in England. I thought you could be a police spy. Forgive also—I did not recognise your name. Sanger's son knows of your work. Now then"—and he took a tight hold of my arm—"you must help me!—we are on the edge of disaster!"

In the most serene voice I could summon up, I suggested, "Tell me what you wish, and I shall do my best."

He hurried on. "A colleague on holiday here has told me General Ludendorff's personal project is a new weapon which creates havoc from the explosion of radium or uranium. It may be a conventional weapon, with radium added to create terrible burns—horrendous idea! But the worst is this: *the weapon has never been tested!* At this time, the break-up, the splitting, of atoms is not even theoretically possible; they are the building-blocks of all matter. God does not play games with the universe—all is arranged in proper order—but we can not penetrate all His laws. There have been cataclysmic accidents over millions of years: one sun moves close to another, and some of its mass is hurled into space—this is probably how our own planet was formed. If this monstrous device should accidentally explode enough atoms, it *could destroy the earth!*"

"How large might this damnable thing be?"

"Who can tell? The magnitude of a cannon or a railway-carriage."

"How can I help you?"

"We must take direct action. I shall draw up a petition among our scientists to end work on this devilish device. And you must do the same in Britain. Together, we can stop this madness!"

I forced myself to conceal the shock evoked by this naïveté. Direct action? A petition urging citizens to desist from

114

supporting their country's survival in war-time would not only be treason, it would be approximately as effective as baying at the moon.

I proposed that the doctor participate in a more concrete and beneficial action by helping me find this weapons plant and unravelling its technical complexities. Since Britain was on an equal level of science and manufacturing with Germany, it could build the weapon, or its counter-measure, if its principles were disclosed quickly. And thus we would achieve an equality of destructive capability—an equilibrium of terror—which would prevent either nation from using the weapon.

"Terror by its nature is uncontrollable!" he exclaimed. "No! No! No!" He took the absolute pacifist's position: he would not assist any country, Britain or Germany, to build such a weapon.

Dr. Einstein urged the driver on; he could not miss his train for the German connexion at Schaffhausen.

And so, in the few minutes remaining, I locked with him in intellectual combat to win his mind and heart. I shall not go into the twists and turns of the argumentation; it was not entirely one-sided. Dr. Einstein spoke in terms of absolutes, the sublime logic of mathematics made somewhat pliable by his kindness of heart and intuitive perceptions, which, as in his grand theory of relativity, had not been proved or disproved. My thinking was essentially more pragmatic, for I had spent years in public debate, propounding causes close to my heart. And in the government of nations, which is the art of the possible, there can be no absolutes, no total black or white—only shades of grey.

Such a weapon, I argued, if developed first in Britain, could demonstrate its invincibility without loss of life by demolishing a deserted island, and thus convince the German people they must rid themselves of the Hohenzollerns, creating an opportunity for liberal democracy and peace in Europe.

Dr. Einstein countered with his conviction that the weapon would be no deterrent to future wars; each explosion could be made more devastating, eventually wiping out all mankind.

I then asked, "Can we not agree it is most sane to prevent hundreds of thousands of deaths by simply sabotaging the explosion of this one weapon now in existence?"

The professor finally yielded. But how could this be accomplished? The weapon would certainly be closely guarded, and he would not be a party to even one person's death.

I replied, "As you have said before, if you do not try, you shall never know."

He nodded ruefully, rubbing his cheek restlessly with his hand. Unfortunately, he did not know the site of the factory or the men engaged in research on the weapon, for he had shunned those who collaborated with the war.

The cab was now in sight of the station. "I implore you, professor—search your memory!"

His soft, small hand reached into the old brief-case on the floor and withdrew a list of members of the Prussian Academy. A name leapt up to greet my eyes: BUCHHALTER. The "Buch" of the charred bit of paper!

"But he is a withdrawn, sick man," Einstein objected. "He was sent several years ago to a hospital near Erfurt."

"Why Erfurt? Berlin and Vienna have the greatest hospitals. And Erfurt is hardly a spa—better air flows in the south, the Thuringian Forest."

"Hm . . . I had not considered the factor of deception."

"This is a project of the military, who are trained in

116

camouflage. Is there any thing of military importance in Erfurt?"

"Nothing that I know."

"Gotha!" I exclaimed. "How far is that from Erfurt?"

"Thirty or thirty-five kilometres. But I fail to see the link—"

"It's a Zeppelin centre. If the bomb is as heavy as you say, it would require the Parseval, lifting twenty tons, to ferry it. Furthermore, since Gotha sits on the main east-west railway line, a train need haul it only a short way from factory to air-ship."

Dr. Einstein slumped back in the seat, shaking his head. "Is it not more logical to build close by Friedrichshafen, where Count Zeppelin's engineers and experimental equipment are concentrated?"

"It's the most obvious place—therefore, exactly what the military want us to believe. But if you and I had followed the most obvious, generally accepted thinking in order to solve our widely divergent puzzles, I would remain a failed physician—"

"—and I a clerk in the patent office. Ah, yes!—the probability favours a factory near Erfurt."

The Hispano-Suiza drew up at the Bahnhof. We embraced each other in farewell, for we both knew that we might never meet and talk so freely again.

"You have my assurance," I told him, "the weapon will be destroyed."

He nodded silently, and his limpid eyes seemed on the edge of tears. "May we again play billiards when this frightfulness is ended. God be with you."

Arachne's reply to my report of the previous night awaited me: AMBASSADOR IN PETERSBURG REPORTS L'S FACTION

117

LAUGHABLE, NO POSSIBLE INFLUENCE ON GOVERNMENT. PM AGREES. WILL APPROVE ANY TRADE DEAL L WANTS. £25,000 AVAILABLE UNION BANQUE DE SUISSE. PAY L HALF ON DEPARTURE, HALF ON RETURN. IF YOUR ISABELLE IS PIANIST, FORMER HUSBAND IS LEGAL COUNSEL FOR ALEX. HELPHAND A.B., SWEDISH TRADING FIRM.

Thus I.A. could have met Helphand through a discarded husband; an interesting link, but it did not prove that my musical cozener was Inessa Armand. I answered Arachne: STRONGLY URGE DELAY VISA."

Over the previous three days I had been calculating the odds in this dire sweep-stake (three to two against me, hardly felicitous, but manageable) and now I made my decision quickly. Despite our mutual abhorrence of the other's politics, Lenin and I stood united on two fundamentals: discovery of the weapons factory's secrets, and the debilitation of German power. Russian withdrawal could make the latter more difficult; never-the-less, Lenin's thrust for power might require months, possibly years, and he could conceivably fail. His success was as much a long shot as mine. In the meanwhile, I was convinced, the United States' munitions and food, possibly their own entry into the fray (propelled by our mutual Anglo-Saxon heritage), would over-weigh the Russian's possible coup in the East.

As to I.A., whoever she might be, she was no danger to me until *after* we had located the weapon, so that if she attempted to wrest its mysteries from me, I would be well prepared. I would stake my life on the certainty that she was not a double agent; if she were indeed Isabelle Andros, I felt a surge of impatience to joust with her again, for she would be the supreme test of my mental and physical powers and it would be unthinkably craven to admit I could not prevail.

118

Friday, 16 March

Lenin demanded that his initial £12,500 be paid at the Botanic Garden, "by the statue of Gessner," at eleven A.M.

On this sparkling spring day the Garden, edged by a row of lovely old houses so similar to London's that they evoked a wistful sigh, glowed with colours: yellow crocus and winter jasmine, blue iris, even white Eurasian hellebore. Lenin had chosen this meeting-place to prevent his café comrades, who never wandered among flowers, from observing his acceptance of a British cheque.

The bronze bust of Conrad Gessner, a sixteenth-century Swiss naturalist, was enshrined in a bower of pleached boxwood, and here Lenin strolled in with I.A. Attired in a nondescript cloak whose drabness was accented by the bright plants around her, she greeted me with a minimum of enthusiasm. Lenin, however, displayed an almost euphoric humour, embracing me to exclaim, "The Tsar has abdicated at last! Now a new world will bloom like the crocus around us!"

I translated this as: Good news from Zimmermann. When I placed the cheque in his hand, he said nothing more about a visa, leading me to conclude that the Germans had secured the documents he required. After stuffing the paper into a rear pocket, he embraced me as a brother. "May this be the start of friendly relations between the peace-loving people of Russia and Britain."

My reply was entirely diplomatic: "Peace among all nations is most desirable."

We stopped to observe the variegated lilies in the pool facing the green-house. "We must agree on ground-rules," I told I.A. "Neither I nor you will carry lethal weapons—quite dangerous if we're searched. And no divided command; I shall be in charge."

119

Lenin stepped between us soothingly. "Our policy is democratic centralism. You and Inessa should discuss all plans and political positions, but you will make the final decision."

"Yes, but there will be no *political* discussions. She will not try to convert me to Bolshevik dogma, and I shall not lecture on the benefits of the British Empire."

"Agreed," she said demurely. "But I trust I shall be consulted on my German identity."

"Most necessary. Meet me in the Bahnhof at nine tomorrow morning, and we shall journey to Bern for that purpose. We cross the German frontier on Sunday."

"I have one more question," she announced, peering into the quaint octagonal wooden palm-house.

"Yes, madame?"

"Will I require your permission to visit the W.C.?"

This evoked a raucous guffaw from Lenin and a ponderous clap on my shoulder. "You see? She's as good as any man!"

Saturday, 17 March

I awakened Plumsoll from whatever grand strategy he was dreaming of to inform him that the die was cast: I would proceed to Germany with Mme. Armand; he would remain in Zurich, serving as liaison between Arachne and Lenin.

"Lenin? Good heavens! What does one say to a Bolshevik?" he sputtered. His head twisted in pain, as if he were a hanged martyr in a cathedral window. "How can you feel safe with that Armand woman?"

"We have a linkage as un-relenting as that of the Siamese Twins. One can not leave the other's side, and as a result, if I do not return—she shall not return."

We were joined together for life—or death—in a sub-cellar at 5 Feldeckweg, our chancellory in Bern. The minister presiding over this un-hallowed ceremony, un-aware of our true identities, was a bearded, hump-backed elf, far from home in London's East End—one Joseph North; he supplied his own ritual music by whistling snatches of "Rose of Tralee" as he forged our German credentials. In this airless room, reeking of chemicals, littered with shreds of half-developed photographs and ink-blotted cards, his mastery of his medium was emphasised by the ability to chatter continuously while he set out his water-marked German forms, ration cards, pens, inks, rubber stamps, pads. ". . . 'prenticed, I was, to 'nengraver—could've been 'nother Cruikshank, ye know, but fell in wi' bad roughs, mollikers an' the like. . . . Now, sir, under the new Kraut law of 5 December 1916"—he rattled it off like a sixth-form boy who had memorised a crib—"ev'ry male, from the end o' the seventeenth to the sixtieth year, unable to bear arms, is liable to auxiliary service in gov'ment offices, war, industry 'n' agriculture, nursin' of sick. . . ."

"We require identities for employment in a munitions factory. To accommodate my Austrian accent, I should have been born there and moved to Germany."

"Yes, sir." He spread out a fat loose-leaf ledger. "I've got a good dead Kraut 'ere, 'bout yer age 'n' size, born Innsbruck, moved to Württemberg, name of 'ermann Grauber. How'd ye like to play 'im?"

"A corporal perhaps, sufficiently crippled to prevent further active duty at the front but with adequate skill to find employment in a munitions works."

"Very good thinkin', sir." With pains-taking precision he filled in a discharge form: ". . . Sixth Ordnance Company . . . expert fusin' shells. . . . Where'd ye like to be crippled, sir?"

"Left leg. The patella—knee-cap—a closed fracture which never set properly. I'll support it bent in a sling with a crutch. Speech and hearing impaired by shell-shock."

"First-rate, sir. Then the beaks can't question ye close. An' where was ye disabled?"

"The Somme, late July, 1916. I've visited the battle-grounds; I know the German divisions."

"Right, sir."

I complimented him on his German script.

"Years of study, sir. Worked in Berlin 'fore the war, with a Kraut 'ngraver named Schimmel. Good draughtsman but 'e 'ad one failin'. *Eyes!* Made the Kaiser wall-eyed, 'n' we seen five years' gaol fer that."

Seating me before an elaborate camera, he parted my hair down the centre—"I'll give ye Kraut moustaches in the re-touch; you can trim yours to match before you cross over."

While he developed the negative he continued his odyssey of life and art un-known to the Tate. "Came back to London, made a few pounds 'ere 'n' there, mostly singles 'n' fivers. Then som'un peached me. Fifteen years in quod."

The negative now hung up to dry, he turned to I.A. and gallantly lifted the cigarette-holder from her lips. "Oh, me dear, ain't ye the beauty! What'll ye be—Frau Grauber?"

"I think not," I said. "I already have a wife."

"Well, we do need some sort of relationship to explain travelling together," she said. "Brother and sister?—not bloody likely. Neighbors? No, make me a widowed—and very distant—cousin."

"Right, ma'am. Widows very num'rous in Germany." He consulted his ledger. "I 'ave 'ere a deceased widow, Elsa Lobegott, born in Baden, fourth-year school-teacher. Kindly take the chair, ma'am." He examined her face critically from several angles, then pulled her hair back in a tight bun and set small, round wire-framed spectacles on her nose. "Now droop yer cheek muscles—think how sad 'tis, yer lovin' husband's killed by the Rooshans."

He peered through the lens of his camera. "Aye, yer a lordy-lady; I'll need to ugly up the negative. 'old it now!" He sloshed the negative in his elixir. "Well, like I said, there I be, rottin' away in Dartmoor, while all me pals be outside, makin' fortunes in war-plants an' ration-card dodges. An' me, shamed I was, me country needin' me, like Kitchener said. Got so I couldn't 'old me 'ead up in the mirror, to set me cap on. Till—"

He produced more forms. "Ye'll need the state labour employment bureau letter, it tells where to go fer a job. Where ye both headed?"

"Erfurt," I said.

He provided an appropriate letter from the Thuringian Central Employment Bureau, directing Herr Grauber and Frau Lobegott to report to a munitions works near Erfurt; we were further outfitted with state sickness-and-accident books, disability benefits for my leg, and ration-cards for meat, bread, eggs and fats.

"—Till one day," the Cockney continued, "in comes this 'telligence Officer, an' asks if I want to serve me country 'stead of twelve more years. I volunteer 'mediately, though I didn't get the King's shillin'—but God bless King George! 'e saved me from the rot! Now 'e be payin' me fer what I always wanted to do—creative work."

In-as-much as he required time to fit our pictures into the various forms, and the papers needed aging, North urged us meanwhile to purchase clothes and travel-equipment to fit our new station in life from the second-hand dealers in the mediaeval quarter of the city.

We acquired properly dilapidated clothing, jerseys, rucksacks, mackintoshes, a German NCO's jacket, and a battered crutch for my crippled leg. A nervously blinking Levantine, stationed before an exquisite sixteenth-century fountain of dolphins, exchanged my sterling for several thousand German marks at a heavy discount. While I.A. busied herself buying under-clothes, I found some heavy wire to re-inforce the handle and cross-bar of my crutch. Later that evening, I sewed my British passport as well as most of the paper marks into the lining of my German jacket; my companion took similar precautions to conceal her money and passport on herself, and we removed all non-German labels.

Our identities, when examined in detail, reflected North's true pride of profession. He displayed several packets of £20 notes. "See, 'ere, just picked up in Basle. I 'ad to put me glass to these beauties."

They appeared to be flawless. I turned a note to the obverse side, where Shakespeare stood, leaning on several of his works. He faced left, but his eyeballs faced right. "Your friend Schimmel," I said.

"Correck!"

"I could use these at the border."

"Oh, they be dangerous sweet. You'll need 'proval."

The embassy's Intelligence Officer agreed that several hundred pounds could be persuasive in our crossing. He provided me with enlarged Baedeker maps detailing roads north, to be memorised, and a tiny luminous compass in a water-proof case that fit into the hollowed-out end of my crutch. Another was set into the heel of I.A.'s boot. She would fix in mind the names and addresses of all her possible contacts along the routes of our secret journey; the three hundred and sixty miles, we calculated, would require eight to ten days. I cabled my wife that I would be visiting the French and Italian fronts and she might well have no word from me for two weeks. Little did I anticipate that contrary to Dr. Einstein's Theory of Relativity, which asserts all bodies are contracted or shortened in the direction of their motion, the weeks I spent in the chase for the weapon would expand.

Sunday, 18 March

Plumsoll was completing his toilet when we heard the breakfast-waiter's tap at the door. I opened to face the Bald Bolivian, his eyes heavy with melancholy.

"Would you leave early, without saying farewell?" he said, leaning against the door.

I mustered my cheeriest "A pleasure to see you, general!" and thrust the fraudulent £300 into his paw. "I trust you won't mind—it's a bit more than a thousand dollars, but our government needs American dollars for imports."

"Of course not, my dear friend." He counted the bills slowly, with the delight of a remittance-man who had deposited his tweeds at Simon Artz's storage-rooms in Port Said, on the way to steaming Kuala Lumpur, and now, twenty years later, recovered them not only in perfect order but pressed as well.

"Muchas gracias," he exclaimed, and as the waiter wheeled in the cart, the general departed with the light, graceful walk of a dancing-master. "The British are the only true gentlemen left."

That same afternoon, an English couple, laden with ski-gear and hand-bags, took separate rooms in the Stag Hotel at Glarisegg, the tiny resort village between Mammern and Steckborn. The hotel, a three-storey Alpine chalet with white, serpentine-carved barge-boards, over-looked the Untersee, the narrow western tongue of Lake Constance. No other guests occupied rooms at this time of year, and the French-Swiss proprietor, who had arrived only a few days before with his *cadre,* was delighted to provide the couple with a skiff, so they might see the castles on the lake by moon-light: Freudenfels and Liebenfels at Eschenz, and Steckborn's formidable fourteenth-century Turmhof.

The tourists enjoyed a hearty dinner of roast beef and pudding near the fireplace of the empty dining-room, then returned to their quarters to change into jerseys and coats against the chill night air.

An hour later, startling transformations had taken place. I had become Herr Grauber, left leg bent back in a sling and hobbling on a crutch; my hair, dyed a straw colour, was so cropped it disappeared into my soldier's field-cap, under which my grey eyes stared off into the distance in a shell-shocked, almost catatonic, glower. A patched black wool jersey covered my old NCO jacket, and I bore the mackintosh over my right arm. I thought it all very effective, for although my polymorphic sleuth had employed fourteen disguises, my only previous attempt, when I dressed as a dragon for a Christmas party, had driven my children to tears.

I.A. truly astonished me by her metamorphosis into the *Hausfrau* who had scrimped pfennigs all her life. She had snipped off at least a foot of her glorious hair, dyed it grey and pulled it back into an ugly bun at the nape of her neck; her wan eyes could barely see beyond the wire-rimmed spectacles. Her entire body slumped in weary resignation under a shapeless old jersey and dun-grey coat, from which protruded high-laced, thick-soled boots. On one lapel she had pinned a metal button: GOTT STRAFE ENGLAND. Each of us carried an old valise under the skeletons of the leafless chestnuts that formed an *allée* from the hotel to the waterfront, a little more than half a mile from the German shore.

I rowed slowly to the northwest, tilting the blade carefully to avoid splashing. The castles, not one window lit, hung above the water like miasmal shapes of a nightmare. Lights flashed off and on, zig-zagging about on the German shore.

"Smuggler," I told I.A. "Sometimes they whistle to each other like birds."

"Then the sentries won't shoot at us—the smugglers have bought them off."

Shrinking down into the skiff, I listened to sounds from the shore, about four hundred yards away; on my left the lights of Wangen glowed dimly. My companion lay almost flat in the boat, her eyes above the gunwhale, methodically sweeping the shore from left to right and back again. She displayed no fear, only the tightly closed mouth of concentration.

After a few minutes, she whispered, "Slowly, now." When we scraped sand, she hitched up her skirt and slipped into the icy water to help pull our craft into a rock-hemmed cove. Above us stretched a line of poplar trees, separated in mathematical precision; the moon flickered briefly through a rift in the clouds to reflect their leafless branches in the water, and their striations, combining with the ripples, created an effective camouflage for our movements.

I handed the two bags and my crutch to her, then yanked out the plugs we had partially sawed through the hull before setting out. With a push outwards, the boat was carried away by the Rhine current.

Abandoning my pretense of infirmity here, I scurried up the shore, holding the crutch at the ready. Our goal was due north to the railway line from Radolfzell, which would guide us west to Singen, where the first of Lenin's comrades lived. It was sparsely populated but hilly country, and I.A. seemed to be in excellent physical condition, scrambling through the coarse brush.

Our three-hundred-sixty-mile expedition to Erfurt had begun at last. I whispered, "Well done, madame!"

"You would do better to call me Frau Elsa," she responded crisply in German.

CHAPTER EIGHT

"God Has Abandoned Us!"

A hard frost greyed the ground as we double-timed up a steadily rising moorland of brush and brambles. Clumps of fir and beeches provided welcome cover. I had been warned of a line of sentries three hundred yards from the border, so that when I heard someone call out *"Wer da?"* I retorted with a non-committal *"Ja, ja"* and whistled a bird-call.

We followed a farm road due north, past the black outlines of scattered houses, from which not a slit of light showed; only the occasional baying of a dog broke the silent night, and whether the animals were howling at shadows or us, we did not stop to enquire. I.A. kept pace with me, even though my stride was a half longer than hers. Singen lay a dozen miles away, and I calculated we could reach it within four hours, permitting three or four stops for rest.

With no warning, a rain-storm burst over us, smothering our view of every thing beyond three feet; the dirt road soon dissolved into mud which sucked at our shoes like a quag-

129

mire. Guided by my compass, we slogged along much more slowly now, for without hedges or fences on either side, there was little difference between farm and road. Crossing a narrow bridge over a swollen stream, I spied a vague light, as if from a window, some six feet above our path.

"Patrol shack!" I.A. whispered. She swiftly pulled me away from the light as a man passed close by in the gloom. I hurried on, turning my head for an instant, to catch sight of a white arm-band on his right sleeve. A torch beam swept across our figures.

"Halt!" he commanded.

I seized I.A.'s elbow and pulled her into a clump of high brush. "Auxiliary guard!" she gasped. A pistol cracked out as we plunged across a deeply furrowed field and rolled down an embankment into a drainage-ditch. Balancing our bags on our heads, I.A. grasping one end of the crutch and I the other, we managed to push and pull each other through the icy water and up the opposite bank.

Scratched by the brush, we sat down to regain our breath, expecting at any moment to hear the voices of our pursuers and their dogs. But the water of the ditch cut our scent off from the latter, and the patrol, like most time-servers, were in no mood to ford icy water. After a few minutes, hearing no sound other than the wind-driven rain, we pushed on.

The icy ditch-water was an affliction. It had seeped into the fabric of our mackintoshes and, combining with the wetness our woollens and under-clothes had soaked up in the ditch, forced us to carry a double burden of weight. I.A.'s valise, made of some carpet-like material, was also water-logged. I offered to help carry it, but she declined with a grim "No favours, my dear Hermann."

We could march only by compass; all place-names and direction-signs fifteen miles from the border had been taken down to confuse escaping prisoners of war, for whom this was a route to Switzerland. During the next hours, we traversed no more than a few hundred yards without resting, under a tree if we found one or simply in an open field. Some of this land had been abandoned, because of farm-labour conscription, and the stubble of previous plantings made for hard going; slithering and stumbling in the gullied fields, occasionally falling into sump-holes hidden by the darkness, I wondered how long my companion could endure. Her face, shielded by a wide-brimmed hat, betrayed no sign of pain or weariness, only determination, her chin jutting forward as if to defy the storm. She continued to match my stride.

Suddenly she cried out, "A barn!" It was a simple, open-end shed, used to store wood for the farm-house about fifty feet away. We sat down gratefully on some logs, but the wretched rain blew in upon us from either end; huddled back to back, we shivered miserably, for no warmth could penetrate layers of icy wool and rubber clothing. After I had checked my compass to make certain of our northern direction, we set out again, leaning into the wind.

She turned to me with a wry smile. "You bloody patriot!—*you volunteered!* You could have been sitting at home in front of a roaring fire."

I nodded. "And you?"

"They promised me I'd be a general."

They? Whoever she was, whatever side she truly served, she was no Kew hot-house flower—she was one of the troops.

Soon we stumbled on to railway-tracks. Another compass check indicated that this was the Radolfzell line; Singen would be four or five miles to our left. We had to take especial care here because the tracks into this town, the junction for a main line north, were heavily guarded, and the tree-covered hills sloped down to the very edge of the rails, leaving only a narrow path. Once again we discerned

131

flashes of torch-light and shadowy figures carrying packs on their backs; smugglers or sentries, they looked alike in the downpour. At length we reached the switching-yard and veered away to find the road into Singen.

I now bent my left leg back and slung the canvas loop from my belt to support it, converting to the crippled veteran again. We passed two men wandering home from a *Bierkeller;* one, with a massive belly, cast his eyes over us bluntly, as people in small towns do when they meet strangers. We must have been a bedraggled sight: dripping water, mud-stained, peering from side to side for street-signs.

A moment later, I heard someone wearing heavy boots coming up rapidly behind us. I.A., without looking back, assured me with a nudge, "It's a woman." We continued on steadily into the old part of town in search of Comrade Schäffer while the footsteps gradually came closer. In a moment I expected a tap on the shoulder or a gun-barrel in my side. But the boots turned off to the left. Glancing over my shoulder, I saw that it was indeed a woman.

"Wooden soles—they're the only ones made for women now," I.A. explained. "Can't you tell the difference between male and female steps?"

"I regret, Frau Lobegott, that I have never been followed by a woman. Have you?"

Under the smears of mud, she grinned. "It broadens one's horizons."

We found the elaborately carved sign

GERHARDT SCHÄFFER

JOINER-CABINETMAKER

hanging from a wrought-iron bracket several doors off the main street. It was a two-storey house with steep, tiled roof; the shattered windows of the shop had been boarded up, and the shutters above were closed. The house, very old with massive beams exposed and filled in by plaster, recalled our Elizabethan style.

I.A. rapped sharply on the door for several minutes before one of the shutters opened an inch. From the darkness came a woman's frightened voice: "Who is it?"

"Inessa," she called out.

"Go away!" floated down in a weary moan, and the shutter silently closed.

I.A. muttered, "Herr Schäffer should've answered. Something's amiss." She led me to a rough-hewn door at the right of the shop and through a narrow passage to the rear. The area had been partly covered over with a roof for the storage of lumber; a wooden stairway ended at a door on the upper storey. She silently climbed the steps and rapped. "I'm Inessa!" she repeated softly. "Where is Comrade Schäffer?"

A small panel in the door slid open. "Shipped off to the front last month. That's what your party has done for me!" And the panel slammed shut.

"Our papers are in order," I.A. said, "and we're wet to the skin. You must give us shelter if you want the war cut short and your husband sent home."

The door opened an inch, but I saw no face or eyes; the room was entirely dark. "Who is *he?*"

"He brings a plan from the Allies to shorten the war!"

At that moment, I was willing to forgive any prevarication simply to be warm again. The voice murmured, "You can stay if you promise to get out after dark tomorrow."

I.A. agreed. "We have ration coupons for you."

The door creaked open on its heavy hinges slowly, reluctantly. "Quick now," the voice cried, and we slipped inside a small bedroom. Frau Schäffer motioned us away from the door, and, shielding the dim light of a small kerosene lamp, held it up to our faces.

133

"This is Herr Grauber, a veteran, shell-shocked," I.A. said. I bowed and thanked Frau Schäffer. "Please, can we dry our clothes and have a hot drink?"

"*Ja.* You can sleep here, in my boy's room. He's in the east. No letter for two months. God has abandoned us!" And she sank into a chair, weeping. A flabby, gentle and pitiable soul, her white hair was drawn tight in a bun just like I.A.'s, and on her right middle finger a thimble still perched—she had been mending clothes to keep her mind off her losses.

We dropped our sopping coats and bags on the floor. Noting the cast-iron stove against the wall, I hurried out to fetch wood; when I returned with the fuel and a hemp rope to dry our clothes over the stove, I.A. had laid out two brown blankets and an eider-down quilt on the bed.

Tears flowed down Frau Schäffer's furrowed cheeks while she rocked back and forth, punctuating the details of her husband's arrest by blowing her nose strenuously into a linen handkerchief. He was one of only two townspeople who received the *Vorwärts,* the Social Democrats' newspaper, which made him a natural target for the police and informers and *agents provocateurs.* They had taken these jobs to be immune from military service, she lamented, and they had to prove themselves indispensable by discovering all sorts of crimes every day.

The neighbouring farmers were incensed because last year the bureaucrats ordered all the milch-cows slaughtered to provide meat; naturally, this year there was a shortage of milk and butter. Two weeks ago, someone had hung a dead cat, its eyes gouged out, above the mayor's door. The police informers automatically assumed it was her husband's work—weren't the Socialists leading the bread riots in Berlin? they said—and he was arrested for "incitement to public disorder." Instead of being sent to prison, he was sentenced last month to the front lines, even though he was fifty-two years old. And she had received no mail from her husband or son. "I warn you, wherever you go, it's wise to talk only *unter vier Augen*." The third pair of eyes could be the informer's.

I.A. returned, wrapped in a blanket, from the bath-tub in the kitchen and draped her clothes on the line suspended over the stove. She had had the good sense to equip herself with winter-weight under-clothes, crocheted at the neck and similar to my wife's, made of Australian lamb's-wool and cotton.

After a heart-warming soak in the tub, I enveloped myself in a blanket, and, finding the door of the front bedroom open, looked in. One entire wall was occupied with shelves of books. Schäffer, the craftsman, was a self-propelled individual who had found his own way to the world outside through reading. Volumes of Schiller and poems by Goethe stood side by side with Marx and Engels, translations of Shakespeare and a rare *Hepplewhite's Cabinet Maker and Upholsterer's Guide*. To the bureaucrat of an autocracy, any bit of writing that does not carry the imprimatur of his own government is confusing, if not dangerous; a reader of the Englishman Shakespeare would be wilfully malevolent.

Frau Schäffer brought from the kitchen steaming *ersatz* coffee and plates of sliced ham and pumpernickel bread, spread with butter. She bartered chairs and chests, made by her husband, for the farmers' products. "They laugh at the people in the cities, spreading *ersatz* honey on that wretched *ersatz* bread."

The coffee, more like barley-water, was warming. We were all weary and spoke little; it was now two in the morning. Frau Schäffer, again pledging us not to depart the house before darkness, closed the door. I.A. settled on the bed, emptying an oiled-cloth bag from her luggage and dumping out jars of skin creams and lotions. Next she opened a waterproof can containing an assortment of cigarettes: Egyptian,

English, American, brands I had never heard of, whatever she had been able to accumulate in Zurich. Producing her cigarette holder, she lit up a Country Life, breathed deeply a few times, and allowed the holder to dangle from her lips as she methodically anointed her entire body with the creams, thereby exposing much of her limbs and bosom.

I turned away and stretched out an eider-down on the floor. Suddenly I heard, "Oh, do forgive me. I forgot you don't have a library to retire to, for cigars and brandy. Please feel free to smoke—"

"Quite all right. I'm not in the mood for a pipe." I wanted to sleep, to blot out the vision of the bereft, sobbing Frau Schäffer. What an inauspicious introduction to Lenin's "dedicated net-work" for which I, or rather the British rate-payers, had already paid out £12,500.

"Will you join me in a brandy, then?" I.A. asked. I hesitated a moment, in which time she un-screwed a flask, separated the cap into two brass cups, and poured.

"Cheers."

"Cheers."

"Oh!" Her tone shifted to incredulity. "Do you intend to sleep on the floor?"

"Of course."

Another shift, to the practical: "Two bodies are warmer than one."

"An un-disputed physiological fact, but irrelevant to our association."

"Very well. Our next stop, if there is only one bed, I shall sleep on the floor."

"No, madame. To me the floor is not a bed of nails."

"I insist on equality in adversity—we shall alternate on the floor." She stated it unequivocally, as if it were a matter of party dogma.

"As you wish."

136

She had let down her hair and was brushing it with long, forceful strokes, counting silently; her face, despite the greyed hair and absence of cosmetics, still displayed the transcendent beauty that had struck me in the hotel dining-room. She noticed my observation and asked in puzzlement, "Doesn't your wife brush every night?"

"I suppose. We have separate rooms."

"But you do meet at night—occasionally?" Not kittenish now, merely mocking.

"Yes, indeed."

"And then you draw straws, and the loser—?" Puffing contentedly, she lay back on her pillow and opened the cover of an Engels tract on the condition of the English workingman in 1863. "You don't object to my reading in bed, I trust?"

"If you don't object to my turning my back."

"You are a dear. This mission may be quite amusing."

"I ask only one small favour—before you fall asleep, be sure to extinguish your cigarette."

"I always have," came the blunt reply.

"Then *gute Nacht*, Frau Lobegott."

"*Gute Nacht*, Herr Grauber."

I rolled over and, without a moment's thought for tomorrow's obstacles, fell sound asleep.

Monday, 19 March

A heavy pounding on the shop-door woke me. Leaping up, I slipped into my blessedly dry under-clothes, threw the mackintosh over all and ran to the front room. Frau Schäffer was peeping through a slit in the shutter.

"Two police!" she cried in terror.

One of them was the fat straggler from the beer-hall; the other, the auxiliary with the white arm-band. "Wait two minutes," I whispered to Frau Schäffer, "then present Elsa as your cousin." I ran to the back room and shook her. "Quick now! The auxiliary policeman's here. He didn't see your face in the rain. I'll hide in the attic."

She opened her eyes slowly, painfully. "*What?* Who?" She stared as if meeting me for the first time. "What do you want?"

I lifted her off the bed, blanket and all. "Wake up! The police are here! You are *Elsa, Frau Schäffer's cousin!*"

She massaged her forehead. "Schäffer's cousin?" She was not in a stupor from the brandy; I realised to my despair that my partner and guide was one of those whose mental and physical functions are adjusted, by some topsy-turvy internal clock, to reach maximum efficiency at night. One theory conjectures that the "clock" is set at the time the infant emerges from the womb. Whatever the cause, it was now nine A.M. and I.A. could barely recall how we had arrived here. I scurried around the room, gathering up my belongings while the shop-door rattled, voices yelled, "Police! Open to the police!" and I repeated to I.A., "You are her cousin, Elsa, on a visit. You don't know me!"

I pulled down the attic trap-door by a knotted rope; Schäffer had rigged a folding ladder ingeniously, so that it dropped as the door opened. I ran into the kitchen for a knife and cut off the tell-tale rope.

I.A. sat on the bed befuddled. "What shall I answer?"

"You met me at the station. . . . You are Frau Schäffer's cousin. Coffee! Give them coffee—give yourself coffee!" I scrambled up the ladder and yanked the trap-door shut as four heavy boots stomped up the back stair.

Stretched out on the attic floor, I put my eye to the crack of the door.

Stumbling about like a somnambulist, I.A. pulled on her coat and set out for the kitchen to prepare coffee, I hoped. Frau Schäffer, on the edge of hysteria, could only shake her head and wail incoherently as the fellow whom I had taken to be a beer-cellar habitué bullied her: Had she sheltered a cripple man? Was this the woman who had fled from the auxiliary in the rain? The beer-belly, obviously one of the *Geheimpolizei*, employed the intimidating technique of poking his pudgy finger to within an inch of her eyes. It was a sticky moment; the *Gepo* could put I.A. and me under protective arrest, simply on the basis of suspicion, while they looked for, and contrived, the evidence.

I.A. was coming alive slowly. "Why, of course I'm the woman you saw," she told The Belly. "I'm a cousin, just stopped off on my way north . . . looking for work to help the Fatherland!" She pointed proudly to the GOTT STRAFE ENGLAND button on her coat and produced the state employment letter. "The cripple I met on the way, poor fellow—shell-shocked, wounded fighting for our country on the Somme—I directed him to the station."

"Where did the cripple go?" the *Gepo* man demanded.

"Sigmaringen." Gulping coffee and puffing a cigarette, she assumed control of the situation. The auxiliary blustered on about two people evading him in the dark, one exactly the cripple's height.

She sniffed at him as if he were a senile, foul-smelling dog. "How could the other man be a cripple and run faster than you?"

The Belly grunted irritably; the two men departed. I lay on the attic floor, relieved but dispirited. If I.A. required at least ten minutes to come fully awake, I could not rely on her in any crisis which might strike before noon. And she should have known that no working-class *Hausfrau* smoked cigarettes in public: it was an upper- or middle-class manifestation. I could only hope that the *Gepo* man would not bethink himself of her blunder.

After darkness fell, I waited under a tree, several hundred feet from the brick and timbered railway station, while I.A.

reconnoitred. "Only a *Landwehr* guard," she reported. The soldier, slouched on a bench inside the station, his eyes half closed, arose slowly to examine our papers. He mumbled, "*Alles in Ordnung*—what's this?" He stared me up and down with an un-comprehending sneer. "Old man, you must get your disability benefits and unemployment cards stamped. Don't you understand that?"

"Oh, yes, yes. I've been travelling to find a job." In truth, I had no intention of collecting these pittances, because I would be required to sign for them inside a police station.

We had decided it was more circumspect to travel in separate carriages; I.A. insisted upon a third-class ticket ("I want to hear the working people"), and I purchased a second-class to Tübingen, south of Stuttgart; we had determined to avoid large cities and their closely guarded stations. The scheduled time for the first stop, Tuttlingen, was one hour and ten minutes, but, the wizened ticket-seller warned, the track was being repaired.

I.A. and I waited at opposite ends of a station bench. She carried a straw basket of sandwiches, bottles of *Einheitsbier,* the watery war-time brew, and some all-important *ersatz* coffee, packed by Frau Schäffer.

Dozens of posters and notices, warning, commanding, cajolling, had been attached to the station walls.

FATTEN PIGS

Fat is most essential for soldiers and factory workers. Not to keep and fatten pigs, if you are able to do so, is treason to the Fatherland.

NO PEN EMPTY!—EVERY PEN FULL!

Another stern note advised women that their country required gold to import food: their gold rings should be brought to the Bureau for Re-usable Materials, where they would be replaced with iron rings free of charge.

At length the train puffed in from its siding; one second-class and two third-class coupés, with half a dozen freight-waggons at the rear. I boarded the train just before it pulled out. I.A.'s carriage of cramped wooden seats was soon occupied by two soldiers returning from recuperation in Switzerland, several elderly men in the clothes of skilled workers, a hump-backed little man carrying a violin, and farmers' wives with baskets of live chickens.

My second-class compartment was as glumly lit and unkempt as the third, but the seats were old plush, worn smooth. I took the space next to a minister with absurdly long feet and ears. Across from me sat a stiff, slender patriarch, the very archetype of the Junker, peering straight ahead as if saluting the Kaiser. On his chest were displayed an Iron Cross and other bronze and gold medals; arms folded and still erect, he fell promptly asleep.

The minister, a thin, garrulous man, introduced himself as Dr. Ekkehard and explained in needless detail that the old gentleman was a Landgraf, fallen on hard times; he had won the medals in the 1870 war, and was journeying to Stuttgart to volunteer for patriotic service.

Stiffening my back, I saluted him solemnly. "With heroes like that *'Und es mag am deutschen Wesen/Einmal noch die Welt genesen.'* " *

Dr. Ekkehard nodded with careful enthusiasm.

The other passenger in the compartment, across from me, was a *Barmherzige Schwester,* a prim sister in loose-fitting blue cotton gown and black apron; from her blue wimple a stiff gauze veil hung down to her chin. She bowed her head into a Bible the instant she sat. When I enquired if she would

---

* "The world may yet again be healed by Germanism."

—R.S.

object to my pipe, she handed to me a worn printed card: I AM OF THE ST. BONIFACE ORDER OF SISTERS OF CHARITY WHO HAVE TAKEN VOWS OF SILENCE AS PENANCE. A SMALL CONTRIBUTION MEANS MORE TO US THAN CONVERSATION.

Returning the card with some pfennigs, I carried my pipe and newspaper out into the corridor. The minister joined me, and we exchanged polite observations on the war reports in our respective newspapers. Mine was the *Kreuz-Zeitung*, the only one available at the station and emblazoned with headlines of the latest Allied perfidies.

I hobbled down the corridor of I.A.'s carriage; through a gap in the compartment curtain I saw her at the opposite corner. Pressed against her was The Belly! He clutched documents in his left hand, and with his right he was poking that confounded finger in a snarling interrogation.

Instantly I buried my face in my paper. He must have leapt on the train after it started, indicating that he had definite information one of us was aboard, and he would, no doubt, come looking for me. I searched up and down the corridor for an escape.

Dr. Ekkehard, glancing up from his *Frankfurter Zeitung*, noted my agitation. "Is something troubling you?" he asked kindly.

"Oh, this wretched news from England!" I grumbled. "The roofs of the biggest stores in London have been converted to prisoner-of-war camps, to scare off our Zeppelins from bombing our own soldiers!"

I limped back towards my own carriage, but Dr. Ekkehard followed, indicating an item in his paper. "One can not understand the working of the British mind. Never, never! Both clever and yet stupid . . ."

Despite my manoeuvres to be rid of him, in order to help I.A. or devise an escape from the train, his thoughtful evaluation of the British pursued me. ". . . Here the wounded, returning from the Western Front, tell that the British on

142

the Somme were so ignorant of the art of warfare that they did not understand they were surrounded and about to be destroyed, and thus terrible losses were inflicted on our brave troops!"

I, too, was surrounded, but replied matter-of-factly, "Strange people, the British. I read that after the first Zeppelin raids, the fashionable London shops sold black lace night-gowns, 'Zepp Nighties' and 'Robes for Raids'—oh, do forgive me!" I lunged into the lavatory. If the track were being repaired, the train would be forced to slow down and thus present an opportunity.

The door was flung open by The Belly. "I want your documents," he growled, thrusting his left hand at me.

I stepped into the deserted corridor and demanded, "Who are you? Let me see *your* identification."

He pointed a pistol to my head. "Hands against the window."

With one hand, he searched expertly into my rear pockets and jacket, shuffled through my cards and letters, grunting with satisfaction at each discovery. "You and that woman, both travelling to Erfurt! So you do not know each other? Liars! And she said you took the train to Sigmaringen. Liar! You will both come off with me at Tuttlingen!"

"She is my sweetheart. Is that such a great sin? For this you bedevil a veteran who's given his limb for the Fatherland!"

"Turn around!" Under the dismal corridor light he held up a well-thumbed copy of *England in Danger,* the back cover of which bore a photograph of my face.* "You are Arthur Conan Doyle—*sir!*" He laughed coarsely.

* Shortly before the war, Conan Doyle wrote a long short story titled "Danger!" as a warning to his country; it depicted, with astonishingly prophetic detail, how Britain could be starved into submission by submarines. British admirals considered it poppycock, but the tale sold a

Although taken several years ago, it was sufficiently clear: my face was on display all over Germany.

I.A. emerged from her compartment and crept behind my captor's back; I concentrated my gaze on the man's gun in order not to betray her with my eyes while I chattered away. "I have brought one hundred thousand marks with me. If you are as intelligent as I think you to be, consider what a hundred thousand marks could bring you—a good house in Switzerland, excellent food, a motor-car—"

"The British killed two of my brothers at Jutland!" he broke in fiercely. "You and the woman will be my repayment."

From her hat, I.A. extracted a long metal wire that had given shape to the brim; grasping each end with a gloved hand, she advanced to within several feet behind The Belly.

The train lurched round a curve into a tunnel. As the engine's steam surged into the overhead vents, fogging the windows and corridor as effectively as a London pea-souper, she looped the wire round his neck and yanked the ends with all her strength. At the same instant I smashed the shaft of my crutch against his bullish head. When we emerged from the tunnel, he was face down, dead.

"The lavatory!" I whispered. I lifted one arm over my shoulder, she hoisted the other, and we dragged him to its door. At that moment, the Sister of Charity strolled into the carriage, a few feet ahead of us.

We manoeuvred behind her. "My friend's had too much to drink," I.A. explained. The Sister did not reply, of course, and continued down the corridor, evidently stretching her legs.

---

million copies under the other title in Germany. Doyle was later accused by some of his countrymen of having thus suggested the concept of submarine warfare to the Germans. —R.S.

"The British killed two of my brothers at Jutland! You and the woman will be my repayment."

"We can't leave him here—they unlock the doors at each station," I said. I dragged the man inside the convenience while I.A. remained outside, guarding the closed door. The window smashed into bits with a kick, and using my crutch as a lever, I managed to squeeze that huge belly through the opening.

In the corridor again, I leaned against the shut door. "We must get off at Tuttlingen—and avoid all trains."

I.A. assented. Her eyes revealed no particular concern or excitement (my wife had shown more remorse in squashing a field-mouse with a broom), but she was scrutinising my face for reactions to this crisis. Except for the perspiration caused by heaving and hauling, I was quite calm; I had justified Arachne's reluctant faith in my ruthlessness, and she had verified Lenin's affirmation that she was the equal of any man in courage and counter-attack.

"Your first one?" she asked sympathetically.

"Yes."

"If I may salve your middle-class morality, my garotte was the primary cause of death."

"Very probably." My mind had focussed not on morality but security. It would not be wise to fall soundly asleep anywhere near a woman who killed so silently.

CHAPTER NINE

Nameless Fears

The only passengers stepping off the train at Tuttlingen, we walked through the silent town towards the Danube and crossed a bridge on the road to Rottweil. I.A. recalled the name of a sympathiser there; this woman, she emphasised, was not a comrade and might refuse us shelter, but we needed to quit Tuttlingen immediately.

We walked slowly, for the clear night and open road required me to play the cripple again. "That garotte was very useful, madame, but we had agreed that neither of us was to carry a deadly weapon."

She exploded into an astonished laugh. "I saved our lives! Do you want to provoke a Jesuitical dialectic on this issue?"

"We *did* make an agreement."

"Very well. That hat was not a weapon—it was an article of woman's clothing, employed for the highly moral purpose of covering my body—and therefore not subject to our agreement."

"Very clever, madame, but—"

"The fact that you raise the question provides the answer—you still fear me. I shall resolve your doubts willingly, Mein Herr, but not as a command from you." She set down her bag, extracted the wire from the hat-brim and tossed it into a copse beside the road. Raising her hands in mocking imprecation to the heavens, she cried, "Oh, Ulyanov!—you married me to an English choir-boy!"

We trudged over the hoar-frosted road in silence. The cold moon illuminated an undulating plateau, occasionally dotted with clumps of pine and the skeletons of tall, slender trees I could not identify, all accented by the frost to resemble a chalk sketch.

"Very Russian," I.A. mused. "Few houses, few barns."

A waggon rumbled by, pulled by two oxen and loaded with fire-wood. I called out, "Two marks for a ride to Rottweil."

The farmer, enveloped in a sheep-skin, a muffler over his head, turned to inspect us. "You live there?" he asked.

"No. We're on our way to Hechingen." (This was some miles to the east, but I thought it wise never to reveal our actual destination.)

The farmer replied, "For a wounded veteran, make it one mark." We scrambled aboard for a prolonged jolting such as I had not experienced before. I.A. un-corked her brandy-flask and opened the basket of sandwiches to make the journey tolerable; we were on the eastern edge of the Black Forest, at about twenty-five hundred feet, but we had under-estimated the windy chill.

The iron-rimmed wheels of the cart grinding against the pebbled roadway raised sufficient clatter to cover our whispered conference, particularly how the death of The Belly might encumber our security.

"He makes no difference," I.A. said. "As soon as you were

seen speaking to Einstein, the Germans knew of your interest in the new device."

"Probably before that. We must move north with all due speed, avoiding trains. The entire police system from here to the North Sea will now have my face under study. I'll shave off my moustaches; it will make my face more commonplace, and that sort is the most difficult to identify."

"Of course, that makes you more suspect if the police look at your identity-photos."

"It is the lesser of my two handicaps."

"The Belly probably reported encountering a cripple and a woman to his superior before boarding that train." She shrugged stoically and lit up a cigarette, which forced me to snatch it away and repeat my warning. After a while she began to speak in a quiet but firm tone. "I also have a caution for you. What I am about to say may disturb you, but it's the result of experience to which you have never been exposed—escaping the police. The fugitive, continually on the run, suffers from nameless fears and doubts; even though you see no one, you will imagine that a *Gepo* or an informer is constantly watching you. And you must be on guard against these paralysing doubts. At this very moment, you may believe that this farmer, carrying us to Rottweil for one mark, is actually a police spy."

"Your warning is valid. However, this man can not be an informer; if he were, he would have ferried us to the police without charge. Most Germans genuinely love their Kaiser and want him to be victorious."

She considered that logic for a moment, then murmured, "I hope you are correct and we won't need that garotte."

The ox-cart stopped a short distance north of Rottweil's walls and towers, at the turn-off to Hechingen. Thanking the farmer, I handed over the mark. He gave it back, saying, "I don't need it, soldier," and drove off.

I.A. and I turned to each other at the same instant; without a word her two hands reached out to grip mine, for we both realised that despite our plans and experience in plotting, fictional and political, we were not masters of our own fate.

"Now, let's find Mathilde," she said briskly. We walked back to Rottweil, high above the Neckar River, one of the mediaeval towns of Württemberg; the houses, huddled wall to wall, rose to impressive heights of five and six storeys, for the space within the fortified walls had been limited and the only way to expand was upwards. The farmers lived within the walls for their protection and worked the land outside, a tradition that continued into the twentieth century.

I.A. tossed pebbles at different windows on the second storey before a shutter opened and a man in a tasselled night-cap called out angrily, "What can it be so late?"

"I am a friend of Mathilde."

"Mathilde is dead."

"Oh, no!—I'm so sorry—we were students together."

Suspicion was obvious in his question: "Where?"

"Paris."

"Wait. I'll open."

The acetylene lamp revealed a sturdy round face, the texture of horse-hide, atop a slender, erect body; he clutched an old flannel dressing-gown.

"We're going north to find factory work," I.A. said. "I'd hoped Mathilde would let us stay."

He hesitated. "It may be good to talk of her." He led us to the two empty bedrooms of his sons in the services. Herr Bessing then offered some eggs and herb tea at the kitchen table and plied I.A. with questions about Mathilde and Paris, eager to envision a portion of her life he had not known: what did she look like then? where did they live?

I.A. lit up the inevitable cigarette and recalled their first meeting, in 1893. Bessing stopped her quickly. "Please, Frau—I don't like a woman to smoke."

Mathilde had been sent to Paris in 1890 to study voice; she could find no professional engagements there or in Germany; supported by her family, she managed to sing in church choirs and finally returned home to do the same in Rottweil and Horb. Rather than sink into the ignominy of spinsterhood, she had become Bessing's second wife, and passed away two years ago.

"How did she die?" I.A. asked.

"In child-birth."

She barely controlled her anger. "At her age?"

"My boys had been called up. I needed sons to till my land."

I.A. excused herself shortly after, and I followed to my room, pleading weariness. Bessing remained seated, unable to comprehend why she had turned cold against him.

When I tapped quietly on her door, she was, as I had suspected, puffing furiously on her cigarette and lathering herself with lotions. "That animal!" she muttered. "He murdered Mathilde!"

I snatched the cigarette from her lips and pinched it out. "This habit will destroy us. If you can not control it, I shall be forced to ration these to occasions when you can not be observed."

Her only reply was a grim snort.

But the date she had let drop at the kitchen table was even more disquieting: 1893, the year she met Mathilde in Paris. I had met Isabelle Andros there in 1891.

Tuesday, 20 March

We departed at dawn. A neighbour of Herr Bessing's transported us in a cart, loaded with evil-smelling rabbit skins and drawn by a wood-fired tractor, to a tannery at Nagold, some thirty-five miles north. Here, at the river-front, I.A. sought out a Comrade Karl (I never heard his last name) whose shallow-draught barge ferried us, atop an un-identified canvas-covered cargo shaped like hams, twenty-five miles up the Nagold River.

Under the welcome warming sun, a young woman in a blue coat bicycled on the path beside the river; I lathered up to shave off my moustaches while I.A. placidly darned our jerseys and socks.

Observing Karl forced me to consider that Lombroso's now-discarded theory of identifiable physical characteristics in criminals might have some validity: squat, thick-set, with sloping forehead, fat nose, prognathous scarred chin, Karl would be marked as a prime suspect in smash-and-grab jobs, maiming for two bob, procuring child prostitutes. Reaching beneath the canvas, I identified the cargo as indeed smoked hams; he evidently had bought them from farmers along the river at above the government-set price and sold them for triple profits to the "back-door market" in cities.

When I reproached I.A. for thus placing us in jeopardy, not only of the *Gepo* but of the myriad informers and bu-reaucrats enforcing the food-ration system, she retorted tes-tily, "We're hardly playing cricket—my comrades are not Gentlemen of England. Work hard, play fair, pay your debts and don't steal—these are values the aristocrats and bour-geoisie have imposed on the common people to enslave them. You are a romantic anachronism."

The amorality of the Bolsheviks or of I.A. was not my central concern; her considerably relaxed views of good and evil confirmed that we were operating on two divergent, perhaps contradictory, levels of basic principle, making it impossible to predict any action she might take against me.

The bicyclist was still gaily pedalling along beside us.

Borrowing the riverman's field-glasses, I discerned that she was another *Barmherzige Schwester*.

Karl turned over his cargo, as well as us, to a confederate, a railway clerk at Calw, who put us on a goods-waggon for Stuttgart with instructions to "jump out when it slows down in the yards."

The train stopped many times for track repairs, east-west troop trains, a rupture in the boiler. When it rattled haltingly somewhere at the outer reaches of the city, we eased open the door to peer into the night.

Suddenly it was pushed open from the outside and in leapt a broad-shouldered six-foot guard brandishing a night-stick. "Thieves! Deserters!" he yelled, and, catching me off balance as I arose, delivered a stunning blow to my shoulder that felled me to the floor. In the half-light, I discerned that this vicious brawler was a woman! The amazon whacked my partner across the head, to which I.A. replied by slamming her valise into the woman's face. I raised my crutch as a lance and rammed the guard in the stomach, pitching her out on to the tracks, where she lay stunned.

Fleeing across the rails, I felicitated I.A.: "The war has opened many opportunities for women."

The yards lay north of Stuttgart; our refuge for the night, a Dr. Kreutzenberg, lived in the south-east, at Degerloch. My leg once again in the sling, we trudged several miles in the dark to the Bopser Brunnen tram-station for the ride up a hill above Stuttgart. The harried little woman conductor ordered a young man in spats, with cane, to turn over his seat to me. Weary I.A. sat on her bag in the aisle.

The socialist physician, to judge by his home, was much more successful that I had ever been. Set back behind a wrought-iron fence and surrounded by trees, the grey-stone edifice boasted a Palladian façade; a maid in apron and cap

153

announced coldly that we were too late for office-hours—the doctor was available only in the morning.

I.A. gruffly ordered her to inform Dr. Kreutzenberg that a Swiss friend had arrived. He apologised for being in the midst of a dinner-party, betraying no surprise at our grubby appearance. He resembled not so much a physician as a butler in a drawing-room comedy: bending only from the waist but ever-flexible in a crisis; about sixty-five, well tailored in pre-war pin-striped suit and a wing collar.

"There is much talk of a new weapon," he volunteered with a heavy sigh. "If true, the working class will keep the wheels turning as obediently as ever, so long as the Kaiser can find a way to feed and clothe them."

He conducted us to a modishly appointed guest-room. "If you wish some supper, ring for the girl. And tomorrow, you must come see the advances we have made in repairing bone injuries." He bowed and left us, standing between a large Biedermeier bed and wardrobe. I offered I.A. first turn at the marble bath, but she insisted on a toss of a coin. I won.

After slogging along mud roads and rolling on bloody rabbit fur, I found the hot bath was a gift from the gods. By the time I emerged, the maid had lit a crackling fire. The mirrored wardrobe was still bare; I.A.'s clothes, invariably tossed about as if she had un-dressed at the epicentre of a tornado, clung to the door-handles and beaded lamp-shade. I swept her boots off the over-stuffed chair in front of the fire and, stretching out my stiff "crippled" leg, lit a clay pipe and pondered how we would insinuate ourselves into the factory developing that damnable new weapon. This, in turn, led to an appalling thought. I had deduced, from Dr. Einstein's revelation of Buchhalter's presence in Erfurt, that this area was inevitably the site of that factory. Thinking back upon the thinness of that hypothesis, I asked myself: Suppose Buchhalter actually *was* a sick old man and in

154

hospital. Could both Dr. Einstein and I have blundered? Had I risked my life and I.A.'s on a fool's errand? I saw no other course but to press on, for we would face the reality of my judgement soon enough.

A half-hour later I.A. emerged, draped in our hostess's silk wrap, trimmed with pink marabou. She stretched out in front of the fire to comb and lotion herself.

"Kreutzenberg's been seduced into the right-wing deviations of Eduard Bernstein, but he provides a good inn. That bath-tub is big enough for two." After a few moments, she asked suddenly, "Tell me, Doyle, have you ever considered the possibilities of passion in marriage?"

"That's a rather peculiar question."

"You're a rather peculiar man to avoid the question. Has passion between husband and wife ever occurred to you?"

"Indeed, yes."

"Can you recall a specific occasion?"

". . . not at the moment."

"Have you considered the possibilities of passion outside marriage?"

". . . not at the moment."

"*Gute Nacht*, Herr Grauber."

"*Gute Nacht*, Frau Lobegott." She was clearly intolerant of a man's indifference.

Wednesday, 21 March

Dr. Kreutzenberg walked us briskly down the main street of Degerloch, relentlessly expanding on the wonders we would see in prosthetics and therapy for the maimed. "You should stay for treatment of your leg," he urged. I.A. made it clear that we were hastening to an important party conference in Berlin and could spare but fifteen minutes.

Degerloch's large summer villas were boarded up; the stucco was peeling; several had been converted to small

155

hospitals known as lazarets. Dr. Kreutzenberg, beyond the age of military medical service, served as a volunteer in the prosthetics section of one lazaret, which consisted of two mansions joined by a wide wooden walkway. The *boiserie* and fire-places maintained some of the former dignity, but I saw no flowers about, no card or board games, no gramophones, as in English hospitals. It was a house of horrors. I was overcome with angry revulsion such as I had not experienced since the loathsome sights in the Boer War field-hospital where I'd served during an out-break of enteric fever.

Here the martyrdom was scrupulously sterile and well organised, designed to re-habilitate soldiers with the most modern equipment, which resembled torture instruments of the Middle Ages. We were ushered into a room where stood a dozen rectangular frames of steel tubing; these, a doctor explained to several high-ranking officers and civilians, *stretched* the injured limbs which had not been properly set at the field-hospitals. One poor devil hung by straps under his arms while similar straps, attached to his ankles and pulled by a cranked wheel, presumably stretched his neck! A similar mechanism stretched a man's legs. The demonstration victims were white-faced and sweating, but they ground their teeth shut to prevent humiliation in front of the guests.

How could German medicine have come to this? The Julius Hospital, situated in nearby Würzburg, was one of the most respected in the world, and even a first-year student of the skeletal system understood that stretching ligaments and tendons was futile, if not dangerous. I could infer only that some doctors, with great influence, were determined to prove a woolly thesis.

In a second room (by this time I was so furious I sat down to calm myself) substitute steel limbs were being exhibited. A doctor strapped on an entire steel arm, flexible at the elbow, with lobster-claws for hands, then ordered the soldier

156

to display how he picked up a cane. One man with two artificial legs and a steel arm could only stumble around in a circle, but the doctor stated he was now ready to work at a factory assembly bench.

At that moment, a dreadful vision blotted out every thing before me. I was in Edinburgh University's laboratory of vivisection (a practice so abhorrent that I campaigned against it for years), and once again I saw the monkeys, cats and dogs bound down, electric wires attached under their skin, and tubes draining them. And I could hear a voice in German lecturing, "We will apply these proven principles of artificial limbs to animals. Not precious steel, of course, but re-inforced wood. They could be trained to pull triggers of two machine-guns with their front appliances, and when these tired, the hind legs could pull two other triggers. Think of it! Hundreds of thousands of useless, stray animals are roaming the countryside, eating precious food-stuffs—let them work for the Fatherland!"

A harsh growl extracted me from this ghastly torment. *"Stand at attention!"*

Glaring down at me from a height of six and a half feet stood a general, wearing the insignia of the medical service. His squared jaw, slashed by the obligatory sabre scar, the crisp hair, intense blue eyes and full moustaches, ending in sharp, waxed points, conveyed the peremptory command bred into the old *echt*-German family.

I rose from my chair automatically and saluted.

"How dare you sit here! Back to quarters!" he ordered.

"Herr Doktor-General," I replied carefully, "I am a visitor here, observing as guest of—"

"*Observing?*" he growled again. "This is not a *Tingel-tangel!*" * He gestured to an orderly. "Have him properly dressed for exercises!"

---

* A vulgar music hall. —R.S.

I drew back in astonishment. "But I'm not a patient—"

Dr. Kreutzenberg, forever the civilian, meekly explained that he had brought me here to see what could be done for my leg. I.A. added that we were on our way to Essen, to seek employment at Krupp's.

The explanations only confounded the general, and that, in men of his rank, could only lead to anger. "You are still a servant of the Kaiser!" he barked to me, then about-faced to command Dr. Kreutzenberg. "Take him to Station One immediately—fill out his forms later!"

Our friend stood paralysed, his mouth open but un-able to speak. The front door was only ten feet away, guarded by a thin little private, and the bovine orderly had a two-handed grip on my right arm. My entrapment was so preposterous that I barely choked down a mirthless laugh.

At this, the general ordered Dr. Kreutzenberg, "And make certain his head is examined!" before he walked away.

"But I'm being married tomorrow!" I exclaimed plaintively.

The general stopped short, as if he had not heard aright. I.A. immediately dropped to her knees in front of him. "I beg you, general—we've been betrothed two years, since he was sent to the Somme. The guests are invited. Be merciful!"

He glanced down at her, bemused. "You want children—*by that one?*"

"Any one! My mother gave birth at forty-six! *Twins!*"

"Well, children are necessary." His scowl became almost avuncular. "Give me your parole that you will return here the day after you're married."

"Yes, general—yes, general!" I exclaimed, saluting on each word.

"Tomorrow night, I hope you at least know what the target is," he grunted, then marched off to greet a newly arrived platoon of newspaper correspondents.

I.A. snatched my arm from the orderly's grasp, and, leaning on her shoulder, I scuttled down the steps to the street. We left the town immediately by tram into the centre of Stuttgart. "Once more unto the breach," I groaned inwardly; the city created a hazard, but it was un-avoidable, because the trams were our only express transport to the north out of this heavily populated area.

At the Schloss-Platz stop sat a Sister of Charity. I.A. stopped short. "The *Okhrana* recruited very few women—they dressed boys as sisters or nuns and covered their faces." She sauntered over to the Sister, donated a coin, abruptly lifted her veil and, taking a round-about way, rejoined me. "She's a woman."

But was that the same woman I had observed on the train and on the bicycle? I moved several steps towards her.

CHAPTER TEN

An Ubiquitous Black Cab

At that moment the Berg-Cannstatt tram rolled in, and I was torn between swift departure and confrontation with a possible informer. Since we had completed one-quarter of our journey on approximate schedule, I felt no pressing need to take chances.

Another tram brought us to Marbach, the terminus of an ancient narrow-gauge railway to Heilbronn, twenty miles away. Finding no sentry at the station, we climbed aboard; our further passage would be provided by a comrade, Otto Frisch, in Neckarsulm, three miles from the end of this line. Darkness had fallen when we arrived there, and to ascertain whether our man was at home, I.A. telephoned to the village post-master, who, after some minutes, brought Frisch to the telephone. She cautiously requested "help to reach Würzburg or beyond." (Our actual destination was Heidingsfeld, a few miles before.)

Frisch's only words were, "Tomorrow, noon, Castle of the Teutonic Order."

"I don't like it," I said. "The post-master over-heard him."

"In these villages, one always meets at a land-mark."

Having no alternative now, we scouted Heilbronn's accommodations and settled on a small hotel which advertised "commended by Baedeker," offering two beds and breakfasts for three marks. The bath-tub delivered only ice-water, and the dinner was so vile that I began to think kindly of the notorious Bedfordshire Clanger.*

"Damn the Germans for their war!" I.A., quivering, wrapped herself in the blanket as if it were a shroud. "And damn the British for their implacable—perverse!—honour."

"I regret my marriage-vow has caused you any inconvenience."

"Thank you, doctor. I regret I must stay here even one night."

Her final mocking rejoinder called to mind Isabelle Andros' fare-well in Paris.

Thursday, 22 March

Otto Frisch rattled up to the castle at noon in a bespattered military motor-cycle with a side-car; he was attired, to my astonishment, in the uniform of a *Landwehr* corporal. When he pulled off his goggles I observed, behind the bushy eye-brows and up-turned moustaches, an utterly worn man, old beyond his years and without hope. He was chauffeur to a captain who did not require him today, he said, causing

---

* A complete meal, encased in a suet roll, once popular in the East Midlands. One started at the end filled with meat and onions, ate through potatoes and assorted fillers, and finished with jam at the other end. Presumably, it all went down with a clang. —R.S.

me to feel for the first time on our mission that we were in safe hands. I.A. and I donned mackintoshes; I jack-knifed into the side-car, I.A. perched on an ammunition cannister behind the driver, and we roared off on a bone-rattling, hill-and-dale road towards Würzburg.

After a long silence, Frisch felt impelled to tell—or, rather, to shout against the on-rushing wind—of his three sons killed in battle, his wife dead of grief and why he'd stolen away from *Landwehr* drill. The man who had destroyed his entire family, General von Hindenburg, would appear this after-noon in Würzburg to dedicate a *Denkmal* * in the Residenz-Platz, and Frisch planned to assassinate him.

I accepted this as the maundering of a deranged mind; for, after all, why should not the Bolsheviks have their fair share of madmen as well as the Conservatives? Soon, a careening skid of the vehicle slapped a heavy metal rod against my leg; I bent down to feel the barrel of a Mauser *Karabiner*.

An attempt on Hindenburg's life would not only make me and I.A. accomplices: it would cause the entire city to be cordoned off instantly, and every hotel and traveller on every road would be intimately searched. The general's safety was linked to ours by an aggrieved fanatic. Nodding sympathetically to Frisch, I manoeuvred under my mackin-tosh with leg and hands to shift the rifle against my crutch. A sign-post indicated we were approaching Lauda, where, as I recollected my map, the road would cross the Tauber River.

I called out, "Your rear tyre is coming loose!"

---

* A gigantic painted wooden statue of himself (the one in Berlin tow-ered fifty feet). It was both patriotic and fashionable to contribute money for the war by purchasing nails which the buyers hammered into this effigy of their leader; the wealthy bought gold and silver nails. —R.S.

I.A., picking up my thought instantly, shouted in Frisch's ear, "Stop! Stop!" and pointed to the wheel.

Frisch side-slipped to a halt some ten feet before a bridge. I stepped out, the rifle gripped to the crutch under my coat. "Must stretch my leg," I explained, and limped to the iron balustrade, through which the *Karabiner* slipped into the Tauber.

We bade Frisch fare-well at Heidingsfeld on a serenely empty street. I.A. lit up one of her precious cigarettes, de-spite my dis-approving frown, and placed it between his lips. "Forget this childish nihilism," she said. "Go home, Frisch—millions of widows need husbands."

His eyes held steady, but revealed no comprehension.

We walked on several yards, then round a corner, where an irresistible impulse, of relief or impending catastrophe, forced me to look back. Corporal Frisch sat on the kerb-stone beside his motor-cycle, sobbing un-controllably, the tears rolling down his cheeks.

The *Goldener Hirsch*, a seventeenth-century timbered inn at Heidingsfeld, was operated by one of I.A.'s party members. Its restaurant occupied the entire street-floor, and I was not pleased to note that most of the diners dawdling over *Mit-tagsessen* wore army uniforms. How could I.A. have neglected the fact that near-by Würzburg served as headquarters for the Second Bavarian Army-Corps?

Comrade Steuermeyer welcomed us rather distantly and hurried us into his office in the cellar. I had the instant impression of a man dis-owned by his family, probably for embezzling their silver-service; the short, slender body, en-cased in skin-tight blue frock-coat, embroidered velvet vest and striped trousers, was topped by the face of Pinocchio, not mischievous but furtive, with an improbable monocle.

"You are staying tonight?" he asked I.A., hoping for a "No."

"Yes. You were informed."

He cocked his head to the side and spoke in a purr. "Always so crowded—"

I.A. assured him any refuge was welcome, as, particularly, was one of his famous dinners.

"At six—we're overwhelmed later."

Little had been changed since the seventeenth century, I observed, as we ascended the quivering stair. The walls, leaning at their own discretion, had been covered with cheap velour draperies, probably to hide the cracks; the doors could not be shut, and the floors inclined at more than three-percent gradient permitted railways on hills. Our triangular room, little more spacious than our host's office, provided only a wash-basin, dresser and bed; but the convenience at the end of the hall was surprisingly new and effective, with a tub in which even I could stretch out.

Dinner was a triumph of illegal enterprise—five courses with the excellent local wines—but the *ambiance* of the dining-room, though charming, struck me as uniquely un-savory. Approximately half the men seated round us were officers: smooth-shaven, carefully pompadoured with a curve of hair over the forehead, their stiffly erect bodies all enhanced by the beautifully tailored grey uniforms; almost all bore duel-scars, and one captain looked as though his face had been seared by a broiling-grille. Of the civilians, those not obviously effeminate had wound bandages or a limb missing, and all seemed in need of a good tailor. (From my travels so far, I was convinced that the German male, no matter how expensively dressed, achieved an air of elegance only in a uniform.) The women were also a varied lot: some bejewelled and in furs; others, quite *hausfräulich* and unwilling to dance, looked like factory workers. Something iniquitous was seeping through the ancient walls of this charming inn.

Friday, 23 March

When I waked, my valise gaped open and my wallet had vanished. Thrusting into the pocket of my NCO jacket, I felt no gold coins. Now I had to rouse I.A., and several minutes were lost in pantomime, persuading her to look for her purse. Although hidden beneath her pillow, it had also disappeared. And when she reached for a cigarette, another scream arose: her entire collection had been stolen. Only our identity-papers and ration-cards remained un-touched.

I.A. fell back in a rage, beating the mattress with her fists, swearing vengeance and mutilation on Steuermeyer.

I dressed hurriedly to fetch up our host. Blear-eyed and surly, in a dressing-gown embroidered with fake jewels, he indicated a small notice posted inside the door: "Inn-keeper is not responsible for valuables unless they are stored in his strong-box. Guests are urged to lock their doors."

I remonstrated, "The doors can't be locked—there are no locks."

His head wagged solicitously. "But you were warned."

I.A. unleashed another of her scatalogical catalogues upon him, from which I ascertained that the inn was actually a brothel, catering to the *à la carte* needs of war-lonely women and homosexuals.

"Why didn't you tell me this before?" I demanded.

"I didn't want to offend your sensibilities." She seized Steuermeyer's lapel: "You filthy whore-monger; you'd best make good on my cigarettes!"

He surveyed her with indulgent concern, such as one displays for naughty children. "How un-gracious. I didn't

166

ask you to pay for meals. Or the accommodation." And he strolled out.

"Rotten Menshevik wrecker!" she called after him. Seated on the bed, she combed through her travel-bag and pockets for stray cigarettes or coins. "I have made an un-pardonable blunder. It will not happen again."

We totalled up our joint cash assets at three marks sixty. "And," I.A. wailed, "not one blessed cigarette!"

"We shall need to raise some money," I said. "I have some valuables—a watch. And you?"

Her face took on a forbidding glare I had never seen before. "There are some things I will *not* do for the party."

"Madame, only your mis-understanding shocks me. Let us find a flea-market. We'll have to chance it in Würzburg."

We could console ourselves with only one bit of optimism in our losses as we portered our bags into the city: it marked the half-way point of our venture, for we had traversed the one hundred and eighty miles in five days, quite close to schedule.

The city sprawled debilitated at every pore after two and a half years of sacrifice. Small shops, green-grocers, even beer-halls had been abandoned (no soldier below officer rank could be served even a glass of beer); the cracked exterior plumbing-pipes leaked filth on to their houses; women in over-alls or baggy trousers, hitched up above thick black stockings, emptied heavy dust-bins into open waggons, where children carefully picked over the refuse for salvageable fats or metals.

We squeezed on to a crowded tram at the Sander-Glacisstrasse, whence it lurched drunkenly over cracked tracks to the market-place. Labourers from an electric-works, a few men but mainly women, sat fast asleep after their twelve-hour shifts; I.A. and I hung on to the car's steps. At

167

the far end of the car, I espied a Sister of Charity, collection-box in hand.

The work-women spoke of nothing but the shortages of the "Turnip Winter," the small-pox vaccinations, the meat ration reduced to one-quarter kilo a week. Their hopeless-ness was leavened only by their certainty that America would never enter the war because of its important German population.

Our tram halted at an avenue while a regiment of soldiers marched by to the railway station; they were the seventeen- or eighteen-year-old classes, each wearing a handful of red flowers at his belt, a gesture honouring those proceeding directly to the front. Young girls and entire families ran along beside them, for the boys marched in a quick goose-step rhythm, eyes front, singing, "In the homeland, in the homeland, we shall meet again."

Several women in mourning-clothes turned their heads away, but I steeled myself with the thought: these were the uniforms that had invaded Belgium and France.

I.A. and I stepped down near the Marktplatz, crowded with haggling buyers and sellers. The Sister took up her stand at a side-street close by.

"There's an amazing prevalence of charity in this coun-try," I said.

I.A. strolled to the Sister with a pfennig in hand, lifted the veil and hurried back to me, retaining the coin.

"It's the same one as in Stuttgart!" she muttered.

"Can you describe her?"

"Vacuous pink face, like all the German country girls."

I turned to look for myself—the Sister had vanished. Here was an untidy piece of bafflement: since we were being surveilled, we had certainly been identified; why then had we not been seized by the *Gepo* for a properly thorough interrogation?

"The police bureaucracy can be just as stupid as the civilians," I.A. said.

"Or our pursuer *may not be German*. British or Allied agents could hardly be following along to protect us. But whoever has followed us here must know our purpose. Given these two known factors, there is one un-known we must consider: our pursuers are not certain of our destination. They hope we shall reveal the site of the factory which they have evidently been un-able to discover. That woman could be the agent for any large foreign power: Italy, Austria, Russia, France." I relayed Arachne's casual comment that none of our allies would help me.

"Then I would nominate the French. Dreadfully chauvinistic."

"Or they may be scouts for one of the many sects who oppose Lenin."

"Most un-likely, my dear Doyle. They don't have the determination or the organisation."

At the moment, our most urgent problems were, first, finance, and second, quick departure. Several *sotto voce* conversations at the market uncovered no one willing to pay enough for my valuables. One man directed me to a mews, some distance away in the Hebrew quarter. Here were the headquarters of the rag-pickers and junk-dealers, Eastern Europeans of the Orthodox faith, wearing full beards and hats or skull-caps.

I sought out the pre-eminent dealer, one Daniel Gelb, a cheerful, rubicund man and the only clean-shaven one, though he wore the cap. He gathered several of his friends round the rear of his waggon, where, in whispers, they formed a consortium to pledge four hundred marks. I now un-wrapped from my crutch the heavy black wire which had re-inforced it. Scraping off the black paint, I revealed solid gold.

"I'll be d——d!" I.A. exclaimed.

"In my profession, I have learnt to expect, far in advance, the un-expected."

I.A. immediately traded a portion of the marks for Egyptian cigarettes from Switzerland; I purchased English pipe-tobacco and a money-belt.

Gelb brought out a bottle of *Schnapps* to seal the agreement.

"We are going north to work in a factory," I ventured. "Do you know of any transport?"

He surveyed me judiciously. "I take the Gemünden road tomorrow, to buy. The informers keep an eye on me because I compete against the Imperial Treasury for scrap. But you have travelled much; you know what makes the wheels of the world turn—"

I.A. interjected a few phrases in Russian, causing his eyes to glow. "But with *die Landsfrau*—no charge," he said.

We passed the night in his stable.

Saturday, 24 March

I sat up front with Gelb on the waggon, pulled by a donkey; a string of sleigh-bells, supported over our heads by poles, announced our arrival through the wooded hills and farms. I.A. reclined on a pile of old mattresses, like Cleopatra on her barge. Very little metal was available, after all the government demands; never-the-less, within a few hours I became expert in ascertaining the difference between tin and block tin, genuine silver and "German silver," which contains no silver at all, being an alloy of copper, zinc and nickel. Gelb also traded cash for butter and eggs, and hummed sprightly Russian tunes, in which I.A. occasionally joined, as he related his life under the Tsar. He had sold potatoes from a waggon in Odessa: ". . . a great city, not a *Dorf*; the best fiddlers come from there! In the Russo-Japanese war, I cut off my trigger-finger, but the Tsar

170

said, 'Don't worry, you can take care of an officer's horse. . . .' "

On the rise of a hill, I.A. tapped my shoulder and revealed in French, "There's a small black car behind us. It slows when we slow, and stops when we stop."

A car was sitting by the stream in the valley below; no one was visible near it, fishing or viewing the scenery. I borrowed her cosmetic-mirror to observe over my shoulder; the black car soon crept along behind us.

"—I wanted to emigrate to America," Gelb rambled on, "but my wife said no, 'who can speak English?' So now the Kaiser has my boys, not the Tsar. And my wife, she studies English."

Our pursuers stopped short as the waggon halted for a poignant sight: the funeral for an old church-bell. The villagers in mourning-clothes, led by their priest, walked slowly behind the bell, bedecked with wreaths and flowers and borne on a heavy farm-waggon. The plain bronze bell, which had proclaimed good news and bad for several hundred years, would be melted down for the Fatherland's war.

The black car had come incautiously close enough for me to discern its outline clearly: a city motor-cab properly labelled and metred. A vague figure sat in the driver's seat, wearing a cap, but I could not see the passenger.

I.A. leaned her chin against my shoulder. "Petrol, oil and tyres are available only to the military, police or bureaucrats vital to the war effort. They would not waste vital resources to follow old Gelb twenty-five miles to Gemünden. Our pursuers *must* be German!"

"If German, they should already know our destination. Possibly it's one arm of government competing against another."

"Then why in h--l doesn't any one hold us for investigation?"

"That, madame, is the Devil's own conundrum!"

CHAPTER ELEVEN

The Mummy's Face

Puffing on a fat cigar, a heavy-set man of some importance, judging by the Mercedes from which he descended,
waddled into the railway restaurant to request the keys for
admission to the Scherenburg castle ruins. I.A. and I, having
just concluded an abysmal *ersatz* meal in the restaurant,
were glumly considering a twelve-mile hike to the nearest
hostelry.

As the stranger bent to enter the motor-car, he asked if he
might give an old soldier a lift to the ruins. By now, one pile
of stones was very similar to another, and I declined, saying
that we planned to go north.

"*Ja,*" the man said, "we are on the way to the waters at
Bad Hersfeld. If you wish the ride—"

I.A. drew me aside. "I have a friend at Fulda, before
Hersfeld. Let's risk it." We climbed into the back seat with
properly servile gratitude.

The man and his wife, overwhelmingly perfumed in a fox

wrap, were returning from holiday in Basle and Lucerne, and he was a purveyor of soap for the military. He offered a Havana cigar, which I promptly accepted, after which I asked if he could sell a few cigarettes to me (actually for I.A.). He presented me with a tin of Egyptians. The black cab followed us faithfully to the bottom of the hill and remained there, waiting for our return from the ruins. Our driver required only five minutes to glance at them and the countryside (his wife did not budge from the car), and we then set off for Schlüchtern and Fulda.

He was a Bavarian, ebullient and talkative, who made it clear, after ascertaining my home-province, that he detested the Prussians. "A black day when we tied up with Bismarck! The Prussians are bleeding our land dry, not only of butter but of men."

His animadversions tumbled out all the way to Schlüchtern as we traversed the Spessart Forest, one of the most glorious spans of gigantic oaks and beeches in Europe. The situation struck me with its grim ironies. Would our benefactor's government contracts be cancelled because our pursuers reported his license-number and connexion with us?

After we left the Bavarians at Fulda, the motor-cab followed discreetly behind us down the dark streets over-hung by trees. Beneath the few lamp-lights, I could make out at the wheel a rather soft, round chin and youthful, thin moustaches under a cap tilted over a nose. The car was thoroughly mud-spattered, effectively obscuring the figure in the back seat as well as the number and city-letter of the license-plates.

Our refuge in Fulda was as confining as a black slave-ship and potentially as hazardous, in-as-much as I.A.'s comrade lawyer, because he had defended the sheet-metal strikers in Würzburg, was subject to continual surveillance. His legal practice had fallen off so precipitously that he was reduced to living in two small rooms, of which the living-room was occupied mainly by a gigantic Beckstein concert-grand piano, retained from the owner's previous home. After dinner in the kitchen, I.A. sat down to the piano, with a glass of brandy by the music, and entertained with several hours of repertoire from operettas and the classic masters. Her playing, of professional calibre, included two of the Chopin *impromptus* I had heard Isabelle Andros practise years ago.

When I expressed my appreciation of her performance, she answered simply that it was the result of years spent in accompanying her father, a mime, in Parisian music-halls. Her reply was immediate and almost convincing.

Sunday, 25 March

Passage to Eisenach, only thirty-three miles from our goal, became available in an ancient, two-horse diligence; the two of us rode in the interior, and a stern matron in the *coupé*. I saw no trace of the tenacious black cab on that sparsely settled route, surmounted in the far distance by the tree-thatched hills of the Thuringian Forest. At the end of the long descent into Eisenach, a road of sudden, shuddering convolutions, the diligence came near to over-turning when, as if by some evil necromancy, the black cab swept past us and sped ahead.

We settled into a small, plain *pension* in Eisenach; the only other couple seemed to be on honeymoon. After a thin supper, we boarded a tram up to the Wartburg, hoping to relieve our taut nerves by a moon-lit stroll round the ramparts and castle of this gigantic mediaeval fortress. Although I could find no surcease from my pre-occupation, being so near my goal, I.A. chatted away, seemingly without a care.

We opened the door of our room to face a pistol in the hand of a captain of the *Gepo*, in grey coat and furred collar, sitting at ease in the open-arm chair. "Do sit down," he said

175

in excellent English, and with a condescending smile, indicated the cane settee.

His was an un-exceptional face, intense, of very pale white skin, almost translucent; his ears were as sharply pointed as his finger-nails, a highly polished rose-colour. I had the impression of an effeminate man of some breeding, who would have been at home in drawing-rooms any where in the world.

"You English do have an excess of brass—we received an alert before you reached Zurich."

"Was that you in the motor-cab?" I asked, quite relaxed now.

He examined the question for some possible ruse and said, "No, I spotted you at the *Landgrafenzimmer*, admiring all seven frescoes. . . . Surely they're not your taste?"

"Ridiculous *kitsch*. Not worth the climb."

"Quite so. Now, if you and the dear lady will join hands." Still pointing the pistol, he held out a pair of hand-cuffs.

The window behind him cracked, and a bullet hit the back of his skull. I.A., peering over his shoulder, screamed in terror; he pitched to the floor at our feet, quite dead.

I.A. had caught a glimpse of our benefactor in the bright moon-light before he disappeared; this, not the shot, had evoked her scream. She sank down, gasping, on the settee.

"That *thing*! It can not be alive—yet it was!"

"Good heavens! What was it?"

"The head of a mummy!"

Most incredible, yet this was the only occasion in my life when I witnessed a person in a true state of horripilation. She gulped a double helping of brandy, and I also took one as we tossed our belongings into our bags. The body we laid out on the bed, a blanket over its staring eyes, then we crept out the rear window and down a fire-stairway.

Hurrying through the city, with the thump of my crutch

The window behind him cracked, and a bullet hit the back of his skull.

magnified by the silence, I wondered, where could we sleep now, after mid-night? An abrupt turn of a street brought us up against the English Church of Eisenach—SERVICES ON FIRST SUNDAY OF EACH MONTH, 3:30 P.M.—but a sign on the door read TO LET.

I kicked in a small wooden opening to the cellar, and we stretched out on the hard oak pews.

I.A. was still in a condition of shock: "Don't be disturbed, Herr Grauber, if I scream in my sleep."

Monday, 26 March

A clatter of hooves roused me shortly before dawn. In the stable behind the church, a bewhiskered feeble man, his left arm amputated, struggled to hitch an elderly mare to a hearse. I waked I.A., and we met the hearse as it rolled out on to the street. To assuage his surprise, I enquired whose funeral it might be. He replied cautiously: there had been some cases of small-pox in Gotha, and the hearse was needed there.

"Two marks if you take us. We're looking for work round there."

He hesitated, then murmured, "Pay first."

For I.A., in her half-awake daze, the thought of being borne in a hearse after the previous night's vision was unsettling; at first she refused to enter the van. "Please wake me before we reach Gotha, dear doctor, and assure me I'm breathing." The driver closed the draperies, and she promptly fell asleep again as we clattered along the rutted valley at the edge of the forest.

Up front with the driver, I enquired casually whether there were any munitions-factories near Gotha or Erfurt.

"Munitions?" He examined me from under a drooping eyelid. "We don't talk about military things here."

I explained that I had served as an ordnance-mechanic and displayed my letter from the employment-bureau.

"Ah? If you're looking for that work, why don't you know where it is?"

The young corporal, eating a *Wurst* alone at the next table, gazed longingly towards my stein of beer in Gotha's Erfürterstrasse Café; even the watery stuff was forbidden to him.

I.A. sipped wine with her fish and turnips and groaned, "Mein Herr, you're growing thinner, even with all the bread and fats rations I give you, and I don't lose an ounce. G-----n this turnip winter!"

The corporal, emboldened I suppose by her rowdy language, came to our table and asked if I would buy a beer for myself and him; he would pay for both. "But pour mine into a coffee-mug."

I invited him to join us and paid for his beer. *"Wie geht's?"*

He sighed. *"Dörrgemüse, trocken Brod, Marmelade, Heldentod."* * His family had not received his telegram in time, and had gone off to visit relatives.

"We're looking for work," I said. "Do you know of a munitions-works round here or Erfurt?"

"There's a big one at Straussfurt, makes shells and ammunition."

I enquired if they were large weapons, for that was my experience in the army. He doubted it; in fact, he'd heard rumours of a new shell called "Little Bertha."

"It must be very tiny?" I.A. asked.

He waved a hand as if brushing away a fly. "People there are ordered not to talk about it."

Arachne had told me that Krupp's "Big Bertha" would be the most far-reaching cannon ever made. The perfect cam-

* "Dried vegetables, dry bread, marmalade, a hero's death." —R.S.

ouflage for the dreadful device I sought would therefore be an insignificant little sister.

"Do they hire women?" I.A. asked.

"Thousands," the boy replied. The factory was about twenty-six kilometres north of Erfurt.

"How can we travel there?" I queried.

"The company runs motor-omnibuses, but they're only for workers."

A Sister of Charity now appeared across the street from us. This was more than co-incidence—it was condescension. I immediately hobbled towards her, and she scurried next to a policeman. She was, assuredly, the same woman who had been following us, for she knew full well that we could not question her in the presence of the police.

I.A. and I departed for the farmers' market in search of transport. Little food was available to the hopeful women, large wicker baskets strapped to their backs, who thronged the square: eggs, chickens, pigeons, some game-birds and, I was shocked to note, crow. The purchased birds were deftly de-capitated over a pail designed for this gruesome task.

One fellow, the very model of a mis-begotten pirate—one eye, twisted face, even a wooden leg—and speaking a Slav-accented German, covertly exchanged cigarettes for eggs. Where did one find cigarettes in this small town?

The same question intrigued I.A., who had reached the end of her tobacco resources. She eaves-dropped behind the pirate, then drew him aside for a lengthy dialogue in Russian. The exchange was warm and animated: I.A. bubbling with surprise and delight while the Russian, overcoming his evident fears, embraced her as an old friend.

She communicated to me in French, showing outward nonchalance in front of the man. "It is *the* factory! Thousands of workers and five hundred Russian prisoners. This one picks up food for the officials' dining-room and also operates for his own profit with cigarettes—they're from Red Cross parcels the POWs receive occasionally. He will carry us to the factory for ten marks, in his closed van."

"Always a danger with these profiteers. Surely the police are aware—"

"I *know* the Russians. Let us do it my way this once."

The Russian drove a creaking, sagging baker's delivery-waggon to a wooded area some distance from the market, where he slammed the doors after us.

The munitions-works was a huge enterprise, he told us, speaking through a panel slid back behind his seat. It was entirely surrounded by barbed wire and had been manufacturing shells and powder from the start of the war. In 1915, before the Russians were brought here, a secret project was undertaken in an area cordoned off from the original factory.

I opened the panel farther to observe the road. We were still in an urban area; my compass showed we were heading south, not north. I demanded, "Why are you going south?"

"Must stop." His fuzzy Russo-German was difficult to comprehend.

"Why?"

"Pay police bribe."

And now the *Polizei* station came into view. My response was, "Halt or you die!" He pulled up his horse instantly. I.A. cried out, "What's wrong?"

In one agonising moment, I sifted a collection of observations and instincts circling in my mind for a decision which meant life or death for all three of us. Some thing overly friendly in I.A.'s manner towards the Russian had given me cause to wonder; now that we had found the home of the secret weapon, she might be tempted to carry on without me. The Russian soldiers, after terrible defeats and suffering, were deeply infected by radical agitators, affording I.A. the opportunity to offer them money, power under the Bolsheviks, almost anything in their propaganda arsenal, in order to collect an army of five hundred men under her command. The bribe for the police could be myself. The pirate would turn me over in payment for some previous transgressions, or simply to curry favour for his future operations. The police-station was about a hundred feet away—I could not run now.

Thrusting my right arm through the panel and round the driver's neck, I seized my wrist with the other hand, creating a deadly, vise-like grip that constricted his throat. "Don't talk or move!" I threatened in German, then ordered I.A. to retreat to the opposite end of the waggon. "Quickly now—and not one word in Russian or I'll strangle him!"

She backed away instantly. "I warned you of this paranoia!"

"Turn north to Straussfurt," I commanded the driver. "Do not stop! Do you understand?"

He grunted a frightened *"Ja, ja!"* and complied. "Madame," I said, shifting my position so that I could see her over my shoulder, "do not attempt to come near me—I can kick with my boots."

She shook her head in a grim reply. "He probably does need to bribe a policeman."

"Who would be the payment—you or I?"

The waggon departed Gotha and veered north by east. We crossed the River Nesse, which I recalled from my map.

"May I smoke?" she asked.

"Sorry. I'd rather you didn't go near your bag."

After some minutes, she spoke again. "You think I will somehow steal this secret with the aid of the prisoners?"

"Precisely."

"But they're infantry--*muzhiks!* Peasants! How could they understand any thing of this complex weapon?"

We passed the village of Gräfen Tonna, directly on course.

182

"I have weighed the responsibilities and taken the risks. If I am proved wrong, I shall make amends."

"You will not need to apologise. Had the situation been reversed, I would have taken the same action—but more effectively." From her boot-top she extracted a pistol, which she skidded across the wood floor to me. She had snatched it from the dead *Gepo* officer, and it was still loaded.

"Your effectiveness re-inforces my doubts. Once again you have broken our pact—once again I insist, *no weapons!*"

"Here is Straussfurt," the Russian glumly announced.

I peered out the panel. It was a town very much like Tennstedt and others we had passed. Soon we reached a barbed-wire enclosure eight feet high, stretching as far as the horizon and re-inforced at equal intervals by elevated sentry-platforms. From these, huge, rotating electric-arc lights scanned the ground, de-nuded of trees and brush. High brick columns, crenellated at the top, supported water-tanks; scores of metal boxes, covered by canopies and screened on four sides (probably air vents), were scattered over the undulating terrain, and a dozen or so derrick structures, such as are employed in collieries to hoist coal and men, ranged in silhouette against the surly skies. Among these and the columns stood high wood poles and cross-bars, like gibbets, from which hung high-tension electric-lines that stretched northwards into infinity. The stockade enclosed a railway siding, wherein sat row upon row of coal-waggons, and, balanced atop these, begrimed women jabbed long metal rods into the black chunks.

I saw no factory buildings, no furnaces or clanging forges. It could have been simply a coal-mine. Had I been lured to this desolate place for my destruction?

In a stab of anger, I cried, "Where is the factory?" poking the pistol into the back of the Russian's head.

He pointed into the earth. *"Salt-mine!"*

True, these ancient mines were scattered over North Germany, but could an entire munitions-works function underground? It struck me as incredible, but possible in incredible times. And then I discerned puffs of smoke issuing from the crenellations under the water-tanks: the brick columns also served as chimneys.

"Say nothing of us," I warned the Russian. "I am German—it's my word against yours!"

Directly outside the main gate, guarded on either side by a sentry-tower, a small shack displayed the sign LABOUR EMPLOYMENT BUREAU. I.A. and I eased out of the van's rear doors, hidden from the gate; in anticipation of a close body search, I dropped the pistol into a pool of mud beside the road as we walked towards our penultimate test.

"Please bear in mind, madame," I whispered, "if I do not come out—neither shall you."

"*Viel Glück,* Herr Grauber." She squeezed my left arm and, glancing up at the electric-poles, murmured, "They do seem prepared for multiple hangings."

Her tone, accompanied by a wan half-smile, was both melancholy and apprehensive; I could not fathom whether it reflected some dire news conveyed by the Russian or an inmost reluctance to enter upon the task before her.

CHAPTER TWELVE

An Eerie City Under the Ground

We formed a queue of two. A *Geheimpolizei* officer in uniform sat beside the civilian functionary to over-see security, for the entire complex was operated by a Krupp-Bosch corporation in behalf of the Imperial Government. They checked over our papers methodically but swiftly, compared our identity-photographs against their files of un-desirables, and impressed our finger-prints. Since this last verification required extensive files, our prints would un-doubtedly be sent to Berlin, where, in view of the pressing business of strikes and food riots, they could rest for weeks, even months. The manager posed a few desultory questions about our previous employment and in less than twenty minutes decided we were both worthy of hire; the essential requirement was, apparently, a moveable, docile body.

I solicited work in the shell-making plant, citing my war experience in ordnance, but most of these jobs were performed by women. I was taken on as a message-carrier, and since they assumed I was already receiving a government pension of ninety-five marks a month (less than £5) for my leg disability, I could receive no remuneration from my employer. However, I would be supplied with a bicycle being developed by a company engineer for leg amputees; indeed, I would be one of the first participating in the experiment. For a moment I had a vision of the torture-racks at the Degerloch hospital, but it was a low, conventional tricycle, on which the drive-wheel was operated by hand-levers instead of pedals. The wooden wheels were banded with iron like a farm waggon's, making for a jolty ride, but it moved me about the works speedily and provided the exercise for my arms and shoulders that I sorely needed in lieu of cricket and boxing.

Best of all, I could use my position as a pretext to communicate daily with Frau Lobegott, who was taken on to teach elementary German at eighty-five pfennigs (one shilling) an hour. The company supplied both food and accommodations in male and female dormitories, for which five marks a month were deducted, and finally, we were provided with passport-like photographs, affixed to identity-tags, to be worn at all times.

Even though I was still doubtful of my formidable partner's true name and motives, when my identification was pinned up directly over my heart, accepting me into the Krupp-Bosch team of Fighters for the Fatherland, I felt a certain pride of achievement.

Tuesday, 27 March

The dimensions of the immense under-ground city in which I now lived were but partially revealed in the following days, while I propelled my tricycle through the electrically illuminated roadways arching as high as the London Underground. The entire Straussfurt works was patrolled twenty-four hours a day by *Landwehr* troops on motor-cycles, and auxiliaries on foot with Alsatian tracking-dogs.

I immediately set about to scout the most closely guarded plant, since this would assuredly be the one manufacturing the secret weapon. I discovered it quickly enough by the simple manifestation of two bayonet-points, one held at my throat and the other at my heart, one hundred metres from the entrance of a tunnel. Four additional guards stood at the portal labelled simply PLANT Z.

While the bayonets kept me stiffly erect on my tricycle, I was informed that all packages and envelopes would be left outside the portal; the ones to be delivered would be opened there; I would be subject to a search of my own person, *et cetera ad infinitum*. I told the sergeant I had made a wrong turn, and quickly wheeled away.

The city occupied only a portion of the Zechstein salt-mine, which had been worked for more than two centuries. Many such deposits lay under the North German plain and Lower Saxony to a depth of four thousand feet, all remainders of a pre-historic ocean which once formed part of the North Sea. The Zechstein area, I discovered after a few days, had been tunnelled to 955 feet below-ground, and comprised forty-six miles of two-way roads, five levels (at least sixteen feet high), un-counted passages and tunnels, huge chambers used for manufacture and storage, a school, a hospital, even a vaudeville-cinema theatre and a ball-room, all carved out of the solid rock-crystal. Moreover, the deeply religious miners, in memoriam to their co-workers crushed in accidents and out of devotion to their patron saint, had wrought a finely detailed baroque Cathedral of St. Barbara, seating fifteen hundred. (She was also, with neat dispassion, the patron saint of artillery.) The city's operations were an eerie conglomeration of scientific advances and primitive labour, exotic colours and fetid smells,

187

ugly starvation and primly neat laboratories, all the dichotomies which men at war can create. It was a cosmos such as I had never viewed before and would never be created again.*

One section of the works, the tremendous Kaiser Wilhelm dome, was still supplying salt for the Empire. I delivered messages and orders to the manager in his office, hewn out of the rock at the top of the chamber. The electric lights, suspended from this height, faded amidst the vast walls of salt, black and glittering as coal. Seen from the bottom, reached in a car lowered by a derrick, the ceiling was as limitless as the heavens and the lights were far-off stars. A tunnel led to the current diggings, another dome round which circled an electric train, on tracks hewn into the sides. From the bottom of this chamber, an icy blast thrust its way in through a crevice in the rock, its ferocity increasing as it circled round and round like a whirlwind to form icicles on the sides of the dome and wreak havoc on the workmen, who laboured in several feet of water at the very bottom.

These were the Russian prisoners of war. Despite the restrictions of international conventions and their physical debilitation—tuberculous, under-fed, crippled, swathed in rags—they swung picks at the rock-crystal and frequently fell, face down, to expire in the black waters. It was a vision of purgatory without hope which shall for ever remain graven in my memory. And how ironic! for salt is an ancient symbol of honour and hospitality; when an Arab says, "There is salt between us," he speaks of having dined with you as his guest, and therefore your friend.

(The prisoners dined on offal. Its stench floated about in

* Hitler's V-2 rockets, which nearly destroyed London, were manufactured in a salt-mine at Nordhausen, some twenty miles from here, by slave labour.—R.S.

188

the corridors, reviving my earliest revulsions in Edinburgh, where the combined reek of glue factories, slaughter-houses, tanneries and gas-works labelled the city Auld Reekie.)

In another chamber, no longer mined, a stream of clear salt-water gushed in to create a small lake, lit up by coloured electric lights; here children and adults paddled about in row-boats to the gramophone music of waltzes and gavottes. Tobogganing provided another entertainment, the wood sleds hurtling down dis-used corridors and tunnels, from which the passengers' squeals and shrieks resonated like the cries of jungle birds or, at times, trills of flutes and piccolos.

In my ears, no music resounded; for the first time, the concrete reality of the enormous impediments to my mission pressed heavily upon me.

Wednesday, 28 March

Some dozen of us, not working on "essential production" such as shells, were assigned to clean up a part of the works for inspection Friday by some "august personages." I swept the roadways and scrubbed walls from the mine entrance leading to Plant Z with a raggle-taggle group of Russians, so sick or disabled that they could not work in the mine. Their only officer, a captain named Karinsky, was a physician who operated their wretchedly ill-equipt hospital, and despite his rank he was forced to work beside them.

Karinsky and I immediately struck a sympathetic chord. Since he had received his medical degrees in Leipzig and Berlin, we communicated in German; I admitted to having pursued chemistry for a year in Würzburg before lack of funds forced me to abandon my studies. He must once have been a man bubbling with energy and wit; now he was a shattered hulk, suffering the final ravages of tuberculosis, symptoms I recognised immediately, for they had stolen

189

away my first wife. He was about fifty but looked seventy: tall as I, stoop-shouldered and thin, with deep-set eyes that still smouldered. Only the luxurious beard, which he kept neatly trimmed down to his chest, remained of the man who had lectured in Petrograd and Moscow. He realised he was dying, yet his mind persisted in its sharpness and vitality. His research had been concentrated in the chemical structure of proteins, and thus, as we swept up the refuse, I turned the conversation to rumours of a "new chemical weapon." Although the Russians were not employed in Plant Z, they laboured beside German women in other sections of the works, creating an effective telegraph-system of facts and fantasies.

From what Karinsky had heard, he theorised that the weapon was a conventional bomb to which radium or uranium was added and somehow made radio-active; it might create burns that would terrorise its victims with the possibility of lingering death. And then, with a sigh that seemed to rise from the very toes of his fissured boots, he said, "What does it matter? We are all doomed. My own life has lingered on far too long."

"Has your government, or the Red Cross, tried to alleviate conditions here?"

"It's impossible." The Germans had captured two million of his countrymen, he explained, and the Russians held only one-fifth that number; therefore, there was no possibility of reprisal to force better treatment, as the British had done. The Tsarist government had simply abandoned the men, without monetary stipends or food packages. Occasionally they received Red Cross parcels with tins of beef and a few cigarettes.

After two years of semi-starvation and deprivation of medicine, they could barely lift themselves from their straw mats. To avoid work in the mine, some inflicted wounds on themselves. Karinsky told me that they slashed their wrists close to the artery, then rubbed in a mixture of bread, soap, mustard and pepper; by frequently applying compresses of boiled paper to the wound, they kept it from healing. But the *Landwehr* NCOs were cognisant of this, and beat them awake in the morning with rifle-butts.

Thursday, 29 March

Commanded to help clean the electric generating plants, I discovered that the military autocrats in control of Germany treated their own people almost as viciously, the women in particular. Germans, many of them mothers, worked beside Belgian women (who had been lured here with promises of high wages: about seven pence an hour for twelve-hour shifts) and a few able-bodied Russians to stoke the huge boilers which fed the generators supplying current for the under-ground lights and ventilating fan system. The women, in shapeless blouses and baggy, short trousers, laboured more vigorously than the Russians, occasionally helping them lift a shovel though they had been ordered not to fraternize with the prisoners. All toiled with heavy iron tools in a heat which recalled my worst days as a battle-correspondent in the Egyptian desert. The perspiration rolled over their faces and arms like a tropical rain; the men stripped to the waist, while the women tore open their blouses and dispensed with under-clothes to achieve some cooling evaporation. For the ten-minute rest-periods granted every four hours, they slept in the dust beside the furnaces.

What a brilliant solution this under-ground city provided for the war government's needs: no precious concrete and steel were required to erect new plants; free of vibration and extreme temperature changes, the chambers required one-third less heat than above-ground factories, and they created an extra bonus for management—workers could not be distracted by staring out windows at trees and clouds or the lucky few disporting themselves in the sunshine. Indeed, Karinsky told me that many Germans who had worked here since the plant opened three years ago had not even wanted to visit "on the outside."

"Have you ever thought of seeing 'the outside' again?"

He studied me for some time with great interest, grinning mordantly. "You could be an *agent provocateur*. Or an agent of another sort; you're far too intelligent to be a messenger. For me, for all Russians, so long as the war continues, there is no hope. Possibly you can help us?"

I replied carefully, "I do not see how."

I.A. contrived an ingenious scheme to gain access to technical information. She suggested to her superior that much of the factory's scrap-paper, letters, memoranda and orders could be used twice, by permitting her pupils to write their lessons on the blank sides, before the paper was carted away to be re-processed. And I, a messenger, would be glad to pick up the scrap on my daily rounds.

"—perusing the obverse side as I go. Madame, you may well be awarded an efficiency commendation for this," I said.

"No. My superior has already forwarded this suggestion as her own."

Friday, 30 March

The cleaning-brigade turned out at five-fifteen A.M.; inspection would take place at noon, and we were required to brighten up the approach to Plant Z. Karinsky assembled his tattered brigade and we straggled over to the forbidden tunnel. As we turned a corner, we found ourselves suddenly pushed back against the wall by guards to make room for a march-past of German women with bright yellow faces, hair and arms, dressed in the usual work-clothes. I took them to be participants in some sort of ceremony for the distinguished visitors.

Not so, said Karinsky. These were the "yellow women," victims of the noxious fumes caused by explosives they poured into the shells; TNT had turned their skins a sharp mustard yellow, even to the roots of their un-kempt hair. They plodded along without speaking or smiling, mouths clamped shut as if to keep out the fumes; their faces, bereft of female attitudes, resembled those of de-humanized, long-term convicts. They were being sent back to their quarters, separate from the other women, so that the plant in which they worked could be shut down for a short time, on the pretext of a mechanical failure. It was not politic to subject the august personages to this dreadful vision of their servants.

We were issued long-handled polished-brass pans with flap tops, like maids' crumbers, and new brooms; the most flagrantly ragged Russians were outfitted in clean clothing. We would be honoured by the task of following the mounted assemblage through Plant Z to sweep after the horses.

When word came that the august personages had arrived at the front gate, the guards installed us in a corridor outside the entrance to Z, to await the inspection.

The band of the Second Weimar Hussars, who had managed to maintain their over-shoulder tunics and gilt-laden shakos even though their regiment had been converted to infantry, led the procession. Behind them a *Fahnenkompanie* of twenty standard-bearers stepped smartly to the music, "I am a Prussian, knowest thou my colours?" This imperial display was only fitting, in-as-much as the two generals on horse-

193

back, Paul von Hindenburg, Commander-in-Chief, and his Quartermaster-General, Erich von Ludendorff, had now taken the place of the Kaiser in the actual government of the German people. Wilhelm II was generally blamed for senile interference and confined to his palace by the military.

The generals, in radiant white and gold, with the Imperial eagle perched atop elaborately gilded helmets, wore the same number of medals on their chests, for they were two halves of one Prussian soul, complementing each other: Ludendorff, the master-mind, and Hindenburg, the executor. Sitting heavily on his white stallion, Hindenburg displayed the long moustaches that had become the model for all army officers, and at sixty-nine, his face still challenged the crystal walls in solidity. Ludendorff, who had planned the recent victorious invasion of Poland and Rumania, possessed the deep-set eyes, square jaws and heavy, wrinkled neck of an English bulldog, which he rivalled in tenacity.

Directly behind them came two shocks for me. First, Herr Direktor Dr. Ehrens, Krupp's foremost technical expért, who had gulled our industrialists into an invitation for a friendly sight-seeing tour of British ship-yards and heavy industries only six weeks before war was declared. The second surprise was Baron Hochwächter, now a colonel but formerly director of Daimler Motor Works in England. I doubted he could recognise me, sweeping the blotches behind him, although we had met several times to aid my campaign of organising rifle-clubs. Both men had been brought along to formulate means of stimulating production.

The Hussars band turned off at the tunnel to Plant Z, and the cleaning-squad were again halted for identity checks, while Ludendorff presented the presiding genius of the works to Hindenburg: Dr. Gerhard Buchhalter, also on horseback, a short, slender patrician, his thin hair receding far back from his forehead. Keloids, the scars of radio-active burns, covered his face with platelets like the shell of an armadillo; these, I surmised, were the result of accidents many years before in radium research, for protection against radio-activity had been known since the pioneer work by Mme. Curie.

From fragments of Buchhalter's conversation with Ludendorff, I gathered that the scientist's early research into atomic structure had been scoffed at by his older colleagues at the Prussian Academy in Berlin; in 1912 he brought his concepts to the attention of Ludendorff through his wife, a cousin of the general. Thus "Little Bertha" had become Ludendorff's personal project, which secured approval of the Kaiser and un-limited funds.

"Now, sirs," Buchhalter announced, "the first plant you will see may astonish you, not only because of its immensity but because, unlike a cannon-works or a saw-mill, there is no noise, no movement, very few people, and you can not even see the product being created. Therefore, to prevent your wondering what has become of the hundreds of engineers and millions of marks spent by the Treasury on 'Little Bertha,' will you spare me a few minutes to demonstrate the years of frustrating experiments and failures before this weapon could be built?"

The two generals eyed each other and, with markedly little enthusiasm, dismounted. They were led to a canopy, open on all sides and well illuminated, which displayed models and diagrams. The *Fahnenkompanie* took up positions on three sides. We sweepers stood beside the horses against the fourth wall, but Karinsky and I took care to move well forward and overhear the proceedings.

Hochwächter whispered to Ehrens, "Oh, G-----n! a physics lecture!"

"Uranium for its very beginnings *belongs* to Germany,"

195

Buchhalter began. "The element was isolated by Martin Klaproth in 1789 from pitch-blende found in Saxony. Small quantities for my early experiments were acquired from our own Erzegebirge. Wilhelm Röntgen in 1895 discovered the X-ray principle—certain particles of matter give off electromagnetic radiation which could penetrate other matter. And Wilhelm Wein, our Nobel Prize winner, found three years later that beams of charged gas particles could be deflected by a magnetic field."

Hindenburg grunted impatiently, shifting his weight from one foot to the other.

"Now, for centuries it has been assumed that energy and matter were immutable; neither could be created or destroyed. But as early as 1905, Albert Einstein theorised that energy could turn into matter, and vice versa."

"He's hardly a German," Ehrens grumbled to the baron.

"Einstein even proposed an equation—Energy equals mass multiplied by the speed of light squared. This means, in effect, that if *one* kilogram of matter could be converted *entirely* to energy, it would create twenty-five billion kilowatt-hours of energy, enough to keep the entire electric-power industry of our country operating for many years! But at that time, of course, it was impossible."

The search for this alternative source of power, Buchhalter continued, had led him to the awesome weapon they would soon see.

Ludendorff now gazed with paternal affection on the models.

"It all derives from the atom, a tiny world of matter which we can not even see." And Buchhalter pointed to the components of a model similar to the solar system. "The nucleus, occupying the position of the sun, consists of one or more positively charged particles, called protons. The electrons, surrounding the nucleus like planets, have negative charges. There is mutual attraction and repulsion, but the

196

attraction is stronger, and thus keeps the universe in operation."

"Thank God!" said Ludendorff.

Buchhalter related his first experiments, bombarding various elements, boron, nitrogen, lithium, with alpha particles of radium. He had observed that an electroscope, set by chance on a table near-by, revealed radio-activity much greater than any of these elements emitted individually.

(This, then, was the significance of the "bombard with X-rays" note left by our murdered agent.)

"It was the boron that was being *ionised* by the radium; that is, one or more electrons had been detached from the boron atom. The eternal entity of the atom had come apart!"

"Good heavens!" said the baron. Ludendorff and Hindenburg nodded to Buchhalter with new appreciation; if he could dissolve God's work, he could loosen mere political frontiers.

But creating changes in nitrogen or boron could produce little energy, because they were low in the scale of atomic weights. Suppose the heaviest element, uranium, could be ionised like boron? Buchhalter achieved this after years of experimentation.

"The next problem was to control the interaction of these variably structured atoms, their attraction and repulsion, so that each particle change would be replaced by particles from the damaged nucleus—a series of almost instantaneous explosions, like one bullet setting off another. This could release the atom's total energy, as estimated by Einstein. But producing sufficient refined uranium to create such explosions was like the difference between the discovery of fire and building a steam locomotive."

Now even Hindenburg was enthralled. He saw the problem as a military exercise: surveying the terrain, laying out the earth-works, spying out the enemy salients, marshalling supplies and weapons against a force whose strength, armour and even uniforms were invisible. He appraised Buchhalter with perplexed esteem: how could this little man do it?

" . . . and then," said Buchhalter, "I had a fateful accident in a small-scale test at the abandoned mine west of here: if the two uranium masses, each of slightly different atomic weight, are not kept a proper distance apart, they create an explosion! Thus the bomb was born. I now invite you to enter Plant Z, to witness the final processing of the uranium."

I judged that Buchhalter, a veteran of the bureaucratic wars, had carefully omitted details of vital intermediate strategies and forces to make certain that no other commander could supersede him. Rutherford and scientists at the Cavendish Laboratory would be able to piece together these processes more readily if I supplied particulars of their complex machinery. As the generals led the way into the all-important Plant Z, I sought a way to put myself within eaves-dropping range. Quickly hoisting a water-filled fire-bucket, I whispered to Karinsky, "Follow me!" and scurried ahead of the generals, sprinkling and sweeping the ground before them; Karinsky immediately caught my purpose and did the same.

Every one, from the top down, assumed that some officer had planned this imperial gesture of polishing the very ground on which the generals walked. To question it now would be *lèse-majesté*. No one stopped us.

We entered an immense and wondrously silent chamber, encompassing one acre and at least twenty feet high, occupied by what resembled two race-tracks, laid out side by side on the concrete floor and connected at one point. Each was approximately four hundred feet in length and one hundred feet across, but only twelve feet high. These, said Buchhalter, were "mass spectrometers," in which the uranium atoms were sent racing around from one track to the other by electro-magnets, in order to sort out the uranium particles according to two different atomic weights. The "grand-stand" of each "track" consisted of twenty-four gigantic, U-shaped magnets, their vertical arms encircled by electric cables as thick as a man's arm. Power for the cables surged through a heavy copper bar, curving around the top of the track.

The uranium was being burned, actually vaporized, by electric arcs, and under the effect of the magnetic forces a particle of one weight sped to the left; another, slightly heavier, raced to the right, each collected by the appropriate repository.

On either side of this immense plant, in balconies hewn out of the salt walls and protected by glass, sat the controllers. They were young women, technicians far different in bulk and perspicacity from the other labourers; they manipulated dials to regulate the current and accelerate the speed of the isotopes round the tracks. Buchhalter said that despite all his technical knowledge, it was not possible to train any one for this work; the women acquired their skill with practice, changing speed and power by intuition, like jockeys riding horses.

One peculiar reason for the great expense of this operation was the war-time shortage of copper for conductors; half the magnets used silver cables, of which about five thousand tons had been obtained from the Imperial Treasury. The total out-put of these two "tracks" was thirty grams of enriched uranium per day, about the weight of two gold marks.

The small bomb produced, "lightweight but capable of laying waste an entire city, is on its way as scheduled for the duty approved by the Kaiser," Buchhalter announced. More than a year had been required to refine the uranium used in it.

I was too late! Only God could help our soldiers now, for

what purpose would I serve to alert Arachne of this over-hanging catastrophe when I did not know the locus, even the size or shape, of the diabolical instrument? A poisonous lassitude, compounded of weariness, anger and futility, coursed through my entire body, and only by stabbing my finger-nails into my palms could I conceal my feelings. I had failed my mission.

Then another blow struck. Buchhalter announced, "Let us now move to Plant Y. The second bomb, twice as destructive as the first, is being assembled."

I stabilised myself; now at last I would come face to face with the enemy, and I found renewed hope in one possibility—sabotage.

It was an awesome moment. Over the centuries, alchemists had dreamed of transforming base-metal into gold or silver, and here a slight, disfigured man had accomplished what the greatest minds of this age had deemed impossible: he had transmuted base pitch-blende into a metal even more valuable than all the gold and silver on earth, because the Prussian war-lords who owned it could now control the world.

"The shell-assembly plant is quite safe," Buchhalter affirmed. "The explosive charge is inserted only after the weapon is in place and—" suddenly he waved me back. "No! no! Enough of this sweeping—the fittings are too delicate for this dust. *Raus!*" Thus I was deprived of the slightest clue to the weapon's structure, doubtless as un-conventional as its fuel.

Karinsky was utterly exhilarated by Buchhalter's demonstrations; in a remote corridor I suggested we might exchange views on these scientific wonders that evening.

"But where can we do it discreetly, without interruptions?" he asked.

"The cathedral is always open for prayer. See you at nine."

CHAPTER THIRTEEN

"Death Is Our Only Hope of Escape"

I believe in God, but I do not accept any of the organised religions for which the acquisition of money, power and pomp, as well as continual warfare among their sects, be-comes an end in itself. Never-the-less, I stood in reverence before this amazing eighteenth-century baroque cathedral of rock-crystal. It was the work not of ambitious princes but of humble miners, craftsmen devoting their individual skills over the centuries to the glorification of their own private deity. St. Barbara's statue welcomed all from the top-most peak of three pediments, rising one above the other on Corinthian columns, confined between two graceful towers nearly seventy-five feet high, each embellished by elaborate scroll-work and topped by fantastic delicate cupolas.

As I entered the vast, dark emptiness, a high-pitched throbbing wail, as if all the souls of hell were sighing, surged over me. It was the organ, reverberating amid the domed ceiling, floors and chapels of quartz which amplified and concentrated each tone to produce nerve-tingling vibrations.

The sounds were not a hymn or recognisable melody but un-earthly heaving and groaning, screams and howls, suggesting that all the miners who had carved and worshipped here had come back from the Other Side to lament the evil uses to which their labours had been twisted.

I approached the organ slowly and, I must admit, reluctantly. Only one large candle lit the entire cathedral: it revealed the face of the organ-player—I.A., eyes closed, swaying like an angel of the Lord through whom the dead struggled to convey their woes. If she were indeed the Isabelle Andros I had known, this occasion had transformed her into a virtuoso.

Silently I retreated to a corner pew near the entrance. Karinsky slipped in, as awed by the sounds as I had been. He murmured with a wintry smile, "A most appropriate elegy for the devastation of Europe."

"Yes, the weapon will be operative," I said. "Buchhalter would not dare make those two generals look foolish if he were not certain."

"What haunts me is this—the bomb may be *better* than he thinks. He has never tested a full-scale version, and when he tampers with the structure of the earth . . ."

That had been Einstein's fear from the start. I sat in silence, contemplating how much I could confide in this man. The music swelled into a crescendo of ear-piercing shrieks, and suddenly stopped in the semi-quaver of a chord. A figure, barely visible, took I.A.'s arm and wrenched her from the seat, then blew out the candle.

"Music at an un-authorized time—serious infraction of the rules," Karinsky whispered. "That means confinement."

"The guard-house? That's a dreadful blow."

"Oh, they firmly believe in the redemption of the God-house. . . . Forgive the wretched pun, but I have so little time to live that even the macabre amuses me. Grauber, at first I thought you were a *provocateur:* I saw you speaking to

One large candle revealed the face of the organ player—I.A., eyes closed, swaying like an angel of the Lord.

that woman before we met, and afterwards you pretended not to know her. But your concern for her now is genuine—you two must be agents of an Allied power. This monstrous weapon must be destroyed. If such is your purpose, I offer my assistance. I have a few men in the shell-assembly boiler-room, the grenade-casting plant . . ."

For an instant I considered the possibility of his being a German *provocateur*. But what could it benefit him? He had not long to live, and each day was a rack of pain. "I welcome your offer," I said, "but at the moment I have no specific plan."

"Could we sabotage the excrescence they are now assembling?"

"All my life I have believed that any goal I desired was possible. But when I consider this one, its impossibilities are limitless."

Saturday, 31 March

How did my imprisoned partner fare? With my un-decipherable script I diverted an envelope, addressed to the NCO-in-charge at the main gate, to the NCO-in-charge of the guard-house where I.A. was held, on the second level of the mine.

While this worthy scurried about consulting the other NCOs on the peculiar orders it contained, I peered through the women's gate at the two dozen prisoners, Belgian and German. I.A., mustering a dismal smile, held up seven fingers—a one-week sentence. I apologised to the NCO for my error, retrieved my envelope and pulled away.

The scrap-paper for the children's lessons I transported, in large baskets fastened fore and aft on my tricycle, to I.A.'s substitute. I had been looking over them beforehand for possibly fruitful gleanings; most were useless. Today's batch came from the draughting department, and one item I committed to memory before I tore it into tiny bits and swallowed them. It was a schematic sketch, without dimensions, of the weapon-assembly, and remarkably simple. As in a cannon barrel, the power-charge at one end, fulminate or something similar to our cordite, smashed one container of uranium (hammer) against the other (anvil).

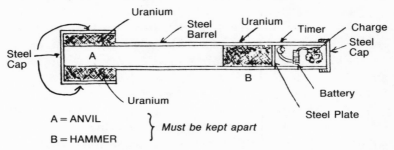

It now became imperative to carry a description of the uranium ionisation process and the weapon-assembly to our specialists in England. I would await I.A.'s release, sabotage the second weapon if possible, or cripple the factory, and then clear out. In the euphoria of the moment, I did not reckon with the relentless power of chance and of sheer stupidity.

Sunday, 1 April

When I delivered the customary inter-office communications to the *Gepo* Chief of Plant Security (not the underling who had hired me), at his side sat a colonel-inspector of the *Gepo* with insignia indicating he was attached to the General Staff in Berlin. He was examining the employee-identity photos; after I entered he glanced up. Keeping my head low in proper servility to the Chief, I discerned in my peripheral vision that the colonel was Charles, Arachne's favourite waiter! What delicious morsels our aristocrats had served up for the German Secret Service: they knew I was in Zurich before our Consul-General had his breakfast.

The Chief, to demonstrate he was operating with the

obligatory efficiency, berated me for tardiness in deliveries. Vowing to work twice as hard for the Fatherland to compensate for my single leg, I painfully hobbled out, but slowly enough to hear Charles lash the Chief: "The weapon is safely on the way to England, despite your bungling. The entire *Gepo* here have been as haphazard and light-headed as our Austrians!—instructions from Berlin are lost, and your employee-files are like pea-meal *Wurst*. I return to Berlin today to check those finger-prints myself. I *know* Conan Doyle and the woman must be here!"

The atom bomb was destined for England!

My plans clarified instantly. The primary objective would be sabotage of the bomb being assembled and then a dash for home, all the while praying that catastrophe would not strike before I arrived. But first I was obligated to release I.A. from her under-ground prison. I set out immediately to institute a direct and regular line of communication.

On my rounds, I had managed to filch several sheets of official stationery from various offices; on one I wrote out an order to the stores department, over an illegible signature, for four slabs of soap, and from the kitchen I snatched a lemon. After hollowing out space inside one piece of soap, I inserted several slices of the lemon with a note, penned in lemon juice:

MUST ESCAPE SOONEST. REPLY WITH LEMON-JUICE ON LAVATORY PAPER. WAD IT UP, DROP NEAR ME. WILL ARRIVE AT DIGGINGS EVERY NIGHT.

Moistening the halves of the soap, I restored it to its original shape. The wad of paper would hardly be noticed on the ground among the grey salt particles, and if it were picked up by a guard, the writing was invisible. She would need to devise a way to escape the obligatory bed-check, the locked doors and the guards. I was confident that her Russian prison experience would stand her in good stead.

For a ruse to see her daily, I forged a note from the Chief of Operations, addressed to Engineer-in-Charge, quoting a fictitious Regulation 120-D which required a written summary of the cube-footage of earth removed by female prisoners, to be prepared each evening at the end of work. Fortunately, since few typewriters were available here because of metal and personnel shortages, most communications were written in pen and ink, occasionally even in pencil.

I found I.A. and the others wielding picks and shovels, enlarging a tunnel-opening at the side of a hill to "the outside," so that rail tracks could be laid to ferry out salt from a new vein.

A *Landwehr* guard sat on his motor-cycle. In the peremptory style I employed for all except my superiors, I informed him that we had received warning that a delegation from the Swiss Red Cross would arrive at any moment, and the women had better be cleaned up.

"Where's the written order?" he demanded.

"This is never put on paper," I sneered. "It's a *surprise* inspection."

He tossed out the three chunks of soap to the clamouring women. In the general *mêlée,* I passed the prepared soap to I.A. with a whispered, "Note inside. Hold over candle."

The second letter I presented to an infirm former civil engineer, now serving as foreman of this project. "What time is this G-------d report wanted?" he grumbled.

"When do you finish?"

"Eight o'clock."

"I'll accept it at that time."

With that night's report I surreptitiously picked up a wadded note from I.A.:

BED-CHECK DIFFICULT. CAN'T SUBSTITUTE FAKE BODY.

To weigh sabotage of the weapon, Karinsky and I met at the vaudeville-cinema theatre's ten P.M. performance. Its acts were too aged for military or amusement service. The performing dogs refused to jump, for there was no food to bribe them; the skinny acrobats, whose muscles had vanished with their hair, swayed ominously on each head-stand. A lumpy flat-faced soprano and a tenor a foot shorter were both off pitch, but they did manage a close physical blending: whereas she protruded above, his belly extended below. When the voices joined in the pavilion seduction scene from *The Merry Widow*, the uproar fairly flaked the gilding off the proscenium.

The noise provided excellent cover for our gloom-laden conversation. Karinsky stated unequivocally that the guard-house nightly bed-check was inescapable; in two years, the best Russian minds, including one grand-master-class chess-player, had not been able to solve that bind.

"There must be a way!" I insisted. "Let us put our minds to it!"

As for breaking into the assembly-plant, the Russian said it was also impossible. "There is only one entry into all those plant-chambers—each has an air-ventilation shaft from the upper surface, and the air is circulated through metal ceiling-tubes by fans down here. Since the air-shafts drop down eight hundred or nine hundred feet, how could any one climb down and through this maze without being decapitated by the fan-blades?"

"Grenades!" I exclaimed. "Drop *them* down the vents! We must ascertain which lead to the assembly and ionisation plants. What of your Russian pirate, dealing in cigarettes?"

"Not to be trusted. He would sell us all for two of them."

The singing ended with a shameless, ear-splitting assault on "Brünnhilde's Battle-Cry" from *Die Walküre*.

"Surely you know a grenade explodes four or five seconds after the firing-lever is released," Karinsky said. "Are you familiar with the formula for the speed of falling bodies?"

"It's .249 multiplied by the square root of the drop." Since the bottom level was at most nine hundred feet, my calculation gave the grenades 7.47 seconds to hit bottom. "We would need some sort of timer to make the grenades go off at least thirty minutes after we drop them, to afford time for our escape."

"You also require a device to pull out the grenade safety-pins *after* they hit bottom. You can not remove those safeties before you drop them. Again, impossible!"

"That word freezes the will. If I believed in the impossible, I would not be here."

We sat, separated by silence, as the finale came on: a variation on a classic pantomime theme—the three inept paper-hangers, with ladders, buckets of paste and brushes, who could not attach the paper to the wall. Their first mad swipes at the wall created a welcome laughter out of all proportion to their conceits.

Even Karinsky smiled. My emotions were utterly exhausted; what had been an exciting task for my country, an intellectual and physical exercise, had now evolved into a painful moral dilemma: I had not calculated on the presence of the suffering workers and my new friend, Karinsky; if the weapon exploded as forcefully as Buchhalter had indicated, many of the under-ground chambers would be destroyed and the radio-activity would seep through the mine.

The paper-hangers had now reached the point where the paper clung to them and not the wall; hands glued together, they rolled about the stage like a Catherine-wheel. It was hilarious farce, but I could not laugh. "Karinsky," I whispered, "many of you would die."

He turned to me and nodded solemnly. "A great favour. Death is our only hope of escape."

I did not relish the rôle of Job's comforter. "It is a terrible decision, to sacrifice innocent people."

"It is a cardinal principle of war: the rear-guard sacrifice themselves to preserve the main forces in retreat. If this factory makes more bombs, they could destroy hundreds of thousands, possibly millions, of troops and civilians. Radio-activity does not discriminate." Karinsky drew his thin prisoner's jacket around him for warmth. "Do this for me. I do not have the courage for suicide."

The vaudeville ended. The three paper-hangers were glued helplessly to one another, un-able to separate, like Laocoön and his two sons, like myself, I.A. and Karinsky. The laughter and applause were over-whelming.

"Tell your men to steal the grenades," I said. And though I lay awake most of the night, plotting I.A.'s escape, the solution eluded me.

Monday, 2 April

Never-the-less, I proceeded with my improvised timing device, which would explode the grenades after they hit the under-ground vent-pipes and still allow us time to flee. Karinsky's man in the sheet-metal shop purloined a small steel shears, so that I could cut the grilles at the ventilator-shaft entrances above-ground. Three barriers remained to be over-come: I. A.'s release; reaching "the outside" with her, for there was a guard at the exit the prisoners were enlarging; and hauling the bulky grenades and materials for the timing device.

We could carry the grenades within wide cloth belts under our loose-fitting mackintoshes. As for the guard at the diggings, I.A., despite her pick-and-shovel labour, was still a beautiful woman; she could distract the fellow somehow while I clubbed him.

I requisitioned a metre of fusing cord and a dozen metres of hemp from the mine workers' supply-room with a fraudulent order.

210

"Why do you need all this rope?" the woman clerk demanded.

My ominous "The Swiss Red Cross is coming!" shut her off.

In Karinsky's dispensary we cut apart the two legs of a deceased Russian's trousers and sewed up the hip sections to form two enclosed pouches. Eight grenades fit into each one neatly. I would wrap one pouch round my waist, over the money-belt; I.A. would wear the other. That night, when I picked up the engineer's report, she again shook her head. Karinsky would assist my sabotage plans sufficiently, yet could I bring myself to abandon I.A.? Unthinkable.

Tuesday, 3 April

I forced myself to press on. The Russians who worked in the boiler-room supplied Karinsky with the location of the electric generating room in approximate geographic relation to my primary targets: the ionisation plant, atomic-bomb assembly and the conventional-explosives storage. One of the boiler-room men, who had been permitted above-ground to help repair the chimneys, specified their location in reference to the main gate. Now, my tricycle wheels had a diameter of twenty-six inches; therefore, the circumference (each revolution of the front wheel) marked off 6.8 feet. Between envelope deliveries, I cycled from target to target, and, employing the compass from the hollow base of my crutch, managed to measure out the distance between my targets in relationship to the electric generator and the front gate. By late after-noon, I had prepared an efficient map of the surface vents to all the targets.

Wednesday, 4 April

Time and good fortune were ebbing away; Charles could telegraph discovery of my finger-prints at any moment, or

211

the *Gepo* chief here could stumble by ridiculous chance upon my identity. Still hoping, I delivered another forged letter to the guard at the diggings, and glanced at I.A. This time she returned a stolid wink, then fell in an exhausted faint to the ground. Before the guard could prod her with his rifle, I hobbled over to raise her up, and she pressed a note into my hand. I re-mounted my tricycle and read it behind a large envelope:

CAN GO TO-NIGHT IF YOU OCCUPY MEN'S WC NEXT TO GUARD-HOUSE AFTER 9.

I.A., now sitting up wearily and drinking water from a filthy cup, caught my eye. I winked.

At Karinsky's dispensary, I coiled the hemp rope round myself above the grenade pouch and stuffed the fusing into a pocket of my mackintosh, which covered all and gave me the appearance of a Japanese sumo wrestler. I.A.'s pouch went into the basket of my tricycle, together with the steel shears and rolls of Karinsky's surgical tape, all under a mass of mail and messages. My valise fitted into another basket, also masked by a pile of mail. As the result of my training with the Sussex Volunteers, I was able to cut the fusing cord here into four lengths that would require forty minutes to burn. When I finished, Karinsky grasped my hands. "And now I shall say fare-well, friend—whoever you are."

"Not fare-well. We'll meet, I'm certain, on the Other Side. My name is Conan Doyle."

He laughed out-right, slapping my back: it was the first moment of transparent enjoyment I had ever heard from him. "I always thought your detective was an outrageous humbug!" I gave him a proper military salute, and cycled away.

I reached the lavatory by eight-forty-five, but—wretched luck—it was occupied. At eight-fifty-five an auxiliary guard and his dog emerged. He surveyed me with a sneer: "Going on the outside to-night?" Enveloped in all my gear, I could barely squeeze through the door. After his footsteps receded, I posted a notice outside on official stationery—OUT OF ORDER—and snapped the latch shut.

A few minutes after nine, I heard I.A. crawling in the vent-pipe. She dropped her nail-file through the over-head grille, so that I could undo the four screws that secured the ceiling-mesh. She pushed out her mackintosh, then a small bundle of belongings and finally her arms, which I pulled to extract her from the pipe. As she kissed my cheek, I fastened the grenades round her waist while I explained the ex-cruciating urgencies now besetting us: the need to sabotage this plant before we were un-masked, and the bomb on its way to England—or already there.

She erupted into a volley of curses. "May the Germans fry in their own explosions! My two children are in England!—evacuated from France to Kent—Maidstone."

She had never spoken of them before, but then women of a certain age seldom emphasised their children.

I exclaimed, "That's only twenty-five miles north of my home in Sussex." I did not add that Maidstone was but twenty miles east of Crayford and Dartford, the giant Vickers munitions conglomeration. "I shall try to alert Arachne despite the cable censorship, but I must proceed to England with utmost haste. First, we must concentrate on this Lucifer's work-shop." Aboard the tricycle I detailed my plans while we sped to an abandoned pit. I pushed the tricycle as well as my crutch (but retained my compass) over the fence here; the water at the bottom of the pit splashed some moments after we quick-stepped away.

We now had approximately a mile to march, weighted with grenades and rope under our mackintoshes and the steel shears in my boot, to the exit the women had dug. I was elated to have the use of my two legs again, but if we met any one who recalled Grauber the cripple, I was truly done for.

213

I.A.'s evasion of bed-check was simplicity itself, and I must admit that I felt abashed that neither I nor all those Russians had thought of it.

"The guards made certain all the cots were occupied," she said. "If a body did not move, they jabbed it with a bayonet, so that I couldn't use the old stuffed-pillow substitute. But the guards never *counted* the beds! I simply dis-mantled the wooden cot, hid the parts behind a clothes-chest, and the women, demonstrating class solidarity of the proletariat, moved their beds apart to cover the space I'd occupied. I hid in the air-vent until the check ended."

Her mind rejected conventional thinking to find the solution no one had ever dreamt of, like the intuitions of inventors of scientists, yet she accepted the stifling dogma of Lenin's Bolshevism.

From behind us came the baying of the Alsatian tracking-hounds employed by the auxiliaries. "Routine rounds," I said.

"Too close for comfort," I.A. replied. She opened her bag and brought forth a small rectangle of folded paper. "I never leave prison without it." At a turn into another corridor, she sprinkled the pepper about, "to confuse the stinking beasts."

The barking and sneezing faded as the hounds scented down another path. In fifteen minutes we jog-trotted to the passage that curved into the prisoners' recent diggings.

"Now, let me take care of this," she insisted, removing her mackintosh and grenades. "Don't try to be noble—just stand back in that crevice." She applied lip-stick and rouge without a mirror, fluffed up her hair and ambled towards the opening of the shaft.

From the cleft in the wall, I saw that the *Landwehr* guard had built a small fire for himself in a metal can just inside the tunnel.

"Keeping warm?" she asked in a husky tone.

214

The guard, a blond, burly fellow, held his rifle at the ready. "Could be warmer."

"It's terribly lonely in the women's dormitory."

"Let's go out to my guard-shack."

"It's warmer here."

"*Ja.*" The guard put down his rifle and un-buttoned his over-coat. Hoisting her skirt to the hip, she kicked above her head, like a can-can dancer, striking the man's jaw with her boot. He dropped to the ground, the astonishment frozen on his face. When I arrived, he was unconscious. I stuffed my hand-kerchief into his mouth; we tied his arms and legs with a length of our rope, then set him down in his shack beside his motor-cycle.

The grenades we assembled in clusters of three, using Karinsky's surgical tape to bind them firmly together. The German weapon was similar to our Mills grenade: a pineapple-shaped metal container of explosive that fit neatly into the hand; a powerful, spring-driven firing-lever was held within a slot of the pineapple by the safety-pin, to which a metal ring was attached. By jerking this ring, one pulled the pin out, thus releasing the lever to activate an internal fuse. The soldier lobbed it over-hand and hoped that within four seconds, when it exploded, it would land on or near the enemy.

The five grenade trios (we saved one grenade for an emergency) were taped so that the safety-pin and firing-lever remained exposed on the circumference. Over these levers, I tightly wrapped a circle of rope to which was attached a forty-minute length of fusing cord. I would ignite this fuse, which burned slowly like a fire-work "sparkler," and remove the safety-pins just before I dropped the cluster. At the bottom of the vent, the fuse would (I fervently trusted) burn through the circle of rope that restrained the firing-levers, the rope would burst apart and the levers would strike their explosive.

My first goal was the generating-plant, in order to shut off the electric-arc spot-lights on the guard-towers. This grenade cluster had a fuse cut to burn only two minutes. I.A. remained in the tunnel to complete attaching the fuses while I sallied out to the vent over the electric generating chamber.

The sweep of the arc-lights, though creating a vivid danger for me, lit up the vent-openings nicely. My running, albeit not so shifty as it had been on the rugby-field forty years before, sufficed to elude the lights, and in a few minutes my steel shears cut an opening through the protective mesh of the vent. My first match did not light; a precious second one was extinguished by the wind. The third finally lit the fusing cord. I pulled the safeties and raced away, crouching and weaving, to our cache at the tunnel. A moment before I reached it, the lights went out on the guard-towers.

Confusion and uproar ensued: sirens shrilled out; shouts, orders and countermands criss-crossed in the dark; motor-cycles and staff-cars collided.

I.A. had fused the four clusters. After a quick check, I wrapped two together with our cloth pouches; I.A. did like-wise and we hopped aboard the guard's motor-cycle, she sitting on the ammunition-carrier and both of us cradling the grenades in our laps. When I kicked the starter-pedal, the engine refused to turn over.

I.A., in a fury, kicked the cylinder-head. That started it, and off we bounced to the assembly-plant. The cloud had passed away, revealing a sharp, cold moon; never-the-less, in the pandemonium of barked orders and shifting, blinding vehicle beams, we raced about without challenge. We dropped two clusters over the bomb-assembly vent: one for the ionisation-works and another for the conventional explosives-magazine. All this required fifteen minutes; another twenty-five remained for our escape. The dash to the fence absorbed four minutes, and cutting the nasty double row of three-level barbed wire required six minutes. We pushed the cycle through—and the engine lapsed into sullen silence. I kicked it to no avail. Screaming one of her primordial curses, I.A. booted it, and we flew down-hill at twenty-five miles per hour.

After fifteen minutes we heard under-ground rumbles, as of distant naval bombardment. Peering back from the rise of a hill, I.A. reported that she could see the earth reverberating, then the top of the mine blow open. "Shells exploding like fire-works!"

"The powder-magazine!"

I.A. screamed, "Look! The sky!"

The heat of a baronial fire-place enveloped my back; I skidded to a stop. An awesome glare turned the moon into the desert sun at noon, forcing us to shield our eyes behind a tree. The fierce golden yellow then faded into the garish white-grey of the magnesium flash used by indoor photographers, lighting up the entire valley before us.

By now, I estimated we were six miles from the mine. We stood transfixed, our arms round each other in mutual protection against this preternatural sight.

Something like a whirlwind swirled over the mine, heaving up guard-sheds, trucks, machinery. On the horizon next to the mine, an entire forest of bright grey trees vanished, erased as though the Almighty had decided to begin a different world. Around us, the brush and trees rustled with sympathy in the wind. Columns of dirt and rubble churned out of fissures in the mine; fires flared up through the vent-shafts as if from the pits of Hell. A cloud of turbulent black-grey dust, about two miles in diameter, billowed and eddied over the surface of the earth, lit from beneath by the fires and from above by the moon.

And now, we were struck dumb by an inconceivable spectacle: a white column of smoke swirled out of that black-grey mass and rose higher and higher, the top expanding and rounding out into what could only be described as a monstrous toad-stool on a long stalk, several miles high!

My astonishment went far beyond the staggering sight, for it was multiplied by my own hope, deep within my consciousness, that the balance of nature could never be torn asunder. Buchhalter, now certainly struck dead in the mine by his arrogance in challenging the Almighty, had indeed wrought what only God could do before.

I.A., the confirmed atheist, cried out, "God help us!"

"We have seen the future, and it is evil."

We re-mounted the motor-cycle and raced south. In the sequence of events, as I reconstructed them, the bomb had been assembled for a final fitting of all its components; the grenades had set off the conventional explosives in the powder-magazine, which in turn propelled the "hammer" into the "anvil."

The suffering had ended at last for Karinsky, but now my torment intensified: the other abominable weapon would inflict the same cataclysm on my beloved England. Indeed, the bomb might already be there.

Soon we encountered ambulances and lorries, jammed with soldiers, hurtling towards the fires. After several miles, our vehicle sputtered and expired, bereft of benzol. We abandoned it to run down a country road, away from the on-rushing soldiers.

Behind us, the throaty whir of a motor-car grew louder over my shoulder. We were over-taken by a large Rolls-Royce Pullman-Limousine, *circa* 1910, which pulled ahead of us and stopped. The chauffeur's arm reached out to open the handle of the rear compartment, and his muffled voice in impeccable English called out, "You are in great danger. Hop in!"

Behind the wheel I perceived, by the light of the moon, the horror that had terrified I.A.—the mummy's face!

CHAPTER FOURTEEN

I Am Offered a Dukedom

"Good heavens!" I seized I.A.'s hand. "Run!"

"One moment, Sir Arthur," the chauffeur said, un-winding his wraps to reveal a grinning Joseph Mombeya. "All to protect you, my friends." He handed a card to me as we warily entered the rear compartment of the limousine. It read, in German:

MUSTARD GAS VICTIM
BATTLE OF YPRES

Gliding the limousine over the pitted road, Mombeya explicated with some relish the purpose of his dreadful disguise: "You see, a gentleman of my colour is quite noticeable in this Aryan land, and their harsh, guttural language does not come easily to my tongue. I could not move about without disguise."

"Did you employ the black taxi and the Sister of Charity?"

"Let us say merely that I learned you were in the mine from the Russian cigarette-vendor."

To I.A., dumbfounded by this acquaintanceship, I divulged the circumstances of our meeting on the train from Devon.

"And you, madame," he said, "are no doubt Inessa Armand, Lenin's agent."

"Now that we are well introduced, would you be good enough to explain where you are taking us?" I asked.

"I offer you shelter and refreshment."

I.A. sank back into the tufted brown leather seat and asked, "Well then, do you have a drop of brandy?"

"Lower the panel in the rear of this seat."

The rosewood and brass bar, with its silver-trimmed glasses, provided fine Napoleon, of which we both availed ourselves. The car was an Athenaeum Club on wheels. The interior wood-trim of Carpathian burl walnut in matched veneers complemented the colour of the upholstery, and the heavy carpeting of the floor displayed an Oriental pattern. At least fifteen feet long and weighing about one and a half tons, the huge vehicle could not operate on benzol but required the much rarer petrol. Mombeya was manifestly performing an important function for the German government.

Mombeya turned off the road into a circular drive to a ponderous two-storey wood and cut-stone châlet, not in the Swiss style but probably the hunting-lodge of a nineteenth-century estate. He led the way into a dark-oak-panelled great hall, surrounded on three sides by a wooden balcony from which boar heads glared down at us. The fire-place, large enough to roast one of these beasts, provided a welcome warmth, and Mombeya awakened a pouting *Fräulein* to serve coffee and strudel at a long oak table. The dough, made flaky by butter, and the coffee, without the slightest adulteration of *ersatz*, testified further to Mombeya's lofty influence.

"Wasn't that explosion stupendous?" he exclaimed, with the delight of a school-boy who has just floored a bully with a surprising blow from his satchel. Relaxed now before the glowing fire, he chose to expound on his purpose in rescuing us, demonstrating that I had severely under-estimated his duplicity and megalomania.

The funds raised in Europe by the Society for the Propagation of Health and Education in the Congo, intended for teachers, physicians and nurses, had been expended mainly by Mombeya to organise the blacks for revolt against the Belgians. This would have been entirely possible, for Belgium lay helpless under the German boot, and the other powers in Africa—France and England—were battling in Europe. But General Ludendorff became desperate for the Congo's pitch-blende, because Joachimsthal in nearby Bohemia could not supply sufficient high-grade ore. He offered Mombeya a huge sum of money, diplomatic status, promise of political position in the post-war Congo, all to delay an uprising so that uranium shipments would be expedited to Hamburg. The tales Mombeya had told me about his compatriots forced to work under slave conditions were un-doubtedly just as true as the brutalisation inflicted on the workers at Straussfurt.

"But German gold," I interjected with scorn, "could not salve your rage over the injustice to your own people."

"Precisely, Sir Arthur. At first I was inclined to refuse Ludendorff, to prolong the war and gain our independence while the Europeans were busy slaughtering each other. But then I bethought myself of a grander strategy. The Congo has a vast population and other valuable assets—copper, diamonds. If Buchhalter's bomb were successful, the wealth

221

of the Congo would provide capital to build our own bomb, using our own uranium. And with this weapon I would not be simply the Kaiser's black governor—I could liberate all Africa! I would lead our continent to its destiny as a great power, equal to all Europe, or England and America combined. And now I have the means to decipher its secret!"

I stared at him, for a moment bereft of speech. "You understand the principles of the ionisation process and the bomb-assembly?"

"Oh, no." He slowly sipped the coffee to savour our astonishment. "But, my dear Sir Arthur, *you do!*"

The immensity of his mania and his mis-calculation confounded me. "But I have no understanding of those complicated processes—"

"Come, come! Surely British Intelligence would not send a man on this mission if he were incapable of mastering such details."

"Our Intelligence is just as renowned for its fallibility as the Germans are for their efficiency. This bomb requires immense research and industrial skill."

He raised his hand in the calm gesture of an auctioneer noting a higher bid. "I offer you a laboratory in Africa, and un-limited subsidy from the sale of Congo copper, diamonds, lumber, if you will guide us to its development."

I.A. boldly interceded. "He has only *seen* the machinery. It demands complex industrialisation, creation of new processes, hundreds of engineers, mathematicians. Even Russia, far ahead of Africa in science, could not build this weapon in fifty years. That is Lenin's own estimate!"

Mombeya ignored her to address me. "You shall become one of the wealthiest men in the world—I offer you a dukedom!—if you supply us with your knowledge."

"I must repeat: I do not comprehend its complexities. I

am not a physicist. Even Dr. Albert Einstein doubted it was possible."

Mombeya's eye-brows shot up in dis-belief, but his tone was quietly discreet. "I have staked my country's future on the certainty that Sir Arthur Conan Doyle at least possesses the intellectual powers of his own detective."

"Only Buchhalter could fathom the intricacies of that weapon—and he is certainly dead."

Lighting up a small blue porcelain pipe, Mombeya warned me with sinister calm, "We Africans have ancient techniques to alter one's thoughts and purposes. I do not suggest torture. I have in mind a prolonged period of isolation, mesmeric suggestion, irregular feeding, until finally you accept our purpose as your most desirable future."

"You dare threaten me with imprisonment?"

"I merely suggest that you shall work for me—or die! And I must have your answer promptly, because I meet with my associates in Hanover tomorrow morning."

I stared over his shoulder, simulating recognition. "Don't shoot!" I cried. A hoary ruse, but he instinctively whirled around, whereupon I leapt to pinion his arms and I.A. snatched his legs. We crashed atop him on the floor.

"Good show!" I gasped to I.A.

From behind us, a thin but determined voice demanded, "Stand up! I have a gun! Both of you—hands high!"

We obeyed reluctantly. I twisted my head to face a Mauser pistol in the hands of a woman.

"The *Barmherzige Schwester!*" I.A. exclaimed.

I recognised the face from the Brighton photographs, in particular her prominent laryngeal cartilage. "Good evening, Cora Matthews."

She corrected me firmly. "Mrs. Joseph Mombeya. Now, both of you lie down—slowly, no more tricks—on the floor."

A wry, albeit puzzled, grin lit up I.A.'s face. "Doyle, you have the most threatening friends!"

While Cora held the Mauser two feet from our heads and Mombeya roped us separately, hand and foot, I analysed the woman's sham death for I.A. She had not dared run off with her lover because Sgt. Matthews could employ the far-reaching facilities of Scotland Yard to hunt them down. The demise was staged on the very day her husband had been ordered to quit London for his testimony, and thus he could not observe her closely when "dead." She had not anticipated Plumsoll's appearance as her guardian, but he, with the excitement of the bloody ceremony and the inexperience of a veterinarian, had mis-judged her pulse-beat. It had been slowed to the very minimum, probably by the drug *Physostigma venenosum,* the "Calabar bean" of tropical Africa.

Mombeya added, with amusement, "It's also known as the 'ordeal bean.' It enables the Obeah to remain underground for days, as proof of his super-natural powers."

"I regret the pain caused my sister," Cora said, "but it is impossible for a white and black couple to go about unnoticed in England. If you should ever return, Dr. Doyle, please assure her that I am happy. We were married in Holland."

"It is never-the-less bigamy. But when did you escape from that coffin?"

"At night," Mombeya interjected grimly, "the most natural camouflage for me."

I.A. added, "And you, madame, with moustaches of eyelid kohl, were the driver of the black taxi. What an ingenious charade."

"I also have an urgent mission," Mombeya said. "You will come with us."

Mombeya and Cora carried me and then I.A. into the rear compartment of the Pullman-Limousine, where we sat surrounded by our captors' luggage, coats, food-hampers, fur coverlets. Our destination, Mombeya said, was Hanover, then Hamburg, from which I would embark on a freighter for the Congo with them. As for my partner, he had not yet decided where to dispose of her. He locked the rear doors, closed the side and rear window-curtains, and drove off.

The black man relit his bowl, and Cora joined him with a matching pipe; when the aroma reached our back seat, I requested permission to light up my clay. My captor agreed to release my right hand if I would give my word of honour not to attack him or his wife, or signal for help. Much to I.A.'s chagrin, I assented.

Soon Mombeya, admitting he had not savoured the aroma of proper English tobacco for weeks because of the successful British blockade, demanded a pipeful. I demurred. "This is the last of it, blended by Ionides of Alexandria."

He was adamant, and I reluctantly handed over a fill; his companion appropriated some of mine for her own pipe.

"So the English still retain a broad sense of honour!" I.A. remarked sardonically to me. "I've always maintained there is a difference between broadening out and flattening out."

Five minutes later, as we approached the environs of Gotha, Mombeya and Cora slumped into a stupor. I lunged over the front seat and twisted the ignition switch with my free right hand; guiding the wheel with my left shoulder, I eased the car off the road into a clump of trees, where I brought it to a stop with the hand-brake.

"Your own Egyptian blend?" I.A. mused.

"A secret of the thugs in Cairo. As Plautus put it, even the mouse never entrusts his life to only one exit."

The food-hampers yielded a knife, which severed our bonds. "They'll be comatose for ten minutes," I explained. After I donned Mombeya's Savile Row great-coat and bowler, we eased him into the rear compartment, where we exchanged bindings with our erstwhile captors and shielded them with a huge buffalo-fur blanket. I.A. slipped into the other woman's splendid furs, hat and scarf.

The couple were travelling on a neutral Dutch passport as husband and wife. Mombeya in addition carried a *laissez-passer*, signed by Gen. von Ludendorff, authorising every assistance for a "diplomatic mission of utmost military importance."

With the knife, I carefully sliced off the couple's faces, as well as the photographs on our original passports. I transposed the heads and glued them with a layer of honey from the hamper; I.A. applied the weight of her boots, and after an hour they were firmly affixed. Having long ago shaved off my moustaches, I became a Teutonic Joseph Mombeya, my hair darkened by his shoe-blacking. And Frau Lobegott tossed away her spectacles to pass for Mrs. Mombeya; as a result, both of us now bore Dutch passports.

The limousine had been thoroughly prepared for the journey to Hamburg. The petrol tank was filled to the brim, the tyres were almost new Dunlops, and the spare-parts box carried every necessity from an electric torch to several types of spanners to a platinum-tipped blade for the commutator.

I.A. conjectured that the Germans would expect us to make for England by the most direct route, north through Holland or Denmark; it would therefore be wiser to motor in the opposite direction, south, to Switzerland. We could cross at several points on Lake Constance by lake steamer.

Her logic was impeccable. Certainly a hue and cry would be raised by Mombeya's henchmen in both Hanover and Hamburg if he never arrived.

I recollected that a 1906 Rolls in a rutty cross-country race had averaged thirty-nine miles per hour. "The Swiss frontier lies about three hundred sixty miles from here; even at thirty miles per hour, we should reach it in twelve or fifteen hours if we alternate at the wheel. Ah!—I do hope you operate a motor-car."

"Certainly. One can sleep while the other drives, and we'll avoid hotel waiters and desk-clerks—they're always on some government's pay-roll."

"Capital! Full speed ahead!—before Charles telegraphs an alert for us."

2 A.M., Thursday, 5 April

We turned south to Gotha, where we were not challenged, and from there continued on a well-paved road through the Thuringian Forest toward Coburg, rolling up hills and down valleys in direct-drive third speed, at a steady twenty-eight miles per hour.

With a profound sense of relief, I made my apologies to I.A. for my long-held suspicions. "And I will tell you, madame, in all admiration, that your daring and intellectual qualities exceed those of any woman I have known."

Wan and exhausted, she succeeded in generating a dazzling smile. "Even your wife's?"

"She is equally intelligent, but I would not depend upon her willingness to kill. As you must have known, I've called you I.A. because those initials represented my doubts as to your identity, Isabelle Andros or Inessa Armand. If you have no objection, I should now like to address you as Inessa."

"You have my permission," she replied with exaggerated formality. "I must admit in turn that your Victorian qualities do have great redeeming virtue: I always know where you stand. Although I was rather startled by your *parole* to Mombeya."

"He merely demanded no attack, and no signal for help. I complied precisely."

"Now that we are in the confessional, I must tell you that

I have always adored England—and I hope to continue on with you to forestall that cursed bomb."

I was taken aback, for I had never contemplated this development. "You have served our venture admirably, madame—"

"—Inessa," she insisted.

"Inessa. But the final decision is not mine to make."

"I must admit I also have a selfish purpose. I have not heard from my children in three months."

"I shall do my utmost to secure this permission, for in all justice it should be granted." True, she had no passion for equal justice at all, but if England could elevate a man like Arachne to high position, it could surely find a place for Inessa. For a vagrant moment, my mind entertained an amusing scene of Arachne interviewing her for a mission.

A far-away booming sound reverberated in our car, a weird other-worldly noise, like a giant bellowing out of a cave. The trees swayed in the shifting winds, and soon a deafening barrage of thunder rattled round the Rolls. A great wind overwhelmed the forest, bending pine branches across the road and buffeting us head-on, forcing us to crawl at four miles per hour; then the heavens dumped wave after wave of water over the hapless car, turning the road into a quicksand. The wheels slipped and sank into the muck and I knew that if we lost our momentum we could well spend the night in this deserted place.

In time, the thunder faded into the distance, the black clouds rolled away and over the hills the moon appeared. It seemed that an hour had passed, but when I glanced at my watch, it was only eighteen minutes and we were on a long road winding down a green valley into Zell.

I concentrated my train of thought on the myriad agonising possibilities for destruction which now hung over my beleaguered homeland. My conviction was un-shakeable that the atomic abomination would be employed at, or near, London, not only for its symbolic value as the vital heart of the Empire but also because the most important producers of munitions, Vickers and the Woolwich Arsenal, were close by. How would it be transported? The newest Zeppelins carried twenty tons, but, in the interviews for my history of the war, airmen revealed that the ships were notoriously inaccurate in their targeting and vulnerable to our anti-aircraft fire and RAF fighters, equipt with incendiary and explosive ammunition. Indeed, by the end of the previous year, seventy-seven of these floating leviathans had been demolished. The more defensible Gotha bombers carried a bomb-load of about one thousand pounds, but our aerial barrages kept them at great heights, and thus their accuracy was un-reliable. Most certainly the Germans would use this one cataclysmic device on one specific target; the carrier, therefore, would require the utmost invulnerability and precision.

My prognosis fixed on transport by ship, a U-boat or even a neutral freighter operated by a tool like Parvus, then emplacement by German agents in London. Thus I came full circle: what was the ultimate target? The munitions-plants near the Thames as well as the most important military or civil leaders seemed most likely. If I could but warn Arachne of this danger immediately!

A soldier strode out of a tent beside the road and motioned with a lantern to halt. We skidded in the mud to the bottom of the hill and stopped, bumper to barricade. The sleepy sergeant demanded our identity-papers. After a routine glance at the *laissez-passer,* he inspected our faces sharply before saluting. "Forgive me, sir—there has been an explosion in a factory up north."

229

"Saboteurs?" I asked idly.

He replied brusquely, "Who knows? Just following orders from Berlin."

It was clear, from this close but blear-eyed scrutiny, that Charles had already telegraphed our descriptions. Equally nettling was the fact that we had progressed but thirteen miles on the road back to England.

CHAPTER FIFTEEN

A Dumpling Is the Key

As we descended into Eisfeld, the southern end of that interminable forest, a team pulling a farm-waggon suddenly reared up at the approach of our motor-car and raced across the road, forcing me to swerve into a ditch. Our two rear wheels, weighted by our captives, sank nearly out of sight into the gummy mud, leaving the front end of the Rolls suspended three feet in the air.

The farmer drove off, entirely un-concerned. I ran after him and insisted that he pull us out of the muck, in-as-much as his horses had forced us into it.

"*Ja, ja,*" he muttered and demanded one hundred marks (about £5). I restrained a temptation to go bald-headed at the rascal and knock him out. Each minute of delay was oppressive, and, further, I did not wish him to see into the rear compartment. I yielded. After a half-hour of straining by the horses, our machine was once more on the way. Shortly after Tremersdorf, the road became fairly level, enabling us to reach Coburg by early noon. Still, we had come only seventy-five miles from Gotha in eleven hours.

Inessa took the wheel here and opened the throttle wide; she was not reckless but, as always, audacious, waving aside ox-carts and scattering flocks of sheep. Some miles later, in the small town of Rossach, I took a desperate chance to alert Arachne by cable. The post-office functionary deferred to my *laissez-passer* but regretted the cable would be censored in any event. My message to Plumsoll at the Hotel Pelikan read: INFORM ARACHNE ORE VERIFIED. REFINED LOT ON WAY DIRECTLY TO HIM. MOMBEYA.

"It's war business," I informed the clerk sternly. "Make haste." I walked out quickly, and we rolled away.

Inessa, cradling Cora's Mauser in her lap, looked into the rear seat and asked, "Isn't it time we disposed of our passengers?"

"Tonight we must change over into their full costumes. Our under-garments and shoes are obviously German, and we may still be searched."

"Exactly. Drop them in a forest without identification-papers."

I could not bring myself to harm the woman I had promised Sgt. Matthews to protect. "We'll discharge them before the Swiss frontier. They may be useful."

"They may be our un-doing. But you are in command."

We avoided Nürnberg by crossing the west bank of the Regnitz River, and below the city reverted to what the map labelled the "main road." We were by no means averaging the thirty m.p.h. I had anticipated. For one, I had not expected that highways between large cities would be little more than English farm-roads, and as we entered Bavaria, the "highways" deteriorated. The small stones used to construct them flew up under our fenders, sounding very much like a hail-storm. They had been macadamised with tar or asphalt, but now, lacking war-time maintenance, they were simply stretches of bare stone, and I was particularly concerned about the effect of these flinty shards on our tyres.

The majority of level-crossings were un-guarded, even by a late-descending gate, so that we never knew which train we might meet. Here also we encountered the *Pflasterzoll*, a toll for the non-existent care of the roads; it was only a few pfennigs, but if by chance the collector was not on duty at the gate of these mediaeval villages, another, smiling gleefully and waving a large yellow flag, halted us before we exited, adding a penalty of a dozen pfennigs. The constant stop-and-go prevented us from getting up speed.

The concentrated efforts of the previous night now weighed heavily on my eyelids, and after turning over the wheel to Inessa, I dropped off into an exhausted sleep. At eleven P.M. I took over again when we reached Neu Ulm and turned south to follow the Iller River and subsidiary roads to Lindau.

Friday, 6 April

In the village of Aitrach, a capped figure, swinging a torch, brought us to a halt at a log barricade shortly after midnight. He was a sergeant of the *Landstürm*, another reserve force which served as armed police, a man in his forties with a lean face and spectacles, a rifle over his shoulder. A corporal held the torch while he examined our passports. After glancing over my *laissez-passer,* he saluted as if I were a general, clicked heels, bowed and begged pardon for the intrusion. The German soldier, when in doubt, always saluted as if facing a general, because it was always wiser to treat a captain as a general than a general as a captain.

The sergeant then pulled open the rear door and reached for the fur coverlet. Instantly, I leapt out to announce that I was pleased to have found someone in authority: I had come to hand over the renowned English spy, Arthur Conan Doyle! Revealing the bound bodies, I told how he and his female companion had attempted to steal my limousine at the previous village, where upon my wife and I had overpowered them. The *Unteroffizier's* astonishment turned to delight, for the barricade had been set up especially to trap Doyle and the woman. He had recently seen a filmed version of *Der Hund von Baskerville* and had read some of the author's other tales in translation. I had to admit I admired Doyle's work and could not believe that such an artist would be an espionage agent.

The soldier examined Doyle's British passport, displaying Mombeya's face, and Mme. Armand's French document, with Cora's face. He studied them for some time, while Mombeya, who knew little German, insisted in English that I had stolen his passport; since the sergeant knew no English, I monopolised attention.

"But Doyle's face is black?" the sergeant grunted.

"Of course!" I replied. "He enjoys those ridiculous disguises. That is why the English are losing this war—they never learn new tactics." Before he could un-scramble this *non sequitur,* I added, "Let me direct your attention to the English tailors' labels in his clothes. And hers."

The sergeant did so, and immediately slipped his hand into the over-coat pockets. From the inner one, he withdrew papers identifying Hermann Grauber, which I had prudently inserted while the captive slept.

"More disguises!" the sergeant exclaimed.

Mombeya was now shouting for "Dutch consul—*Ich bin holländisch!*"

The sergeant replied with *"Raus! Raus!"* to Cora. In her hand-bag he discovered papers of a Frau Lobegott and, worse, a Central Employment Bureau letter, directing her and Grauber to a munitions-works near Erfurt.

234

"Twenty kilometres from Straussfurt!" Inessa cried. "The British stupidity surpasses their arrogance!"

The sergeant held an embarrassingly accurate photograph of me up to Mombeya's face, then shook his head, bewildered. "Must consult an officer."

"That picture was made years ago," I countered.

He ordered the corporal to guard the four of us while he ran into the inn, their headquarters for the road-block.

An officer approached with the sergeant, carrying another torch, and flashed it full on my face.

"The game's up, old boy!" It was Charles, his *Gepo* uniform indecently dusty. "Fortunately, the servant-girl at Mombeya's châlet was in our employ, and when we received reports of a large Rolls racing south instead of north to Hamburg, it struck me the game's not afoot—but awheel! And as you see, my Mercedes is still a speedier motor."

"When you don't pay that blasted *Pflasterzoll!*" I retorted.

"Not very sporting, Doyle. Will you and Madame Armand join me in a spot of brandy for the interrogation?"

Arachne had dissected me all too well: the speedy return to England had been snatched away by my sentimental refusal to cast off Sgt. Matthews' wife.

Guarded by two NCOs, we were marched into adjoining rooms at the inn, over-looking the stables, and ordered to remove the garments we had appropriated from Mombeya. He flung them over his arm, glaring wrathfully at Charles, as though the German had stolen his spoils of war, and refused his offer of supper.

"I really must hurry back to Hamburg," Mombeya explained. "You certainly have all the evidence you need." He turned to me: "You bungling fool! You deserve the firing-squad!"

Under Charles' supervision, the NCO confiscated my identity-papers, ration-cards and books, money, compass, shave-kit, tobacco-pouch, match-box and pipes "for detailed analysis."

"Surely," I said, "you will permit me the consolations of my pipe and razor?" Charles there upon examined these articles minutely, in particular the stem of the pipe, and returned them.

I was then stripped to the skin, and my ears, nose, mouth and other parts of the body were investigated. Charles tore open the linings of all my clothing, exposing them to the concentrated light of two torches, seeking anything written with secret ink. The sergeant even sponged me with water, to which citric acid was added, to make visible any writing on my body!

"If you know me as well as you claim, Charles, you must realise that I do not need notes to jog my memory."

"We have our methods," he said. My valise was measured inside and out to detect false compartments, and Charles examined every article in it for notes, poisons or weapons. I was both astonished and a bit flattered that Charles as well as Mombeya believed I had mastered some secrets of the atomic weapon.

Chagrined to find nothing, Charles returned my clothes, now utterly in shreds, and informed me that Inessa (who had been subjected to the same search) and I would both be taken to Berlin tomorrow for further questioning—"and, no doubt, execution. You may have a final meal here. Be prepared to depart at zero seven hundred. I wish you a good night's sleep."

A guard took up his post outside our contiguous rooms. Two *Landstürmer* nailed tight the shutters of my one window, adding wooden bars across it. They hauled up from the barn what must have once been the portcullis of an old fortress, then nailed and screwed it over the window; the neat, efficient job led me to surmise they had been carpenters.

I immediately inspected the room for escape. It was an old building; from the depth of the window I judged the stone-and-stucco walls were at least a foot and a half thick. My door to the hallway and the locked one to Inessa's room were ancient two-inch oak, nearly petrified—my finger-nail could not make a dent in it.

The serving-girl, a dull, amiable sort, carried in the tray behind a corpulent sentry who stood beside me, bayonet pointed at my heart. The ring on a length of braided cord, attached around her waist, held but one key. This suggested two possibilities: all the locks in the inn were the same, or this was a master key; its operative end revealed several precise notches. She set the supper on a small table, with cheap bent utensils and a soiled napkin, then waddled away; the corporal backed out, watching me intently for a suspicious sneeze. The girl now locked the hall-door with a complete turn of the key. I examined the brass lock scrupulously—and admitted I could never pick it.

The meal consisted of the inevitable soggy boiled fish, potato dumplings and black bread. When I split one of the heavy grey dumplings with the fork, it had the consistency of clay, revealing the grooves made by the fork lines. The utensils, as I had learned on my journey with the junk-collector, were white metal.

My escape plan materialised in an instant, complete with opening exposition, crisis, climax and resolution, as so few of my own tales did, even on a felicitous after-noon. I gulped down all the food, hid the spoon in my pocket and rapped loudly on the door to Inessa's room. "Send the serving-girl in here!"

She entered with surprising promptness, preceded by the ferocious corporal. "Young lady, I am a large, hungry man. Bring me more of those dumplings and bread! I am famished."

She indicated Inessa's room with her thumb. "I'll bring hers. She doesn't want it!"

She and the corporal returned with the entire meal, which she set on my table. "You like the dumplings?"

"Magnificent!" I exclaimed, rising to express my compliments. My long legs upset the table and splattered its contents over the girl. I apologised, wiping the beer off her skirt with the napkin in my left hand while in the ensuing confusion—the girl giggling, the *Landstürmer* ordering me to sit down—my right hand squeezed half of a dumpling over the key at her waist. I helped pick up the food, assured her I would eat it anyway, and she walked out, still giggling, followed by the corporal. The door was locked once more.

The pattern imbedded in the dumpling was quite clear and not overly complex. I tested my razor on the white-metal spoon; the Sheffield-steel blade whittled slivers as easily as if it had been wood.

I slipped a note under our mutual door: "Can make key. Prepare escape."

Inessa replied: "Understood. Did you save pepper?"

"Sorry." I set to work shaping the spoon to the dumpling pattern. Within an hour, I was ready for the first try. Inessa swabbed the interior of the lock with hair-oil, and after two adjustments in the key, the door opened.

Inessa swept in, folding her arms around me. "I really must steal an Iron Cross for you!"

I cautioned silence, and searched her room for a long rod or bar of metal. Failing that, I quietly pried off the leg from the wood table in my room. The corporal, pacing his rounds on the squeaking bare wood of the hall, un-wittingly covered whatever sounds I made as I levered and jemmied the portcullis bars with the table-leg.

Inessa tore up her mattress-covering into cloth strips; knotted together, they were strong enough to support my fifteen stone and, combined with my cover, made a cord twenty feet long. After a half-hour at the window, two bars bent to permit passage of my chest; by whittling the end of the table-leg to a wedge, I opened the shutters and raised the windows.

I estimated a ten-foot drop to the stable-roof below, and another ten from there to the ground. Our escape-line was tied to the bed, jammed fast against the window wall. Inessa and I lowered ourselves, hand over hand, knees gripping the fabric knots, to the stable-roof and then to the dirt without a sound.

We had no identity-papers, no money, no map, only the compass Charles had over-looked inside the hollowed-out heel of Inessa's boot. Our route was south by west across the open country to Leutkirch, eight miles away, where Inessa knew a comrade, Rosa, "an elderly woman, a fire-brand—she exiled herself from Munich to avoid arrest." Here we would be hidden, thirty miles from Lindau, a port one hour by lake steamer from Switzerland. But without passports we were still fugitives a world away.

It was now five in the morning—four o'clock in London, if it had not been destroyed. We would have about two hours, on a bright, star-lit night, before our absence was discovered and Charles mobilised the far-flung resources of the *Geheim-polizei* and the army against us. And neither of us had the slightest clue to a plan for crossing the German frontier.

CHAPTER SIXTEEN

Three Hostile Borders to Cross

Out of the densely massed trees on the slope of a low mountain, Leutkirch materialised. There was no mistaking the cottage of Inessa's friend: it was the only one on the road at the edge of town, and a large sign had been nailed across the door: CLOSED BY POLICE—ENTRY FORBIDDEN.

Inessa grumbled, "Preventive arrest. D--n her, couldn't keep her mouth closed!"

"But a perfect hiding-place," I said. In the rear yard I pried open a shutter. A rubbish-pile provided old newspapers which, smeared with thick mud from a roof-drain puddle, stuck to the glass tenaciously so that a kick of my boot created scarcely a tinkle.

Inessa picked up a candle bit and some matches in the kitchen, and we explored the house. Chests and wardrobes were flung open, their contents scattered about the floor; a thorough, angry search had been made by the police. Somehow, they had ignored a large tin of Danish *Pflanzenfette*, a solidified vegetable fat, which we re-packed in small glass bottles. It would keep our feet from blistering. Scattered about were three marks and a few pfennigs, several tins of Norwegian sardines and "fish-balls," stale biscuits from Switzerland, a jar of preserves, and a packet of camomile tea. That, at least, would warm us a bit.

Smoke or sparks up the chimney could not be risked; I broke up a chair which produced a tiny fire in the kitchen sink, and an iron grille from the stove, placed above the fire, supported the metal tea-pot. We set our boots beside the fire, and hung our dew-moistened clothing above it.

From the photograph on her desk, Rosa B. was in her sixties, a burnt-out comet: white hair tumbled over the worn, sharply lined face; the eyes shone fiercely, even in the half-dark, but I diagnosed that palsy had taken command. On the wall a coloured decorative map of early-nineteenth-century German states depicted every little duchy with its coat of arms. It showed the rivers and main cities, however, so I removed it from the frame.

A second bedroom offered a helter-skelter selection of male clothes, to fit a gentleman about a head shorter than I. "Her lover," Inessa said. She immediately decided that the trousers, jacket and shirt could be cut down to provide a boy's costume for her, and thus frustrate the *Gepo* alarm describing a woman and a tall man.

While she stitched, we breakfasted on tea and a few biscuits lathered with jam. Map in hand, I pondered our course from here. The only southern frontier exits from Germany had been established at Friedrichshafen, Lindau, and Konstanz, all on Lake Constance. A western route, through the wooded mountains and valleys of the Black Forest, was popular with British POWs and therefore well guarded. A third passage was the one we had taken when we entered, and certainly Charles would anticipate that. The fourth

242

course turned the eastern corner of Lake Constance where the frontiers of Germany, Austria, and Switzerland crowded together; this was perhaps the most difficult way because it required crossing the Austrian frontier twice.

Our nemesis had un-doubtedly telegraphed an alert to all frontiers on this route, but here I had the advantage of him. At the age of sixteen, I had attended the Jesuit academy at Feldkirch in Austria, some twenty miles south of Bregenz but only five miles from the Swiss frontier across the Rhine. Aside from some crude football and puffing into the huge brass bombardon of the school band, my recreation had consisted of long walks along the Rhine and boating on it. In short, I knew every yard of the Austrian-Swiss frontier north and south of Feldkirch.

After stealing over the German line, we would enter and exit Austria, then cross the Rhine into Switzerland. Recalling Charles' excoriation of the mine's Security Chief as being "haphazard and light-headed as the Austrians" (indeed, Gen. Ludendorff had complained of them, "We are allied to a corpse"), I felt certain that the route through Austria, although the longest, was safest.

Inessa agreed. "Do you plan to cross to Switzerland from Feldkirch?"

"No. Somewhere below Bregenz. It's mostly low-lying farm and marsh land, perfect for concealment."

"Good. As to evading the police without identity-papers, I should like to convey some personal experience in this art. We must move only at night, avoiding cities and terminals. Long before dawn, we must locate shelter for the day—a hay-stack or barn, a copse, a dry ditch which can be covered over with branches or brush. When we pass a local citizen, let us be whistling a German song, and wish him a good day. Most important, we must weigh alternatives and always take the most *cautious* path."

243

"Excellent. Except for 'cautious.' It has been my experience, in fiction as well as in sport, that audacity and surprise are the most un-settling elements to your opponent."

"Forgive me, Sir Arthur, but how many times have you escaped from prison?"

"I concede the point."

Inessa, having completed her costume, aged it by dragging it around the dusty floor. She cut the brim of the gentleman's soft felt hat to the edge of the crown, leaving only three inches at the front to create a "peak" for the boy's cap. Now she took up the scissors and without a touch of remorse cut even shorter her lustrous hair. Donning the cap, she became a young but beautiful boy. What an incredibly ageless face! I thought. Her creams had helped, of course, but whatever concatenation of genes had made her beauty possible, it could not occur often, in any land, in any decade.

When I stood beside her, I became even more aware of my height, an obvious target for Charles' alert. I sifted again through the drawers and wardrobe, the remnants of a lifetime of accumulation. A woman's long black cape caught my eye—a cassock of the Jesuit fathers! My cover tale would be simplicity itself: returning an incorrigible run-away boy, Otto Pfanzler, to Switzerland because his parents were too feeble to attempt it themselves. In Catholic South Germany and Austria, the police would be much less concerned about the identity-papers of a priest than those of a common workman. I could draw up my own *celebret*, the Latin document certifying that I was authorised to conduct masses.

My plan met with a reverent *"Dominus vobiscum"* from Inessa. The next three hours were occupied in clerical work. She let out the hem of the cape so that it reached to my ankles. The required buttons down the front edge of the cassock were detached from a coat of Rosa's, and the cape's matching scarf converted into a three-inch strip for my cincture. The gentleman's white shirt, minus the collar, was adequate—the short sleeves would be hidden by the cassock—but his black trousers presented a problem: they fit me like plus-fours. I made do with my workman's trousers, which Inessa pressed out neatly with a brass pot heated over our kitchen fire, and the card-board foundation for the square *biretta* came from the back of the frame that had supplied my map, neatly covered by black material from our socialist comrade's petticoat. Her vellum stationery I elevated to an impressive *celebret*, in my best Latin calligraphy, identifying me as Father Johannes Beschling, and signed by Luders, my Provincial at Feldkirch. For a Bible and a breviary, I substituted black-bound volumes from Rosa's library, flaying the heresies of the German right-wing socialists.

It was now four-fifteen P.M. and Wangen lay but eighteen miles away. While Inessa slept, I spent my watch in plotting stratagems and counter-moves for our first crossing, the German frontier. I slept fitfully when she stood guard.

At nine P.M. we set out along a road paralleling the railway south. I carried our imprisoned hostess's small black leather bag, into which I'd stuffed our belongings and the tins of fish. The few people still awake I greeted with a benign *"Guten Abend"* and received a respectful *"Guten Abend, Vater"* in return.

Saturday, 7 April

At about three in the morning, we came to within a mile of Wangen, turned off the road and found our hide-out for the day: a substantial barn with hay-loft, well ventilated by a round window of slanted wood strips; below us rested a waggon, tools and a sway-backed dobbin. We burrowed into the rear of the hay, and I.A. took the first watch.

"Wake me when they come for the waggon," I said. *"Gute Nacht, Otto."*

"Gute Nacht, Vater Beschling."

What seemed to be only a few minutes later, she agitated my shoulder, her hand over my mouth. In the dawn mist, the farmer at the front of our loft was pitching fodder into the waggon below, while his squat wife berated him for lubricating its wheels with her fresh butter. He pitched the hay into her face, growling, "There's no axle-grease to be bought."

After some moments of suspended breathing, we heard the waggon jolt out and the doors creak shut.

I rolled over and fell asleep. Once more I was awakened by Inessa, as she leaned over me and pointed to a bright red spot at the base of her neck; the sun now streaming through the ventilator-slats cast a theatrical glow through the thin boy's shirt hanging open over her nakedness. "A *flea!*" she cried. "I've got fleas!"

Turning my head, I demanded that she cover herself. "You'll catch cold." After she had buttoned up, I examined the spot in the sunlight. It did resemble a flea-bite.

"Am I infested, doctor?" she groaned.

I scrutinised the hair of her head, strand by strand, while she poured out a flood of billingsgate between declarations. "In prison twice! Never caught them! I'll be G——d if I take a kerosene bath!"

I could find no culprit.

"Of course," she wailed. "They hop around. Tomorrow I'll be covered with spots like measles! *German* measles, the swine!"

"I doubt it, Inessa, even at your tender age."

"Spare me your pawky humour—just give me the diagnosis."

246

After a re-arrangement of the skimpy shirt, I examined under her arms. "Nothing."

"But you haven't—"

I interjected, in my most comforting physician's manner, that she now continue the search herself.

"But I haven't the faintest notion what the little b——s look like."

"Tiny little insects, no wings, all legs. If you see anything crawling, simply squish it."

"Ugh!" Then, suddenly, "Have you ever been consulted in a flea case?"

"Never."

"Then I am willing to offer my body to science. Just think of it as extracting a very tiny . . . child."

"That is not the medical profession's code."

"But you're not a doctor now—you're a priest."

"Inessa," I said firmly, "you must do this for yourself." I turned away and picked up Father Beschling's costume while she continued grumbling about British perversity. Soon I heard her exclaim triumphantly, "Nothing! Not *one!*"

"Thank heavens. It may have been simply an ant or mosquito."

As I donned the cassock, shirt and *biretta,* I heard her rummaging through the hay for her clothes. Suddenly I felt her arms about my neck. "I must confess, when I was a child I often had dreams of being seduced by a priest."

I had by now so completely entered into the habit and soul of Father Beschling that I felt an instant twinge of grievous sin. She locked her hands round my waist from behind: "Consider how this would avenge all the beatings the good fathers gave you at school. . . ."

"Come, come, Inessa!" I wrenched myself free and whirled about, discovering that she was utterly naked.

"Good God! You are determined to provoke a most unseemly contretemps."

Entwining my neck, she nodded with a hoydenish grin. Where upon, recalling that scene in the Zurich café where she had castigated me for holding women in low esteem, fit only for prostitution or breeding of sons, I felt duty-bound to demonstrate the fallacy of her accusation.

After sunset, considerably refreshed by our rest, we approached Wangen. Suddenly, Inessa exclaimed, "A torch! We can never make our way without a torch—and money!"

"How do you propose to acquire that?"

"Steal from the rich. Marx proves all un-earned income is stolen anyhow."

I had never stolen any thing in my life except some chocolate biscuits intended for my sisters, and I did not propose, at my advanced age, to play hapless Oliver to a female Fagin. "But you've proposed the most cautious course. A theft will bring us to the attention of the police."

"I know a trick—purse-snatching. It makes the victim look so foolish he never reports it to the police. It's quite easy at night. You greet the person as a benefactor, a long-lost friend, throw your arms around him, and I do the rest."

"I insist, I wish to go to England, not to gaol."

She glanced down the tree-lined street. "Well, if you really believe in God's grace—here is our benefactor!"

Into the shadowy circle of the single street-lamp ambled the cane-swinging proto-type of the man who had done himself proudly in this war: under a homburg, a rotund face, alternatively swinish and ingratiating, puffing a fat cigar; his fur-collared coat, open to the cool breezes, revealed grey-stripe trousers and spats to match.

I greeted him with a hearty *"Guten Abend!"* and a great smile of recognition suffused my face. "What a pleasure to

248

"When I was a child I often had dreams of being seduced by a priest."

see you again. What joy your contribution has brought to the seminary!"

He blinked, his head twisting away dubiously, but turned on a smile with a *"Guten Abend, Vater."* As he passed by, Inessa tripped him.

I immediately helped him to his feet, pinning his elbows, while Inessa, apologising volubly, brushed the dust off his suit and coat. I introduced Otto as a student. The stranger was considerably non-plussed, but thanked me for my assistance and sauntered off. We strolled at a judicious pace in the opposite direction, into the darkness, where we broke into a run. Some distance outside the town, we examined our loot by the light of a match.

The contents, dumped into my hand, totalled twenty marks and some pfennigs—about one British pound. "Why, the fellow's a fraud!" I exclaimed, before I realised that all three of us were the same.

Inessa laughed. "Marx did not foresee this: all un-earned income is not worth stealing!"

We continued southward through the pine trees and meandering streams with somewhat up-lifted spirits. The proprietor of a village grocery and farm-supply shop was up late, playing pinochle (a game similar to bezique) with his cronies, and as surprised to see us as we him. He produced an excellent Swiss torch, a cake of smuggled Margarison's White Windsor soap, and a water-canteen, which he filled while I explained my return of the run-away boy. Since I needed to know our proximity to the un-marked German border, I changed our destination to Feldkirch. The proprietor was exceedingly helpful; he pointed out the near-by town of Hergatz to the south, on the Leiblach River. "The Austrian frontier lies across the river." Otto stood off in the shadows, his head low in appropriate shame, and we departed with no feeling of apprehension. Our costumes and characterisation had passed a second test.

The good fortune continued, for soon afterwards rain began to fall, a spattering at first that embellished itself into a splendid spring down-pour. Inessa pointed out that in such rain the frontier sentries, wet and weary, retired into their guard-shacks.

Sunday, 8 April

Some time after midnight, we skirted Hergatz on a zig-zag farmers' road, where the mud sucked at our boots. At the bottom of a hill, a wooden bridge arched over the Leiblach, but before it stood a shack from which two German sentries emerged, each toting a *Karabiner*, and blinded us with their torches.

I explained my purpose, but they were only interested in my passport. I had left Feldkirch in such great hurry, I affirmed, that I had neglected to secure one because I had never set foot out of Austria. I produced my *celebret*, which caused some consternation because it was in a strange language, Latin.

All the while we stood in the down-pour the sentries grew more restless and un-yielding. I rambled on: after all, I found this run-away boy inside Germany and I had been permitted to enter at Konstanz, where the officials, recognising my Provincial's name, had agreed that further papers and identification were not necessary. This decision immediately lifted all responsibility from the sentries' shoulders, and they passed us through the barbed-wire gate to the bridge.

The sentries on the Austrian side, without waiting to hear my tale, escorted me into the well-heated guard-room. Their lieutenant, an extremely tall, pinkish young man, with the obligatory moustaches but still pimpled, puffed an aromatic cigar over a chess end-game with a portly older gentleman. This worthy, a few years older than I, smoked the same brand of cigar; his dark clothes, formal collar and self-

251

assured importance evidenced a town official. Looking up with a victor's smile, he extended a pleasant *"Guten Abend, Vater."* The lieutenant pushed a pawn in a futile delaying action, and, obviously nettled by our intrusion, auto- matically held out his hand for our passports.

I repeated the unhappy tale accepted across the bridge, but the lieutenant remained short-tempered. "From what city did you depart Germany without a passport?"

Whatever my reply, it would provoke a telephoned inves- tigation.

The older man interrupted. "Permit me, lieutenant. I am familiar with Feldkirch—I graduated from the school in 1880." He expelled a puff of smoke and gazed calculatingly at me. "I am Herr Geheimrat Köhler, Father. Perhaps you recall some of the teachers at Feldkirch?"

I was delighted to revivify those exciting days. Convinced, Herr Köhler did not think it fitting for a priest to travel under such wretched conditions, and announced he would pay for our fare to Feldkirch. That settled the passport question for the lieutenant. Herr Köhler went further: he would drive us to the Bregenz station in his motor-car, as an additional contribution to the church.

My objections were most polite but firm: the rain had stopped; the boy and I could walk the fifteen kilometres, *et cetera*. I assuredly did not want to be deposited in Bregenz; as the official Austrian departure-point for lake-steamers, it was un-doubtedly under observation by at least four branches of the police.

But Köhler was a man whose devotion to good works could not be denied. He escorted Otto and me into his Benz touring-car, which rolled up to the Bregenz station on the Lake Promenade at two-fifteen in the morning, and, in an irresistible torrent of philanthropy, he insisted he would buy our tickets.

The moment he was out of sight, we abandoned the station and crossed over to the dark side of the Seestrasse. From behind us a voice commanded, *"Halt!"*

It was the ever-smiling Charles. "Surely you did not think we would over-look this station?"

I replied in a garbled accent, "You have made some mistake, Mein Herr."

"Come, come!" He ripped off Inessa's cap. "This is the notorious Madame Armand. Can Sir Arthur Conan Doyle be far away?" He attempted to tear open my cincture.

I cried out loudly, "How dare you attack a priest!" The street was bare at this hour, and we could attempt a dash, but in the next instant I realised that Charles would certainly have men at his call inside. We were truly pinned in an end-game.

Charles drew his pistol. "You will come with me," he commanded.

Inessa, who had slipped beside him, delivered the same high kick that had incapacitated the guard at the mine. It smashed the pistol out of Charles' hand.

CHAPTER SEVENTEEN

The Blistering Run

Charles stood transfixed, gaping at his empty right hand. Whirling about, Inessa snapped her boot-heel into his stomach, and when he still did not fall, she dropped to a handstand and kicked both feet backwards at his face, hammering his head to the cobble-stones. The manoeuvre resembled a mediaeval war-horse's capriole. Manifestly, she was an expert in *savate,* that vicious French art of kick-fighting. Her attack, so surprising that Charles had not cried out, ended in several seconds with Charles stretched out un-conscious, bleeding at the mouth.

Inessa, coolly re-claiming her cap, took up his head, I his feet, and we trundled him into a near-by shadowed alleyway. A half-open door beside a house led to the rear yard; we dropped Charles under a bush, hands and feet bound in my cincture and mouth gagged with the sleeve of my shirt.

We fled through the back-streets of the city's Old Town, rising up the side of the Gebhardsberg, and on the run we gasped out possible solutions to our crisis. We had been marching from Wangen with only a few rests for more than seven hours, eating an occasional sardine or biscuit on the way. Both of us were near to exhaustion, and worse, our feet, alternately wet and never quite dry, were chafing; Inessa could scarcely walk, so oppressive was the heeling in her boots.

We rested for some minutes on a church-yard fence, to salve Inessa's blisters with the Danish fat and cover it with another bandage ripped from my shirt. Leaning on my arm, she hobbled down-hill, south of Bregenz, with as much speed as we could muster, traversing three-quarters of a mile to the foot of the Gebhardsberg. On the way, I snatched up several turnips from a garden for emergency rations.

After a five-minute rest, we pushed on to a girls' school which, I recalled, was situated near a bridge over the River Ach. Crossing here, we turned outside the village of Riedenberg and followed a farm road towards the lowlands on our right. Our objective, the bridge to Höchst, across the Fussach Cutting, would bring us to one more bridge—and freedom.

It was now four A.M. The road to Höchst was in wretched decay; its mushy surface, together with the ever-present mist, created the curious effect of our sliding through clouds. To bedevil us further, all sign-posts had been removed from this area, just as they had disappeared from the German-Swiss border; I relied on memory alone.

At last, I recognised a curiously gabled church, and close by was the Höchst bridge. I assumed it would not be guarded, since it neither bore a railway nor crossed a frontier. In this I was mistaken. An older reserve, face deeply lined and feral-grim, halted us under a single electric bulb at the approach. I had lost my *biretta* and cincture, and the cassock under my mackintosh was torn and muddied; the priestly pretense would no longer suffice.

256

"Wie geht's?" I asked with a semblance of cheer.

"We'll stick it out," he replied coldly. "Where are you going?"

I entered into a long circumlocution about farm jobs awaiting me and my boy at Fussach, a half mile north, and we would need to reach it before dawn.

"Where are your residence-cards?"

I replied that we had walked all the way from Schwarzach in the Vorarlberg, fallen into a drainage ditch, lost our papers, and our feet were bloody.

"Must have documents," he insisted.

At this point, Inessa started to sniffle. She drew her handkerchief from her pocket, and several of our German marks fell onto the metal flooring. He instantly covered them with his boot, and waved us on.

"Very neat, my dear," I said.

"Prison is a great educator—if one escapes."

Höchst, a cluster of houses in a marsh, lay only a half-mile from St. Margrethen in Switzerland. Now came the last bridge out of Austria, the most challenging of all.

From behind us in the distance, rifles cracked and dogs bayed. Could the alarm for us be out so soon? The sun was piercing the mist; it was six A.M., Sunday. *Sunday!* A fearful remembrance filtered through my brain: on Sunday the Austrians, like the Germans, shot for the pot! They were out early, hunting the marsh and lake birds around us. Inessa, half asleep, huddled down under her mackintosh in the moist grass, murmured wearily, "Are they shooting at us?"

"No, no. Don't worry."

I was worried. Even more, I was chapfallen and angry with myself. Although the brilliant improvisations of my invincible investigator had demanded hours of research and planning, the success of this mission had lulled me to believe in my own instant inspiration, over-looking the cunning and resolve of my partner. Thus, at this climactic stage in our

257

venture, I had not a glimmer of a scheme to cross into Switzerland! Only two factors were certain: Inessa was in no condition to make a run for it, and the atomic bomb was fused for England, seven hundred miles away.

Above the mists floated the bridge, a conventional steel truss-span built many years ago and, I estimated, approximately a thousand feet long. On elbows and knees I crawled through the marsh-grass towards the river to reconnoitre. The line of six Austrian sentries was posted about three hundred feet before it, and distanced so that each could patrol within the other's vision: ten steps to the left, ten to the right. The relaxed Austrians had, however, dispensed with the barbed wire. A red and white striped wooden barrier, counter-weighted at one end, marked the exact frontier-line on the bridge. One Austrian and one Swiss guard, rifle on shoulder, paced their respective sides; both smoked cigarettes and occasionally chatted.

A dozen feet ahead of me, at the water's edge, stood a metal shack, the size of a small garage, possibly the bridge maintenance-shop or storage-room. The rear was out of the sentries' sight, and there I crawled to peep through a door window. On a wooden rack hung the round, black-peaked cap and black, brass-buttoned jacket proclaiming a minor state railway official: this was the maintenance chief's headquarters.

I inched back to Inessa and shook her vigorously. One eye opened in a wary slit. "That shack." I pointed. "We must break in."

Several rifle shots snapped over our heads.

"Get on with it!" she cried. "I'd rather be shot in Switzerland."

We snaked through the tall grass, flat on our stomachs, to the door of the shack. The glass near the handle broke under the heel of my boot, and its sound went un-noticed amidst the crackling of rifles.

258

The functionary's jacket was somewhat tight on me, but no one at that level wore bespoke tailoring. From the desk, I picked up a note-book and pencil, and discovered in a drawer a rule and small hammer.

"Inessa," I said, "you are once again the boy Otto, but now you are my assistant." I adjusted her cap low over her eyes.

"*Ja, ja,*" she muttered. "What is your plan?"

"We shall simply walk across the bridge."

A bitter, startled laugh escaped through her gritted teeth. Then: "I wish I had a cigarette. . . ." She limped behind me towards the sentry at the bridge-approach, where I raised the functionary's note-book to display it prominently.

He saluted and asked pleasantly, "Working on Sunday, Mein Herr?"

I drew myself up stiffly, and with the studied insolence of the Central European bureaucrat, I snapped, "Of course. I am a servant of the Emperor, just as you are! And when I'm despatched from Bregenz, I do my duty, whatever the day!"

"Yes, Mein Herr." He saluted sharply.

I strode on to the bridge, Otto hobbling obsequiously behind with the hammer. He tapped the bridge-railing and floor crisply while I listened to the sound and made notes. A metre beyond that spot, he tapped again. And thus we proceeded across the bridge, metre by metre, at the pace set by my assistant's swollen feet. When the Austrian guard advanced from the centre barrier towards me, I growled, "Remove that cigarette—you're on duty!" He did so, saluted smartly and enquired, most politely, "Repairs at last, sir?"

I continued making notes, refusing to reply to his unwarranted intrusion. After a while, I answered in steely, overly precise tones, "If I recommend it to Vienna. And *if* the Emperor can spare the steel. The war comes first."

Otto tapped and measured, occasionally dropping to his knees as we neared the barrier. Behind us, I heard a growl-

259

ing, insistent motor-car horn. A glance revealed a German staff-car, rifles poking out at the sides, racing along the road to the bridge. We were two hundred feet from the border barrier, and I needed this last Austrian sentry to shield me from that car.

Pointing my thumb over my shoulder, I indicated the Germans now at the bridge-ramp. "This bridge is dangerously rusty. The vibration that car sets up could crack the metal!"

He looked at me incredulously.

"Stop them!" I ordered, in the harsh voice of the *Feldwebel*. He ran to meet the on-coming car, pointing his rifle. I seized Inessa's hand, warning, "Don't look back!" and pulling, half-carrying her, I raced for the barrier.

The car rumbled on to the bridge; then came snaps of rifle-fire. We accelerated directly towards the Swiss guard, shouting, "English! English *Gefangene! Echappées!"*

The Swiss held his fire, and now the Germans lowered their rifles for fear of hitting the other Swiss guards who had rushed out of their shelter. We dived under the barrier a few seconds before the car skidded to a halt, cracking into the wood beam. Seated beside the driver, Charles stared malevolently, to which Inessa replied with extremely impolite descriptions of him and his parents.

I waved good-bye to our obdurate pursuer. "Possibly we can find a position for you after the war—as a waiter?"

The formalities of entry were expeditiously solved by our Vice-Consul in Zurich, who vouched for me and even persuaded the French Consul to do the same for Inessa. Mr. Angel also telephoned to an English couple in St. Margrethen who took us home for a bath and change of clothes (from a box that had been set aside for a charity bazaar) and even lent us several pounds for train-fare. We reached Zurich at noon.

There was no word of a London explosion in the newspapers, so my heart was still buoyant. And we were considerably cheered by news that the United States had entered the conflict three days before, and promised voluminous, immediate aid.

"Well, now the Krauts must capitulate," Inessa exulted.

I was not so sanguine. From my conversations with British officers I knew the Americans had a minute standing-army, and as for their air-force, there was none: it was a section of the Army Signal Corps with fifty-five training (not combat) planes and only thirty-five officers who could fly.

At the consulate, Arachne's wireless bulletin made clear that it was the Germans who demanded capitulation: ULTIMATUM CLAIMS THEY HAVE SEVERAL ATOMIC BOMBS. DEMAND PEACE TALKS OR WILL DESTROY ENGLAND. POSSIBLE?

I replied: THEY HAVE ONE, REPEAT ONE, WEAPON LEFT. FACTORY AND ONE BOMB DESTROYED. EXPLOSION EFFECTIVE ONE-MILE RADIUS. RADIO-ACTIVE WIND-STORM CAN CREATE PANIC. RETURNING SOONEST, PLEASE INFORM WIFE. I.A. VERY ESSENTIAL, REQUEST PERMISSION FOR HER TO VISIT CHILDREN IN ENGLAND.

A telephone call to Plumsoll revealed that he had received no cable from Germany; the censor had intercepted. I repeated my warning in another note to Arachne, adding, SEARCH ALL SHIPS IN LONDON.

We awaited the answer, but it came from an underling: A. UN-AVAILABLE. REPLY PROBABLE 0900 MONDAY.

I arranged to meet Inessa for lunch Monday noon at my hotel café, when I hoped to have Arachne's consent.

"I look forward to seeing sweet old moral London," she said blithely. "Until tomorrow then." She clasped my hand and stepped into a cab.

Plumsoll had kept excellent vigil over our possessions at the Pelikan, and he had even attempted to meet Lenin once, "to take his measure," but had been rebuffed. He was all

261

aquiver to hear particulars of my journey; pleading that I was not at present permitted to reveal anything, I urged him to pack, for we would take the after-noon train to Lausanne, then the express to Paris.

Shortly before midnight, a consulate-courier bore a wire-less from London. It was utterly shattering: CABINET RE-QUESTED KING OPEN PARLIAMENT EARLIER THAN USUAL TO DEAL WITH WAR LEGISLATION AND BOMB THREAT. START NOON 10 APRIL.

I bit hard into the stem of my pipe. The King's Speech from the Throne would be the perfect target for Buchhalter's "light-weight" bomb! It was probably already in London, and could be emplanted in the huge expanse of Parliament buildings, thus destroying the King and Queen, the House of Lords, Members of Parliament and the Cabinet, and if any of the royal family remained at home in Buckingham Palace, the radio-active cloud would over-take them, too. In short, this cataclysmic explosion would annihilate our entire governing class and much of the civil and military leadership, create terror and despair by its radio-active burns and probably snuff out Britain's will to fight on.

After all I had endured to eliminate this demonic menace, and now to find its power and my warnings simply ignored, I could only think, *"Quos Deus vult perdere prius dementat!"* *

Noon 10 April would afford me only thirty-six hours to reach London. The pre-war Simplon Express bowled along from Lausanne to Paris in eight and a half to eleven and a half hours; with war-time delays, an ordinary express could consume twice that time.

My vehement rejoinder to Arachne read: BOMB WILL BE

* "Whom God wishes to destroy, he first deprives of reason." Attributed to Euripides. —R.S.

SET OFF INSIDE HOUSE OF LORDS. POSTPONE! POSTPONE! CAN YOU ARRANGE PLANE PARIS-DIEPPE-LONDON?

Monday, 9 April

This was Arachne's answer: KING REFUSES TO POSTPONE, CONSIDERS IT PUBLIC ADMISSION OF COWARDICE. ALL FORCES IN SEARCH. FIVE ANTI-AIRCRAFT SQUADRONS AROUND LONDON. PLANE TRANSPORT ARRANGED FOR YOU PLUS PLUMSOLL. TEMPORARY VISA GRANTED I.A.

I wound up my affairs in a flurry of motor-cab rounds, first authorising the Swiss bank to transfer the remaining £12,500 to Lenin, due under our agreement, and arrived at the Pelikan Café a few minutes before noon, knowing I.A.'s penchant for promptness. An hour later, she had not yet appeared, and I feared some peril or accident had overtaken her. Another cab raced to her *pension*, where I rang insistently before the rachitic proprietress opened the door.

"Madame Armand?" I demanded.

"Left an hour ago."

"Did she reveal her destination?"

"Took two bags in a taxi, the fine lady."

"Did any one wait for her, or go with her?"

"No, no!" She shut the door in my face.

I urged the cab on to maximum speed to my hotel. No message from Inessa awaited me, and I was deeply perplexed—yes, troubled. She had solicited my aid for immediate passage to England, and disappeared. Something entirely un-anticipated and extra-ordinary was afoot.

CHAPTER EIGHTEEN

King and Parliament in Peril

The porter loaded Plumsoll and me into the waiting motor-cab, and we whirled off to meet the three-fifteen train for Lausanne.

A most peculiar sight greeted us at the Zurich station. The local to Schaffhausen, the Swiss town at the German frontier, was surrounded by a shoving, yelling mass whom I took to be Russians and other European revolutionaries, screaming imprecations, coarse epithets, beating on the windows of one carriage: "Traitors! Spies! You'll never get out of Germany!" Their fury was directed at a file of about thirty men, women and a few children trudging stolidly through the up-roar to board a carriage at a single door, where Lenin, in a bowler hat and a heavy over-coat, scornfully ignored the demonstrators to welcome the voyagers.

They were dressed in their best clothes, worn and threadbare, almost all of them in black: the men, some in coats with scruffy velvet collars, had donned ties, even wing collars, and soft felt hats or homburgs; a few of the women wore wide-brimmed hats, tied under their chins with scarves, but most had wrapped the familiar peasant *babushka* over their heads. Among them I discerned Lenin's wife, helping the women lift their bundles of blankets, pillows, baskets of food, even samovars, into the carriage. The women clung to one another, averting their eyes from the protestors, who spat upon them. One comrade shouted in German, "Lenin's insane! Who approved this policy? The party will toss you out of Russia!"

Lenin's return had finally been arranged by Zimmermann. The Germans were wagering that this cell of revolutionaries, like a plague bacillus, would destroy Kerensky's debating-society and put an end to Russia's participation in the war. The expediency of German support did not trouble Lenin one whit; as he had told me, "Any enemy of my enemy is my friend." *

At two-forty Inessa arrived, in the same fetching yellow costume she had worn when we met on the tour-launch. She stood last in line, refulgent, like a cockatoo among sparrows; her eyes met mine, and I tipped my hat slowly, albeit stiffly, in fare-well. A rueful smile quivered on her lips; she turned on the train step, as if to approach me, but instead brought two fingers up to her mouth, blew a graceful kiss in my

* The Germans attempted to conceal his dependence by transporting the Bolsheviks in one carriage and a baggage-waggon, labelled a "sealed train," an extra-territorial area. A neat but fraudulent twist of international law, it made the occupants immune from ordinary border controls at Sweden and Finland, where local engines would be hitched to the cars. An important co-ordinate purpose was to ensure that the Russians did not infect any Germans with peace propaganda while passing through. A German engine was attached at the frontier beyond Switzerland, and two German officers accompanied the radicals to enforce the "sealed" carriage.

—R.S.

direction and, without a backwards glance, entered the car as it slowly rolled away.

Her swift change of plan was startling, a disappointment, but not entirely surprising. She had consummated her pledges to my mission, and now she had made her choice: she had embraced her true religion, the Church of Marx, a theology as fulfilling and comforting to its believers as Christianity or Islam. *Das Kapital* was its Holy Book, and Lenin its St. Peter. All her doubts would now be answered without question, and un-like other religions that promised eternal bliss after death, hers vowed to create a paradise on earth. She wanted to stand directly at the shoulder of Lenin, and, if audacity and intelligence could rule Russia, she would.

I felt it my duty now to warn Arachne of Lenin's threat to the Allied cause, for the removal of Russian troops from the East would enable the Germans to concentrate their entire fury in France. From the station telephone I dictated in code to the Intelligence Officer at our consulate, exhorting Arachne to stop or delay the train at the Swedish or Finnish frontier.

Our new vulnerability, coupled with the impending threat to London, pressed heavily on every moment as Plumsoll and I paced in the warmish spring air outside the Lausanne station, awaiting the Paris express. Around us, school-children in pairs, one carrying a money-box, the other a basket of silk poppies in the red and white colours of the Swiss flag, solicited francs for the Red Cross; in accord with ancient Swiss neutrality, a week of rest was provided in their mountains to nurses of both the Allied and Central powers. I accepted a red flower from a pert, flaxen-haired youngster, who eagerly pinned it to my jacket-lapel; a white one was affixed to Plumsoll's, and shortly after, we settled back into the worn plush of our compartment.

The coach's jiggles and wavers soon made me aware of an

irritation under my shirt. I extracted the poppy pin to discover the end stained a blood red; a closer examination
revealed that it was actually a fine, hollow needle. The Swiss
child (upon recollection she appeared somewhat older than
the others) could hardly have thrust the "pin" through two
layers of cheviot by accident. My immediate reaction was:
poison! The maleficent enemy were still grappling to prevent
my knowledge of the bomb from reaching England

Behind the locked door of the lavatory, I ripped open my
shirt and found the minute puncture in my skin, topped by
a spot of the brownish-red liquid. It could have been blood
or any of a dozen deadly infections: *bacillus botulinus,*
bubonic, typhus or influenza virus, snake venom, *mytilotoxin*
of shellfish, curare (not so far-fetched, for there had been a
frustrated attempt to attack Mr. Lloyd George with it).
With my razor I cut out a square inch of skin and sufficient
sub-cutaneous tissue surrounding the needle-prick. The
blood I stanched with a hand-kerchief, which I held in place
under my jacket when I returned to my seat. Plumsoll,
outraged by the effrontery of the assault, supplied two additional linens.

Heaven only knows what frightful forebodings of suicide
or assassination my hidden hand produced among our fellow
passengers; as for myself, I could only smile re-assuringly
and pray that I had arrested the malignancy until I reached
London. At length, the blood congealed, and I experienced
no symptoms of paralysis, shock or internal pains; never-the-
less, since poisons kill by intense local action, or by their
effect on remote organs after absorption, or by both methods, I accepted the fact that the continuation of my life on
earth was now beyond my control.

At the Dijon stop, a British courier passed an envelope to
me. It was the reply to my "sealed train" alert:

BUCHANAN [our ambassador in Petersburg] REPORTS SOL-
DIERS EAGER TO CONTINUE FIGHTING. DISCIPLINE RESTORED
BALTIC FLEET. PM AND CABINET AGREE LENIN'S FUTURE
DESTROYED BY GERMAN TIES. ALL ACCEPT BUCHANAN'S ES-
TIMATE LENIN HAS NO FOLLOWING IN RUSSIA. DON'T MED-
DLE IN POLITICAL MATTERS.

The sinuosities of international diplomacy are not without
some exasperation.*

Finding it nerve-wrenching to carry on a meaningful conversation with Plumsoll at this time, I re-newed the cultiva-
tion of my moustaches, and stared out the train window: the
billowy clouds over-head suggested bomb sizes ranging from
torpedo to barrage balloon.

Tuesday, 10 April

After the most chafing delays, we reached Paris at eight-
thirty in the morning, three and a half hours before the
King's speech was scheduled. From the Gare de Lyon, a
British staff-car rushed us to an air-field where a peculiar
three-wing plane awaited: the newest Sopwith three-seat tri-
plane, assigned to the Royal Naval Flying Corps at Luxeil
for testing in combat. I climbed into the gunner's seat at the
leading edge of the top wing, and Plumsoll occupied the
rear gunner's place, behind the pilot. Within fifty-five min-

---

* At the Finnish frontier, Russian border-control had dis-integrated to
the point where British officers, stationed there under an Allied agreement, searched Lenin's party and could have easily sent them back to
Sweden. Eight months later, Lenin signed an armistice, permitting Hindenburg to transfer hundreds of thousands of troops to the Western Front;
his 1918 spring offensive very nearly smashed the Allies. Thus the bomb
demolished in the factory would un-doubtedly have decided the war in
Germany's favour. —R.S.

utes, we landed at Dieppe. Here I took over a Navy 1½-Strutter reconnaissance bi-plane, fitted with floats, which I piloted to a landing on the Thames, adjacent to the Houses of Parliament. The clock now showed ten-fifty.

Arachne and several naval and army officers met me on the terrace, which we reached by a Jacob's ladder. I motioned Arachne aside: "Have you considered forcing a postponement with a small fire?"

His vacant eyes revealed a flash of pleasure at the audacity of it, then faded in an instant. "You're playin' home ground-rules now. We've combed every inch of the buildin's. And Westminster Hall, roofs, cellars, crypts, under-croftin'. Even pried up that carvin' behind the Throne, the ceiling-panels, all six wall frescoes—what a to-do that raised! Net result—zero. I'm convinced they'll drop the deuced thing from a tandem of Gothas."

"Mind if I stroll round a bit?"

"Do be quick. The old dear starts speakin' at noon."

Dogged by Plumsoll, I walked rapidly through the limestone and marble corridors westward, then proceeded under the lofty vault of the Central Hall to St. Stephen's Porch. On the lawn, already green under the spring sun, Members and distinguished visitors were greeting one another with the chatter and smiles of a college re-union. I detected no feeling of urgency or alarm. The Lords and Commoners arrived in civil dress and army attire, several of the latter on crutches or in wheel-chairs. A few, summoned in such haste that they carried golfing-bags and tennis-racquets, retired directly to the robing-rooms to change.

This huge conglomeration of buildings, begun nine centuries ago, burnt in 1834 and rebuilt with the Victorians' indomitable confidence into a veritable Gothic city, to symbolise the enduring glory of Britain and display their innumerable works of art and historic mementoes, was now under siege by the Germans, imminently facing the destiny of Ypres—obliteration.

Shouts arose of a sudden on the river-front roof next to the Clock Tower housing "Big Ben." Peering up, I saw a constable and an army man in hot pursuit of someone scrambling from the Tower over the steeply pitched iron plates towards the south; then abruptly he veered in the direction of Westminster Hall.

" 'Big Ben'!" I exclaimed to Plumsoll. "Diabolically clever! It's the timer for the bomb!"

We raced through several hundred yards of corridors to the Clock Tower, and up the oblong stone stair-case—a short flight, a right turn, another flight and another, hanging on to the balustrade to swing round the turns. From a long-ago tale, read me by my mother, the number of steps popped into my head: 292. By the time I counted 89, I knew we could never reach the clock at that pace.

We slowed to half-time; the climb, never-the-less, seemed to draw upon un-willing muscles I had not employed before. At 125, I leaned against the balustrade, my heart pounding, to gasp for air. Plumsoll was in worse straits: he had to sit. After a minute of rest we surged upwards again, not swinging round on the balustrade now but pulling ourselves up by it. At step 180 I felt such weariness in my legs and arms as if I had bowled an entire match at Lord's, where upon I slowed to a walk, breathing deeply with each step. Nearing 200, we found a room wherein two doors opened on a shaft, through which the weights that drive the clock-works descend nearly to the bottom floor. I found no possible timing-device here.

At step 292, we staggered into a dazzling white, square gallery, behind the four enormous clock-faces; now I sat down to rest. "Where's the clock-works?" Plumsoll cried.

Half-blinded by the sunshine streaming through the opal

glass dials, almost four times my height, I discerned a small door. This opened into the clock-chamber, un-expectedly quiet despite the huge iron and brass apparatus of wheels and gears spread out on a rectangular frame, about fifteen feet long and reminiscent of a flat-bed printing press. Dozens of oiled gears in a succession of diameters revolved slowly, creating the discreet tick of a kitchen clock.

On my knees now, I inspected the under-side of the machinery which operated the dial hands as well as the cables pulling the famous bells. The gears were driven by weights hung on long cables, extending down the shaft we had seen many steps below. The timer would consist of two wires, I assumed, each attached to a gear or escapement, so that when they met, an electric circuit would be completed, as in a conventional home light-switch, and ignite the bomb's explosive charge. The essential problem was—which gears? The bevel gear, driving the hands, revolved most slowly, once an hour; there were no wires here.

We could hear the pounding of boots on the stone steps, and military commands; others had made the same deduction from the pursuit on the roof. A startling click resounded through the room. Instinctively, we dropped on our stomachs to the floor, as if for a shell attack. Four cables were yanked abruptly by the mechanism, and from high above in the belfry we heard the quarter-chime bells ring out, providing the exact time, eleven-fifteen, and a great relief to us.

I turned my attention to the smaller gears, which made a full revolution in half or three-quarters of an hour. Directly behind the centre of the horizontal girder, where an oval plate read FIXED HERE 1859, I found two rubber-covered wires tied to adjoining gears, neatly insulated from the metal so that only the bare ends would meet--in approximately five minutes. I stripped off my coat, waistcoat and tie, to avoid being caught up by the moving mechanisms, and, contorting my body between the wheels of the weight-lift motor and the revolving gears of the clock, I felt carefully for the wire closest at hand. It had been firmly attached to a spoke by a heavy iron wire which, at that very moment, was revolving out of my sight. Now I could work only by touch to un-twist that heavy knot. It was slow, finely strung work, for I could not allow the bare end of one electric line to touch any of the gears or platform; these were entirely metal and might inter-connect with the gear bearing the second wire, thus un-wittingly completing the electric circuit. Several harrowing minutes dragged by before I jerked the line loose. The other end of the insulated wire, which would connect to the bomb's detonator, dropped down the weight-shaft.

"The room below!" I cried. "Doors to the shaft." We raced down the ninety or so steps, pushing our way through the investigators gasping and staggering on their way up, and I flung open the doors. High up, where the shaft entered the ceiling, I detected the two wires. They were simply attached to a nail!

We had been duped! decoyed by a fiendishly inventive mind. The man on the roof had diverted most of the security forces to the Clock Tower, while his accomplices had set the actual device in place and fused it. And time was now distressingly short: eleven-thirty.

In the Royal Gallery, the Prime Minister and Cabinet, even the Queen herself, gathered to persuade the sovereign of the advisibility of holding Parliament in another building, possibly St. Paul's Cathedral, until the Houses could be searched again. Just as he had refused to evacuate the city, he stood firm here; indeed, he explained, to reveal that the enemy could threaten the inner sanctum of government would be tantamount to admitting he was no longer in control of his country. He ordered the ceremony to proceed.

I moved ahead on my own initiative. The weapon would now be close to, or within, the House of Lords, since the King would deliver his Speech there. Followed by Plumsoll, I hastened into the Peers' Lobby. The engraved clock face here drew my inspection.

"Another timer?" Plumsoll asked, desperately hopeful.

As I turned away, a robed peer sauntered out.

"That face seems . . . unfinished," I speculated, stroking my upper lip from habit, even though the moustaches had not yet grown back. The peer was also stroking his upper lip, which bore no moustaches at all. He walked on to the Central Hall.

"Unfinished?" Plumsoll repeated in a bewildered whisper.

I exclaimed, "It's *Charles!*" and hurried after him. How could he have slipped by all the security safe-guards?

He had turned off to the left, in the direction of St. Stephen's Hall. When we reached the Central Hall, he was no where in sight.

"Where the devil—?" Plumsoll groaned.

"We mustn't waste time pursuing him—probably another ruse in his master plan! To the Peers' Cloak-Room!" I set out at a run; Plumsoll puffed along, still demanding explanation.

"The non-existent moustaches, my dear Plumsoll, are one key to the puzzle. The other missing element completes the solution: the golf-bag he carried into the House when he arrived."

"What has a golf-bag to do with it?"

"The bomb must be in it!"

"Really, now, you've gone too far!" he snorted.

"Why else, tell me, should Charles walk in a direction opposite to the Throne, where the King will speak?"

I searched among the coats and hats hanging on the iron

Contorting my body between the wheels and gears, I felt carefully for the detonating wire.

275

stands in the cloak-room and discovered two bags stuffed with conventional clubs.

"Good heavens, this is heavy!" Plumsoll exclaimed, tugging at another.

It was actually a double bag and shoulder-strap, heavily re-inforced and resting on the usual cart but equipt with heavy steel wheels. Inside was a steel cylinder, approximately three and a half feet long and a foot in diameter, sealed by steel caps. The shape corresponded exactly to the sketch I had memorised in the factory. Inside the cylinder, a timer ticked faintly.

We hoisted this accursed burden on to our shoulders and made the best speed possible through the corridors to the Terrace. The two of us labouriously manoeuvred the cylinder down the ladder into the sea-plane's rear cockpit; Plumsoll squeezed in beside it and I took the stick up front.

The plane skimmed along the Thames out to sea, but try as I might, I could gain only a futile three feet in altitude because of the bomb's weight; the 1½-Strutter had been designed to carry two men and petrol for three and a quarter hours, and although we had consumed a substantial portion of the fuel in our flight from Dieppe, we were still over-loaded.

We now faced the life-or-death question: when would this cylinder explode? It must have been set to detonate after the King began his speech at noon; but I required the precise minute in order to stop the timer with some margin of safety. Based on my experience with Charles' personal traits and ingenuity, I needed to penetrate his thought-processes, just as surely as he had burrowed into mine; thus we were engaged in a long-distance, blind and lethal gambit and counter-gambit. I had not only to anticipate what he might do but also to consider the reverse action, just as he had deluded me with the "Big Ben" diversion. The German spy could be certain that his man on the roof diverted us so that the bomb could be hidden somewhere in the building; most important, he knew that this discovery would not prevent the King from speaking as scheduled, for George V, being of Saxe-Coburg descent, was just as stubborn as his German ancestors.

Arachne had informed me the King would start precisely at noon and speak for twenty minutes. If I were Charles, I would set the device to go off in the middle of the speech—twelve-ten. My watch now showed eleven-fifty-four, and thus my margin of safety to defuse this complex mechanism encased in armour-plate was sixteen minutes.

Plumsoll rapped my shoulder and pointed to the tail. A motor-launch was gaining on us, and crouched in the bow was a man aiming a rifle. We could not hear the shot; we saw only that a section of the vertical fin had splintered, and it flapped uselessly. Our plane, skewing erratically, had gained about four feet above the Thames when a man leaped from the launch to the tail. Charles had come to complete his mission, crawling forward, hanging on like a lobster-claw.

"What the devil does he hope to do?" Plumsoll shouted.

He would attempt to release the weapon over Parliament, or, if unable to manage that, would no doubt dive directly into the buildings, as the twentieth-century incarnation of Siegfried, hero of that preposterous Götterdämmerung myth which has such a fierce hold on the German soul: riding forth to perform great deeds, so bloody and obscure neither he nor the gods understand why, he brings the entire world down in flames round him.

If the Hun insisted on jousting in mid-air, I could not refuse his challenge. I motioned Plumsoll to crawl forward and take the controls.

"Impossible!" he yelled into the propeller back-wash. "I've never flown a plane."

"Just hold the stick steady on!" I replied. By a most careful balancing and timing, reminiscent of circus acrobats, we switched positions as the plane wallowed and bucked. It continued on its spasmodic course as Plumsoll struggled to master the controls and the intruder's weight forced us dangerously low to the water again. I managed to stretch out on the fuselage, gripping the wing struts, to offer a minimum target while I employed my booted legs to maximum advantage.

Charles eased forward with reptilian grace for a fight to the finish; both of us knew that no quarter could be given because in a very short time the atom device would disintegrate us. Suddenly, he snatched a German field knife, concealed within his left shirt-sleeve, and plunged it deep above my boot. The blood-spewing shock to my muscles, together with an abrupt tilt of the wing, loosed my grip on the struts. I rolled off the fuselage, clutching wildly for any finger-hold as I dropped into space. My hands seized upon one of the vertical struts supporting a float and I hung there, suspended between clouds and grim water. Curling my legs up on to the float, I rolled my body upwards, where upon the strut broke loose—and came off in my right hand. Desperately, I swung over to the opposite float, careful now to hang on its steel cable braces and still grasping the disjointed strut.

Utterly beyond Plumsoll's control, the plane revolved forty-five degrees, bringing the wing into a near-vertical position. The unrelenting German leaned down and under for the *coup de grâce;* his brow wrinkled in concentration, lips fixed in a tightly curved satanic grin, he slashed at my face and eyes. Eluding his fierce thrusts, I surprised him behind the ear with my metal club, a ferocious blow that caused his eyes to open wide, then harden into an opaque stare. He plummeted head-down into the drink with scarcely a splash.

Relieved of his weight, Plumsoll levelled off while I crept with the agonizing slowness of a slug into the rear cockpit beside the bomb. Peering below, I saw that Charles had not surfaced.

"Well done!" Plumsoll called out. "Back to Woolwich Arsenal?"

"No! No! We don't dare approach it with this explosive. Stay on course east."

"But that's the sea!"

"Exactly! We don't want to be over land if it blows."

My watch revealed I had but eight minutes to doom. I asked him to call out the minutes remaining, so that I could gauge the timing required for the multiple steps in defusing. The caps of this atrocious bomb had been forcefully screwed shut—I could not un-wind the timer-end. Opening the tool kit, I found an oil can and a hacksaw, and bore down on it with all the strength at my command to hew away at the steel casing.

"Six minutes!" Plumsoll shouted. "We have enough petrol for Woolwich after you defuse it."

I had no intention of turning the bomb over to the experts at Woolwich. Dr. Einstein's logic and humanity had affected me profoundly. This dreadful weapon would not bar future wars; the great nations would invent more powerful and ingenious devices using uranium, and with the development of aeroplanes, they could move through the limitless skies over the entire world.

"Five!" Plumsoll called.

Even worse, if Buchhalter could create so small and simple a device, soon every self-respecting despotic ruler of a desert water-hole would feel impelled to acquire one or two

279

bombs in order to assert his potency and importance. In a few years, the German myth would be truly realised: immolation of the planet.*

By now I had cut a sufficiently wide and deep slit in the casing to insert a knife. Resurrecting some surgical precision which I had not employed for many years, I lifted one of the wires through the cut and yanked it loose. The demon was at last exorcised.

"Three!" Plumsoll announced. He turned in dread to observe my progress, and found me levering the cylinder over the fuselage.

"Careful!" he cried. "This could win the war for us!"

Killing, even when licensed by a King, was still evil; I would not bear on my conscience the incineration of the human race. As the plane yawed wildly, I heaved the weapon into the sea, far off Foulness Point.

It sank slowly, with what seemed like a protesting gurgle.

The sea-water, seeping in through the cut, would effectively neutralise the detonating charge. Most fortunately, Plumsoll had no understanding of the plane's instrument-readings, so that he would never know where the bomb lay.

I directed him in the technique of steering a full turn; we flew once more along the Thames to London, a task made enormously difficult by the ineffectiveness of the tail-fin in the soupy fog blowing up before us. Plumsoll fought gamely to hold course, and though I could not see his face, I had the certain impression he was praying.

---

* Dr. Einstein had abandoned his pacifist position by August 1939, when he sent a letter to President Roosevelt urging intensified studies of the possibility of an atom bomb because he feared that German research could build a weapon first. This was the impetus for the Manhattan Project, which produced the American A-bombs. Could Einstein have been influenced by Conan Doyle's argument in 1917? —R.S.

In the mirrored red foyer of the Café Royal, Plumsoll and I bade good-night to Arachne, while the doorman searched for a cab in the pitchy night. Our supper had been a savourless affair. The mission completed, Arachne seemed to have already dismissed me from his memory, though he did impart a few desultory words of appreciation in my direction. I considered this most magnanimous, in view of the fact that Arachne had heedlessly served Charles almost as well as Charles had served him.

Before we stepped into the cab, Arachne fished a letter out of his waistcoat pocket and handed it to me without a word of explanation. The ancient hansom, resurrected to over-come the shortage of petrol, and its spavined horse swayed in opposite directions. Stifling fog swirled over empty streets, where windows were blacked out with flannel against the Zeppelin nuisance; Regent Street and Piccadilly looked abandoned, and only wardens walked about with shielded torches to guide the occasional pedestrian across the invisible kerb-stones. There were no motor-cars in sight, no electric lights, no telephone-lines; we seemed to have been transported back to the previous century, clip-clopping through the streets of London in 1887.

". . . Madame Armand had scope, a sense of magnitude," I mused, a tincture of esteem lightening my un-accustomed melancholy. "She had no children over here—that was a ruse to gain entry. She probably planned to worm the bomb's 'secret' out of me somehow, or make off with the weapon itself. Sympathetic scientists here might have helped her attack its complexities."

"And hand it all over to Lenin?"

"Of course. He has the Pisgah vision."

"Still, how can you be so certain she was not Isabelle Andros?"

"My dear Plumsoll, surely you must agree with my detective's un-impeachable axiom: whenever one excludes the impossible, whatever remains, however improbable, must be the truth."

He nodded reluctantly. I borrowed the cabman's torch to look over the letter passed on by Arachne. Tearing open the envelope, addressed in care of the consulate at Zurich, I extracted a note:

Thank you again, Dr. Doyle. I regret I can't stay a few more days. —I.A.

ENVOI

I would not let the matter rest there. Continuing enquiries were made, in which I discovered that the astonishing woman known as Inessa Armand had been Lenin's lover ever since they had met in Paris, in 1910, and they had maintained over the years, with the assent of his wife, a *ménage-à-trois*. But the closer Lenin approached supreme power in Russia, the more remote he and I.A. became. While his wife stayed by his side, I.A. threw her prodigious energies into nursing victims of the civil war and famine that accompanied it; she dressed in rags, neglected to eat, took to living in freight-trains. She was caring for refugees on one of these trains when she was over-come by typhoid in the Caucasus; hungry, cold and alone, she died in 1920.*

* Details of her relationship with Lenin may be found in "Lenin and Inessa Armand," by Bertram Wolfe, *Slavic Review,* Vol. XXII, No. 1, March 1963 (published at the University of Washington, Seattle), as well as in *Lenin in Zurich,* by Alexander Solzhenitsyn (New York, 1976), which also unveils fascinating aspects of Parvus's manipulations. —R.S.

I have often speculated, on the basis of information brought Up Here by new arrivals after I crossed over in 1930, what the world might have been had Lenin never reached Russia. Untouched by the ordinary emotions of friendship, honour or mercy, only this charismatic theologian could have consummated the Bolshevik Revolution, and he set in motion stupendous forces, causing deaths so innumerable as to shrivel the mind. Reputable historians state that ten million Russians died in the civil war and famine; in the 1930s, Stalin liquidated twenty million more; and Mr. Solzhenitsyn, I am told, estimates that fifteen million kulaks, who could not see the virtues of giving up their own plots of land, should be added to the carnage. Thus, the total deaths in Russia attributable to Bolshevism reached forty-five million!—the greatest catastrophe in world history since the Black Plague very nearly wiped out all Europe.

Mr. Somerset Maugham, who crossed over to us in 1965, believes he could have prevented Lenin's accession if only he had reached Petersburg sooner. In a chat we had recently, exchanging memories of those tumultuous months of 1917 (incidentally, he *had* paid that Bolivian assassin in full), Maugham revealed that his secret mission to Petersburg differed considerably from the tale he presented in *Ashenden.* After my plea to restrain Lenin in April had been negated, Maugham was approached in July in New York by Sir William Wiseman, ostensibly director of the British Purchasing Commission in the United States but actually chief of MI-1C (later known as MI-6), in order to persuade the Russians to stay in the war. Someone in the government had at last recognised the danger of Lenin.

Maugham embarked at Vancouver on the *Empress of Russia* on 2 August for Japan, thence to Vladivostok and across six thousand miles on the Trans-Siberian Railway to

Moscow, and on to Petersburg. He carried in his money-belt bills of exchange, not for the un-specified staggering amount he mentioned in his book but for a paltry twenty-one thousand dollars, to stop the Bolshevik Revolution!

The enormity of this second Intelligence miscalculation helps one understand why England is now less than merry.

ACKNOWLEDGEMENTS

For assistance in clarifying details of the atom bomb, I am deeply indebted to Dr. Philip Morrison; for German and Russian history of the period, to Prof. Aaron Noland and to Herbert Robinson; and for medical matters, to Dr. Benjamin Singer. Paul W. Benson and Maxwell E. Siegel urged full speed ahead from the start of the communications, and my wife, Gloria, my constant editor, even verified the ingredients of the Bedfordshire Clanger.